D0867431

JEMIMA'S LEGACY

MAXANNE EZER

PIQUANT PRESS

Cover and interior design and layout: Sue Reynolds

Cover art: High Park Gate, painting by John Howard

ISBN 978-1-987813-49-4 paperback
ISBN 978-1-987813-50-0 ebook

Published by Piquant Press
13240 Mast Rd., Port Perry, ON L9L 1B5
piquantpress.ca

Printed in Canada

1   2   3   4   5   6   7   8   9   10

Dedication

For my grandsons,
Jasper, Quinn and Sebastian

Before the Beginning

I am not mad.

I know what they say. John, my nieces, the servants, the doctor with the little silver spectacles.

I have a nurse now, like a child. Like the child I never had.

Do they not think I see them, their worried faces, their troubled looks? Do they not think I hear their whispers?

Don't think I don't know what is going on, that I have always known what is going on.

Perhaps, that, really, is the cause of what has happened to me now. The time when I knew, before I knew. The looks, the whispers. The conversations that stopped when I walked into a room. And then, to pretend I didn't know, which perhaps was even worse.

I know about the locked doors. I know about being chained like an animal. Do they think because I can't talk to them, that I don't know about what is going on? Doors without door knobs. Windows that are sealed.

I have been trying so hard to fight what is happening to me. But more and more, now, I know there is nothing I can do. I disappear. Time passes. Is it hours, even days? Sometimes, I don't know where I am. I seem to wake up and know only that time has passed. It is dark when it was light. Cold where it was

1

warm.

The memories collide, a door opens. Sometimes, there is only darkness. Feelings come first. The tang of salty sea air on my lips. The slap of the sails.

There is a moment I remember, I am standing on the deck of the Emperor Alexander, the ship that is carrying us to Upper Canada.

I have been so seasick; days and days of lying on the hard bed in the cabin, John, more ill than I, moaning in the other berth. Heavy winds blow constantly and huge waves toss the little ship like a toy boat in a child's bath. The waves swell up and crash against the portholes. In the cabin, objects fly across the room. Then the winds die down. The storm passes. I am well enough to go outside, to marvel at the grandeur of the sea and the freedom.

For a long time, I have been thinking about writing my story. One day, when I was in town, I slipped into Rowsell's and bought a stack of notebooks, some new pens and several bottles of ink and hid everything when I got home.

John has been talking about writing his story—one of his many projects, and knowing him, he probably will do it. One thing about John, he doesn't just dream about doing things, he follows through. Our house is filled with his ideas and experiments. "People will be interested in what I did for this city," he says. "What I did!" As if he did it all alone. As if I wasn't there.

I don't often let myself dwell on this, but then, there is so much I won't think about. All these years, I have schooled myself to put my thoughts and anger aside, but the anger has been there, always festering.

I don't know if anyone will ever read what I write. Maybe I am writing for the girls; for Ellen, and Eliza, and Clara, my clever, talented Clara. Perhaps I will be able to give it to them, secretly. Maybe I will hide it away and someone will find it later, when it doesn't matter anymore.

I push back, far into the past, to a little girl in England.

It was an unusually pleasant childhood; I see that now. A happy family, a comfortable house, not wealthy, but never in need. How often, during our first terrible year in little York did I dream of our cozy home in Staines. The warmth of the fire when John and I had none. The busy hum of the household there, when we huddled in an attic, snow seeping through holes in the roof.

There were four of us at home, each with our own special place. My older sisters, Mary Ann and Martha. Fanny, my little sister, the giggly, sometimes flighty one, but loved and cuddled by all. Father was a surveyor by trade with his own quite successful business, but he was a man whose true great love was his paintbox and he was never so happy as when he went off with his paint box and sketchbooks, with all of us in tow. And as for me, I was Father's special one, the serious artist. I cannot remember a time when I wasn't making pictures.

I must have been very small when my father would let me "work" in his office. I loved to help him tidy up, to poke around with his tools, to draw sometimes on the drafts he was about to discard. For a special treat, Father would lift me up on a stool beside him in the office. I can hear my endless questions.

"Papa, what are those lines there?" I asked, peering at the survey maps. "Please, can I make some." I pestered him until he gave me paper and pencils and let me "work" at his side. Later, I so proudly showed him my work. "Look Papa, I made a map, just like you."

"When you grow up, I will hire you as my assistant," Father used to say with a laugh as he sent me off to play.

Of course, it was common for girls in good families to learn to draw and paint a little. It was like playing the piano and doing embroidery, learning to ride, all pleasant things for a young gentlewoman to know. But in our household, it was quite different. Mother was a serious and talented artist and for her, our little projects were much more than simple past-times.

"You never know where life will take you," she used to say. "You girls have talents you might have to use one day. There is no time to be idle."

Although we all went to the local school where we learned to read and write and do basic arithmetic, it was Mother who pushed us further. She encouraged us to read widely and to learn about the world beyond our little town. The home she created was filled with laughter and a love of adventure.

As I grew older, I began to spend more and more time with Father in his office. I soon learned to draw plans, make detailed and finished copies of the surveys. Father let me set up my easel and paints in a bright corner of his office so that I could paint and keep him company.

And then, one day, everything changed. Father's young assistant was ill and he needed a detailed survey for an important client.

"I could do that, Father." I said, eagerly.

He looked at me carefully. I could almost see him turning the thought in his head. "Yes," he said, "I suppose you could."

And after that, there was more and more serious work. Without anyone really noticing, I began to work along with Father's clerks and apprentices, taking on more of the routine tasks of the office. No one ever questioned my presence there. Sometimes, I even accompanied my father on visits to sites, discussing the work on the way.

And that, of course, was how I met John Howard, or John Corby, as he was then, when his work as an articling architect brought him to my father's office. I don't actually remember being introduced to him, but somehow, very quickly, it seemed that he was always there. At first it seemed quite natural that he had many reasons to come by, to pick up surveys or to discuss projects and somehow, I found myself drawn into conversations he would have with my father. One day, as he was leaving the office, he stopped and looked at my latest painting which was resting on the easel. I can still hear the words of that first, stilted exchange.

"Miss Meikle," he began, stepping back from the work. "I, um, have noticed you painting here. You are really an excellent artist."

I remember being quite flustered. I mumbled a thank you and then, asked, rather hesitantly, "Do you also paint, Mr. Corby?"

"A little," he answered. "Perhaps we might chat about our work another time."

Soon we were spending more and more time together. John was quite unlike anyone I had ever known. He was tall and, I thought, quite handsome; pale skin, light brown hair, blue eyes, a sometimes questioning, almost amused look on his face, as if, he was always sizing up everything. He was so full of energy that sometimes it seemed as if he could barely manage to sit still long enough for a cup of tea. He had an insatiable curiosity, interested in how things worked, in new ideas and new machines. At the same time, there was something very open and unassuming about him. He didn't tell me much about his childhood, but I gathered that it hadn't been easy. Instead of being bitter however, John seemed to have a tremendous optimism.

"I don't have a farthing now," he said, "but I have great plans. Give me half a chance, and you'll see."

Sometimes, we went to London together, John with notebook in hand, jotted down his thoughts about the ancient Westminster Abby and pointed out features of St. Paul's Cathedral. We were excited to explore the newly built Regency terraces designed by John Nash. John even sketched out the plans of the elegant, curving streets which he would turn to many years later. I think he enjoyed having someone who would listen to him carefully, sometimes even challenge what he was saying.

I was not as outgoing as my sisters. Young men would cluster around Fanny when we went to parties and dances, but I usually hung back, almost afraid that someone would try to talk to me and I wouldn't know what to say. My older sisters married quite young and Fanny, who had many choices, finally accepted Sidney Mountcastle, a young man who had been courting her for years.

At twenty-five, I was beginning to see myself as the spinster of the family, the one who remained forever at home, looking after the aging parents. At first, I was just intrigued by my friendship with this fiery, young man with whom I shared so many interests. Often tongue-tied with other people, I marvelled at how easy it was to talk to him. I think others noticed before I did that our friendship was beginning to grow, but it wasn't long until we began to talk about a future together. When John asked for permission to marry, however, Father made it clear that he had hoped for something better for me, better than this penniless young man of questionable background.

Rumours about him made their way around the sm&
society of architects and builders. He was hot-tempered and
impulsive. He had left a good position working on the rebuilding
of Leeds Castle when a workman had called him "that little
Cockney." He had articled with a number of firms until he finally
settled with William Ford in London, an arrangement made a
little easier perhaps since that Ford had married John's sister,
Sarah.

But it was my mother who took me aside and talked to me
about the questions surrounding John's background, cloudy
stories about his birth that would follow him all his life. "Born
on the other side of sheets" was whispered by one of my aunties,
sniffing over her mending, with little attempt to hide from my
hearing.

It was true that John was really quite poor, having just his
salary from his work, no money of his own, and no family
connections. "All I have," he said, "are my hopes and dreams."

I was quite caught up in his dreams and very happy about
the idea of marrying him.

"Are you very sure?" Father asked me as we went for a long
walk together. "You're still young and you'll have other
chances."

But I chose to marry John Corby, in St. Leonard's Church,
Shoreditch, witnessed by my mother and father and my sister
Martha.

Our life together started off so well. While we didn't have
much money, John was young with boundless energy and was
already beginning to make his way as an architect in London.
Then times changed. After the wars with France, people thought
everything would be better. And it was, for a time. But now,
everyone was worse off than before. There were poor harvests

almost as if he was looking at me for the first time. "I've seen your work. It's... it's very professional," he said slowly, working out the idea. "And it won't be all work. When we get settled, you'll have time for your painting too."

I hadn't really thought that John had paid much attention to my work on those visits to my father. But he had noticed. He didn't laugh at me at all. That night was really a beginning for us. Emigrating would be more than just moving to another place. It would be starting an adventure, a new way for us to live.

After the meeting, things began to move quickly. Fanny and Sidney, her husband, made their decision and settled in a town called Goderich. They wrote glowing letters about their new life in the colony, and soon, we were planning to make the journey and join them. It was all arranged that we would go to live with them until we got established.

What a flurry of activity there was then. We were used to living in London, a "city of shopkeepers" as it was said, where shop windows were filled with everything anyone could want. We knew even though we were planning to settle in York, it was a small town with few shops and long waits to have things imported from England. With a list from the Canada Company of things we should plan to take with us, we began to shop for our move. We would need everything; clothing for every season, bedding, dishes, cutlery, pots and pans and everything we would need for the kitchen.

With this list in mind, we began our packing. We didn't think we had much, living in a few rooms with our wedding gifts and what we thought of as the necessities in life. But it all added up quickly; everything John would need for his work, his gun collection, my paints and sketchbooks, our books and keepsakes, the gifts that our families insisted on giving us. But John, ever organized, developed a system for packing: labelling our boxes hair hung down over my face. I could not even imagine what we looked like climbing up a rope ladder in the wind. What a way to meet the people with whom we would spend the next two months. It was June 26, the start of our new life!

After all these years, I remember standing on the deck of the *Emperor Alexander,* desperately trying to catch my breath as the ship moved away from the land. Somewhere deep inside me, although I tried to ignore it, was that nagging, little thought. Was this a warning? What if we weren't meant to be doing this at all? Still, I kept telling myself, hadn't my own sister Fanny and her husband Sidney made the same decision? Leaving a short time before us, they had written glowing letters about their new life, and it was all arranged that we would be able to go directly to live with them until we got settled.

The ship sailed slowly along the coast, stopping to pick up passengers as we went, the stormy weather making us seasick and filling me with dread at the prospect of weeks out on the open sea.

The Voyage

J ohn was not a good sailor. At fifteen, he had been sent to sea as a boy "before the mast," as they call it. Being sent to sea so young had always seemed cruel to me, but it was the way to begin a career in the navy, and John had been lucky to get the position. However, it was not to be.

"I never got my sea legs," John said. "The Navy just wasn't for me." Constantly seasick, he had to abandon the sea life. Once, telling me this story, John had remarked with little bitterness, "Nothing is ever wasted. Think of what I learned—navigation, practical geometry, marine surveying. You never know when that will come in handy."

Nothing had changed in all those years. John was still seasick and I was not much better. We kept to our cabin a lot of the time and I wondered how we were going to manage living like this for two whole months. It was a tiny space with two berths, a dresser and a little wardrobe. We had brought our own bedding and had been told to bring only a small bag each while all the rest of our luggage would be stored in the hold. The space was crammed, and after a few days of illness, the air was fetid and almost suffocating.

Slowly, our ship sailed around the south coast of England,

tossed in the stormy channel. For much of the first part of the journey, we were confined to our small cabin, only venturing out when the ship stopped along the way to pick up passengers in Margate, then Dover, Portsmouth and the Isle of Wight. We welcomed those stops along the coast where some days, we could leave the ship, explore the port and stop for cream teas in teashops on the high streets or even a decent meal. All along the way, the stormy weather continued to make us seasick and filled me with dread at the prospect of weeks out on the open sea.

Sometimes, when the storms ceased, and the winds died down, and John was feeling better, we ventured out of our room, explored the ship and made the acquaintance of some of the other passengers. Much later, when we were settled in York, we would hear from other emigrants that we were really very fortunate in our choice of ship. Our fellow travellers, people very much like ourselves—young couples, who, faced with hardships at home, had decided to strike out their own in a new land—became great company as the voyage dragged on. Other ships, we would later find out, had only one or two cabins for passengers, which meant that except for the captain and the officers, the passengers were forced to spend the harrowing months of the sea voyage virtually alone.

Our cabin opened onto the saloon, a large, quite attractive space where we would take our meals with the other passengers and pass the time when we began to feel well enough. At the beginning of the voyage, we ate well. There was beef, cabbage and potatoes, vegetables and fruit for supper. Hens were kept in a long boat and, at first, we had fresh eggs every day. The men gathered in the salon, smoking their pipes and talking of their plans for life in the New World. We women, many with their children and even their maids, had a salon of our own.

Of the long, dreary two months on that ship, my memories

are but fragments. I remember the storms and the sickness. Sometimes I can still smell the sea and the growing stench of the crowded ship and the rotting food. I remember the sunsets and the grandeur of the sea. But one terrible day early in the voyage has remained fixed in my mind forever. July the fourth dawned sunny and clear. The ship made another stop, and while it was at anchor, John and some companions decided to go out on a small boat to do some shooting. With several of the other wives, I watched from the deck.

Suddenly the wind came up and, soon, without any warning, the *Emperor Alexander* began to be blown out to sea. Watching from the deck, we were horrified. We screamed to the captain to turn back as the waves grew higher and higher, and the small boat with our husbands in it disappeared from sight. We ran to the mate and begged him to look back for the men, but even when he went to the masthead and searched through his telescope, still he could see nothing.

Then, strangely, as quickly as it had come up, the wind began to subside.

I ran to Captain Boig and cried out, "Please, please turn back! You can't leave them to die!"

The others gathered around him. "Please, please, turn back," they begged.

And finally, as the sun began to set, the captain turned the ship around and went back in search of the men. We waited on the deck, terrified.

At last, we could see the tiny boat bobbing in the sea, the men rowing furiously as they tried to reach us.

The *Emperor Alexander* drew closer and closer to the little boat. Again, we gathered around the captain, begging him to stop and take the men aboard. Slowly, the great ship came to a halt, still pitching and tossing in the sea.

Slowly the men were hauled on board one by one, so benumbed by the cold they could hardly stand.

Shaking with relief, with exhaustion, John and I embraced, little caring if we were making a spectacle of ourselves.

Back in our cabin, after John had finally gone to sleep, I lay staring out of the porthole at the stars, wondering, worrying if this was yet another omen, a sign of worse things to come.

That strange adventure had a least one good outcome. United in our desperate attempts to rescue our husbands, I finally came to know some of the other women with whom I was sailing. We had been somewhat wary of each other at first, quite self-conscious about living at such close quarters with strangers. Although we had our own cabins, we felt already that people were seeing us at our worst, often desperately ill and scarcely able to maintain any semblance of privacy. Now, having shared our adventure, we became true friends at last. As we began to get used to being at sea, we were able to find a place to sit on the deck on good days, sewing or knitting, gossiping as if we had known each other all our lives. I still remember when we discovered that one of the families in the neighbouring cabin was also planning to settle in York. Richard Tuton, a pharmacist travelling with his wife, Sarah, was planning to open his own apothecary and had even investigated possible locations. Stephen Ducat, who was going on to settle in Niagara, had not decided what he would do in the young colony, but he and his wife Elizabeth were brimming with optimism and enthusiasm and were always able to cheer us over the difficult weeks ahead.

Our first adventures on the Emperor Alexander would become the stuff of shared memories for years to come.

"That first day, when you and John came rowing wildly to the ship," someone would begin years later in Toronto over a dinner or at a party. "*Such a frivolous pair!* I thought."

And then someone else would add, "Who would have thought we'd become friends for life?"

Slowly, we began to adjust to life at sea. People organized activities to pass the time. When some of the men volunteered to give talks to entertain us, John chose to speak about his adventures at sea as a young lad and later he talked about architecture. On days when the sea was calm, even he was beginning to feel a little better. We had readings, shared the books we had brought with us and even gathered a group to present a short play. On sunny days, I took my sketch book out on the deck and tried to catch a sense of the sea, the play of light on the waves, the endless, arching sky.

How different our life was from that of the poor people in steerage below Some of the passengers had brought their maids with them, young women who were eager to accept the offer of free passage and the luxury of having a position in the new world. From them we heard about how the travellers there were suffering, in terribly cramped conditions, darkness and filth. When there were storms, their quarters were often swamped with water, their meagre possessions often ruined. The people had to bring their own food and somehow manage to prepare it. Fresh water only lasted a short time. At night, often, we could hear their cries.

No one ever spoke about illness, but rumours were everywhere. In steerage, without help, some poor women died in childbirth, but even so, the maids reported, others were, almost miraculously able to give birth and feed their newborns who were able to survive the voyage. Those who began the voyage old or weak or already suffering from illness had little chance of surviving.

And there was always the threat of the dreaded cholera.

There was a doctor on board, but there was little he could do when sickness came. We knew that several infants had died and many people were severely ill, but no one ever talked about what was happening. Funerals were quite simply a dumping of the body sewn in a sack for the poor or a perfunctory service for the others; the less said, the better.

I remember so clearly the morning when everything changed for me. I woke up to the gentle rocking of the ship. After so many bleak, grey days, sunlight was streaming through our grimy little porthole. Quietly, so as not to awaken John, I climbed down from my bed, dressed quickly and slipped out of the cabin. What a beautiful morning it was! After all these years, I can still see the brilliant, blue, cloudless sky. I can still feel the sting of the salty spray on my skin. And I remember that moment when I looked out over the sea, the huge empty sea all around us. Behind me, invisible after all those weeks, lay England, the Old World, everything we had left behind. Ahead, to the west, the New World, a world of freedom where everything would be possible. Something, almost imperceptible, had changed in me that morning. I realized that I loved the sea. It was almost as if in those moments, I shed something then, a dark cloak that had been enveloping me, filling me with dread, making me see omens and dangers everywhere.

After that, I was up early every morning, striding happily on the deck, walking easily with the roll of the ship, singing to the wind and the slap of the sails. The sailors would smile as I walked by. One tipped an imaginary hat and called out, "Morning, Ma'am. I see you've got your sea legs." And indeed, I had. Looking back, it seems that those magical mornings were some of the happiest of my life.

And I remember the sunsets. Sometimes, there would be an incredibly clear and cloudless sky. In the evening, wrapped in shawls against the cold, we would gather on the deck. A silence would settle over our little group of travellers as we watched the western sky turn pink and gold as the red ball of the sun began to sink slowly into the endless, empty sea. Somewhere, there, beyond the after-glow stretching across the horizon was our destination, that strangely named country, Canada.

The time passed. Supplies dwindled. Tempers frayed. Rumours began to spread that passengers were becoming ill with the cholera. There were times when the ship was becalmed, and it seemed as if we would never sail again. There were huge storms when we despaired for our lives. One time, the captain and his sailors got drunk and quarrelled. and if not for the intervention of John and some of the other men, it seemed as if a dreaded mutiny might have taken place. Food supplies started to dwindle; the hens had long since been slaughtered, fruit and vegetables had disappeared, and although we still gathered for meals in the salon, we were managing on hard biscuits and what was left of mouldy food.

Just when everyone teetered on the edge of despair, we drew near the grand banks of Newfoundland. Chattering excitedly, we gathered on the deck, marvelling at the sight of huge icebergs in the distance. Not far away, many fishing boats were bobbing in the waters; our first sign of people after so many weeks at sea. Some of the men went off in a boat and came back with fresh cod, the first fresh food we had eaten in weeks.

All these weeks, we had been following our progress on a map posted by Captain Boig. We knew that we had entered the Gulf of St. Lawrence and had been disappointed to discover that it was such a huge body of water that there would still be days of sailing until we crossed the gulf and would actually be able to land. This would only be the first of many times when we would realize the immensity of this new world. The sea journey was almost over, but there would still be long days of travel until we finally reached our destination in the city of York.

Finally, the Gulf began to narrow and the *Emperor Alexander* entered the St. Lawrence River. Overwhelmed with emotions—excitement, relief, gratitude, curiosity—we all rushed to the railings to get a glance of our new land. Beside me, I heard whispered prayers of thanks for our safe arrival and I found my own lips moving as well.

It was only much later over dinner that night we learned that our arrival in Quebec City would be delayed because of the cholera. The ship would lay anchor outside the city, where a quarantine centre had recently been set up on a small island called Grosse Ile. No one would be allowed to disembark in Quebec until an inspection had taken place and it was clear that there was no illness aboard. The steerage passengers had to leave the ship, and wash all their bedding and clothes on the island before being allowed to continue. How frustrating after all those weeks at sea, to anchor at the foot of those huge cliffs of the city, but to be unable to disembark. We reached Quebec on the 29th of August, but we were not allowed to finally disembark until September the 4th.

"Be careful when you first walk on dry land," they warned us. And sure enough, when we walked down the gangplank and stood at last on the shore, it seemed as if everything was still rocking. Eventually, the strange feeling began to subside, but for days afterward, it returned every so often, as if our bodies, so long accustomed to the rocking of the ship, could not easily adjust to the solidity of the land.

We had agreed to travel with the Tutons and the Ducats since we were all going to York. We three women gathered together while the men hurried around making sure that all our luggage had arrived safely. John eventually collected all those thirty-eight boxes and pieces of luggage of various kinds that we had so carefully packed months ago.

Then we had to go to the Custom House. The Customs officer looked at us dubiously, and at first it seemed as if they were going to make John open all the boxes we had brought with us.

But John was ready for him. He opened the notebook he had cleverly brought with him and being at his most polite, he offered a suggestion. "Sir," he said. "I have itemized everything in the boxes and I have here a system for identifying them. Perhaps you might allow me to demonstrate."

The officer nodded somewhat warily, and allowed John to identify one of the boxes, open it and prove to the officer that indeed the inventory was exact. One more box was opened and then, with a sigh, the officer wrote up a bill, charged us two shillings, sixpence duty and let us go on our way.

Arriving at Quebec was only the beginning of our journey in Canada. It had been decided that the boxes were to be shipped directly to Toronto, but we had to board a steamboat which would take us to Montreal. The great river became narrower as we approached the city nestled at the base of a mountain we could see in the distance. How tantalizing it was. At each stage, when it seemed as if our journey was over, we would discover that there was still so much further to go. We stayed overnight in Montreal at an inn, went by another coach passed by the rapids at Lachine and finally boarded the steamer, *William the Fourth,* which would carry us, finally, to York.

How long? How long has it been since the last time I was writing? Hours? Days? Somehow, I hold on to my story. In my dreams, I see myself, that young woman, pale, worn from the long journey, but filled with hope, Oh, so filled with hope.

It is the end of summer, and yet on this day, the heat is so oppressive. After all these years, it is so often on days like this, that I remember what it was like on that first morning in York.

The Arrival

September 14, 1832

I t was horribly hot. I was dressed in the stylish, grey travelling outfit I had chosen carefully in London and packed so that I could find it. Something fresh and clean for the new world. Now my heavy clothes clung damply to my skin. Beads of sweat trickled down the back of my neck.

"Heat!" I remember thinking. "Nobody told us about the heat."

We had heard about the cold and the snow, but this heavy, oppressive heat was a shock, almost as if I had been struck by a heavy weight. It was to be only the first of the many surprises and disillusionments I would experience during that wretched first year.

I was sitting on the deck of the steamer, surrounded by all the belongings we had brought with us from England. The moment we docked at the little harbour of the town of York, porters swarmed onto the boat, pushing and shoving, shouting, competing with one another to help the passengers unload their luggage. Runners from the hotels also hurried aboard. They carried signs and called out, trying to lure guests to their inns. It was all very loud, noisy and confusing.

Our new friends were all ready to disembark; the Duckets travelling directly to Niagara, where they had planned to settle, and the Tutons going off to find a hotel in town. With so much baggage and not being exactly sure of how to proceed, John decided to go ashore and find out the best way to get to Goderich, where Fanny and her husband had settled.

"You had better stay here, Jemima, and watch the luggage," he said, "until I get everything settled."

"Are you quite sure you will feel secure waiting alone?" Sarah asked anxiously as she prepared to leave.

"I will be quite fine, and John will be back very soon," I assured her with a bravado I really didn't feel.

"Just sit here, my dear and watch everything," said John. And with that, he left me on the deck in the hot sun while he strode off into town.

The bay behind me was very busy. There were barges and steamers and schooners with two tall masts.

"Look over there, Ma'am." One of the sailors pointed out a timber raft.

It was a floating camp of logs so large that it had sails and a shack built on it. Later we would learn that this was the way they brought timber from the great forests to ships like the one that had brought us to Canada. The bunks where the steerage passengers had slept were stripped away and the holds filled with timber and furs for the voyage back to England.

Restless, I looked out at the little town in front of me. It was so small! Was it possible that we had come so far for this? Not far away, I could see a small fish market. Even on the boat, I could smell the fish, much of it already left too long in the hot sun, and hear the fishwives calling out their wares. I sniffed again. It was not fish, that I was smelling, but something rank and heavy. A stench that I would soon discover permeated the whole town.

One of the porters noticed my reaction. "Terrible isn't it?" he said, grimacing. "Yah never get used to it, ma'am. But don't worry. It'll disappear once cold weather sets in and all the stink begins to freeze."

There were several other wharfs beside us and beyond them, a little row of buildings strung along the shore; one quite large and impressive, built of brick. But as for the rest, just little, one storey wooden houses and even some huts.

Several streets were laid out, leading away from the harbour, and lined with more small buildings, and beyond that, there was nothing but trees. In the distance, the land rose up from the flats near the shore, the trees blurring into a gentle, hazy blue.

Soon most of the passengers left the boat, and still John had not come back. The crew had gone ashore and the porters who had swarmed onto the deck when we first arrived had gone as well. A strange quiet settled over the ship. In spite of myself, I began to worry. All those dark thoughts I had tried so hard to ignore returned. I was so shocked by the smallness of everything, by the emptiness. Had we made the wrong decision to come to this strange, wild place?

I was tired and thirsty and hot.

Then, all of a sudden, I saw John, equally hot and dishevelled, coming up the gangplank.

He was not alone. Behind him, a woman who seemed at first oddly familiar walked, almost stumbling, slowly. I arose, shaking, not wanting to believe what I was seeing.

It was Fanny! A thin, pale, defeated version of the beloved sister whom I had last seen setting off for Canada in such high spirits. There were great dark circles under her eyes.

She clasped a thin little boy by the hand.

Behind her, his head bowed in shame, Sidney boarded the

ship.

We stood facing one another on the deck, at first in such shock that neither of us was able to say a word. My stomach was churning. I struggled to catch my breath. Then I leaned forward and took her in my arms.

My words, when I was finally able to speak came out in disjointed bits. "Fanny—Oh, Fansi!" The name we called her when she was little tumbled out of my lips. "How?... What happened? You're here... in York..."

Fanny began to cry, burying her tear-stained face on my shoulder. She was so thin that as I held her, she felt almost like a little bird. Her voice was muffled. Between sobs she began to speak.

"It's been so terrible, so terrible. The baby took sick, there is no money for a doctor. He... he died. And you see little Alfie, I'm so afraid for him too..."

"But I don't understand, everything was all arranged. The letters you wrote...."

"Lies, all lies." She was crying loudly now. I could not comfort her.

John came and drew me away. He spoke in a low voice. "Leave her. I'll tell you all I know later, when we're alone. Now we just have to find a way to deal with all of this."

"But what on earth happened to them?" I gasped.

John shook his head. "I have no idea. But there'll be time enough to find out once we get settled."

Reeling with the shock of the meeting, I tried not to stare at Fanny. She was so weak. She could barely stand, while I kept thinking of the pretty, vivacious sister I remembered. Her skin had taken on a sickly, yellowish tone and her once lustrous hair hung limply to her shoulders. Their child was so ill and Sidney and Fanny were so shaken that I later found out that John's first task was to set about the new town to find a doctor for him.

It was difficult to even sort out what I felt, as if I had been dropped into the middle of something I couldn't begin to understand. All our careful plans were shattered. Our world was turned upside down. Now far from going on to Goderich, to stay with the Mountcastles, we were now faced with trying to look after them as well. They were so truly devastated that it was impossible to be angry with them, but I could barely suppress that sense of foreboding that I had felt at the beginning of our journey. Were my worst fears for our future coming true?

The porters had long since gone off with other passengers, but John managed to find some of the crew still lounging around the wharf. Somehow he was able to cajole them into helping unload our luggage, sent one of them to find some porters, and, at last, finally, with the dejected Mountcastles in tow, I was ready to take my first step unto my new home.

It was worse than anything I could have imagined! The heat was still so oppressive. With porters carrying our luggage, we straggled up a dusty path to the street I had been able to see from the boat. Fanny and Sidney followed us holding the weeping little Alfie. John had been able to find lodging for us in a hotel and to get there, we walked along another dusty and crowded street. There were no sidewalks and everyone crowded together, people, horses and carts, mangy looking dogs searching for food and farmers bringing their animals to market. And the stench! The mingling of waste—animal and worse—things were rotting in the relentless heat! I still remember how I felt myself recoiling in shock. It was difficult to breathe.

Shaking my head sadly, I remembered, a moment on the *Emperor Alexander*. Becalmed on a warm afternoon, we had been sitting on the deck sharing with other passengers our hopes for life in the new land.

A sailor, overhearing, had teased us in his strong Cockney accent.

"Cor, lady," he had laughed. "Wot ever 'appens, you'll be breathing clean air, at least."

Little did he know how awful this air would be! Later some of the townspeople we met explained that it was the rapid growth of the little settlement that was causing the problem. It's growing too fast for us to keep up with, they said. And soon, into the future, John would be one of the people who helped to find a solution. But for now, that first impression of York would be forever tainted with that appalling smell, and the wailing of little Alfie, tired and hungry and sick.

At last we came to Grey's Inn, a solid-looking two-storey, white frame building near what we later discovered to be Market Square. There was an inviting, well-furnished parlour off to one side of the entrance where John settled Fanny, Alfie and me while he and Sidney looked after the luggage.

A tall woman whom I judged to be the innkeeper's wife greeted us and then disappeared into one of the back rooms. Shortly afterwards, a young girl with flaming red hair in pigtails brought us some tea. There was a large teapot with a bright crimson tea cosy, pretty, pink, china teacups and a plate of warm biscuits with jam and butter. A loud sigh escaped my lips at the familiar sight. After the shock of finding the Mountcastles, the smells and dust of the little town, at least, somewhere there was a touch of home.

Fanny sat, holding and trying to comfort the little boy, as she drank her tea. At last, I got up my courage to ask her what had happened. Tears welled up in her eyes and she just shook her head. At last, she began to speak in bits, in garbled sentences as if even she could not make sense of it all.

"It... it wasn't what they said—Goderich—it is nothing. A

handful of houses, a tavern, a port that was started and never finished. We had nowhere to stay. We had the land, you see, and ...” She stopped, overcome and unable to go on.

“We... Sidney... it cost so much money... And then came the winter. The baby took sick. We had to find a doctor. ... We have nothing left. All the things we bought. So foolish. What need did we have with your beautiful carving knife in a hovel in the woods? We had no food to carve.”

I didn't press her anymore. John would probably learn the story from Sidney, and somehow, we would piece everything together. I thought also that John would be very angry about what had happened, but much to my surprise, and relief, it was quite the opposite. He was very sympathetic and immediately made arrangements for the Mountcastles to stay in the hotel with us until things became more settled.

Grey's Inn turned out to be a very fortunate choice. There were a number of clean, comfortable bedrooms, a warm parlour and a large dining room. With great relief, John and I finally settled in our own room with a chance to talk. I was so anxious to learn everything that had happened.

“I asked someone where to find some transport to get us to Goderich and they directed me up a street called Church Street,” he began, “a busy street with lots of shops.”

“As I walked along, I glanced in one of the windows. And, suddenly, there in the window of what turned out to be a pawn shop, what did I find but a very handsome carving knife and fork that looked somewhat familiar. I went over to have another look and I realized with a shock that it was the one we gave the Mountcastles before they left England. The very one! I knew it by the unusual marking on the handle. I'll tell you, Jemima. I can still feel the shock of it. Of course, I had to go inside and there I found Fanny, looking half starved, the poor child and Sidney! I stood there staring, like one transfixed. They looked at me blankly at first, scarcely believing their eyes. The child was so ill I immediately asked someone to find a doctor for him and there was nothing to be done except to bring them with us."

"It's so strange," I said. "Meeting that way. Almost as if it was destined to happen."

"Almost as if it were meant to be," John agreed.

"And, what now?" I asked, "We've just arrived ourselves. How can we possibly look after them as well?"

"We'll manage somehow, Jemima. Give us time to get things sorted. It'll all work out you'll see." I remember, at that moment, feeling a great sense of pride in John. He could have been angry about the way things were working out and our having to take on the burden of looking after the Mountcastles, but he seemed to relish the challenge and his optimism helped to calm me a little.

It took me a long time to fall asleep that first night, Fanny's thin, drawn face and the sad eyes of the little boy haunting me. But I must have fallen, at last, into a fitful sleep because I woke suddenly, confused, wondering at first where I was. I got up, opened the curtains and looked out for the first time over my new home.

I remember that first morning with such clarity, almost as if I am watching a play taking place before my eyes.

The Tutons were also staying at Grey's and John and Mr. Tuton had planned to get up early and set off to visit the office of the Canada Company to get advice about finding lodging. Fanny was busy looking after Alfie and quite honestly, after our harrowing meeting the day before, I felt almost reluctant to see her until we had all calmed down at little. So Sarah and I were left on our own and we were just beginning to discuss our plans when the innkeeper's wife approached us with the young girl who had served us our tea.

After greeting us with a cheery "Good morning," she drew the girl close to her and said, "This is my Jennie. If you ladies would like a walk around our little town, Jennie can certainly show you around."

What a lovely idea, we thought. We immediately agreed, returned to our rooms, put on our bonnets and met Jennie who was eagerly waiting for us at the door of the inn. She was a slight bit of a thing, with piercing blue eyes, freckles and that red hair tied in pigtails from which wispy strands of hair kept escaping. We set off, with Jennie almost skipping along beside us.

The heat seemed to have broken a little and the morning air was quite fresh. Even the odours I had noticed the day before didn't seem quite as pungent.

"This here is the east end," said Jennie waving her hands around. "And that's Front Street, 'cause it's at the front." Jennie seemed to have done this before and waited for some kind of response to her little quip. We just sighed and glanced at each other, but she continued undaunted.

"Well, it is the front of the town on the bay, and those are called front lots—where all the big mucky-mucks live."

What have we gotten ourselves into we wondered.

"Governor Simcoe, you know, gave all the best land to his friends so they could look out at the nice views."

Sure enough as we walked west along Front Street, we noticed several fine houses with lovely gardens. Jennie told us the names of the owners, but at that time the names meant nothing to us.

Opposite, in the harbour, were the wharfs we had seen on our arrival with all the activity of a busy port.

Jennie continued her chatter as we walked along.

"Did you know this town used to be called Toronto? It's an

Memories of busy London, with its two million people; the shops on Oxford Street, their windows filled with enticements, flitted through my mind. I tried hard to push those thoughts away. We had chosen to come to this place to start a new life. There was no use to dwell on memories.

We were quite weary from our walk when Jennie finally brought us back to the Inn.

"Anything else you want to know, just ask me," she said, as fresh as she had been when we started out. She had certainly given us a lot to think about.

After Jennie left, I sat in my room thinking about what we had seen. Somehow, in my imagination, while planning our journey, I saw York as a little English town, something like Staines, where I grew up. Instead, it was, in reality, a little outpost on the edge of civilization, a ramshackle collection of houses, a few imposing buildings, and a handful of shops. It was, I had read, only forty years since John Graves Simcoe had moved the capital of the little colony from Newark near the American border and had laid out the plans for the new settlement. And then, it wasn't just the parliament; much of the older town had also been burned by the Americans as well. I just hadn't expected it to be so small, so empty.

There was little time for such reflection. The important thing we had to think about was finding a place to live and very quickly the plan we had made on the ship with the Tutons was put into action. John and Mr. Tuton found a suitable property on King Street. Tuton would open his pharmacy there and we would take the second floor for our flat until we could find a proper house. The only problem was that this flat had been rented separately and the lease wouldn't be up until the spring. There was, however, a large kitchen and an attic, and having no idea what a Canadian winter would be like, we agreed to make do with those two rooms until the spring. John found a small flat for the Mountcastles and we agreed to help them out until John could help Sydney sort out his affairs. What an about-face it was! Our plan was to join our family and settle with them in Goderich, and now here we were, responsible for them and trying to find our way in York.

Still, it was a comfort to have Fanny nearby in this strange little town.

We found a place to store most of our belongings and cheerfully moved into our new lodgings.

Looking back, I see how willfully blind we were. We saw it as an adventure, little realizing how horrible our choice of housing would be.

It was a strange time. We didn't really have a home, so there was little for me to do, no boxes to unpack, no household to set up. Fanny, too, was living in a tiny flat, feeling uprooted and restless. We spent much time walking about the town, visiting the little market daily, almost for something to do. Little Jennie also seemed to make herself a part of our life. If she saw us passing the inn, she would often coax her mother to let her leave her work and come along with us. She would regale us with her lively stories and gossip about the people in the town.

In no way was I prepared for the filth of the town. The stench had literally struck us when we first arrived on that sweltering day in September. At every street corner, we saw stagnant pools of water so filthy they were covered with a slimy, green film from which dreadful smells arose. Local writers wrote articles about the horrible conditions in the town and danger of the cholera which had followed us across the sea, but it seemed that little was being done to make improvements. As the days passed and the weather began to cool, the stench seemed to lessen a little, but it still pervaded everything.

After London, it was so difficult to get used to the dirt roads. There were no sidewalks. The roads were dust when it was dry and after a rainstorm, they simply turned into streams of dirty, churning mud. No wonder they called it "Muddy York."

Soon it was autumn. Nights became cooler and that oppressive heat we had experienced on our arrival finally disappeared. All at once, the leaves began to turn; maple trees became a blaze of red, crimson and scarlet. There were incandescent yellows and deep golds and the sky on sunny days was a brilliant blue. It was wonderful, so different from the gentle, misty autumns we had known. John and I felt invigorated and optimistic. We went for long walks, together, happily exploring the new town and venturing out into the woods outside the town. John took a notebook with him on our walks, making sketches and jotting down ideas.

"This is going to be quite a town soon, you'll see," he said. "There's only nine thousand people here now, little more than a village. But emigrants like us are streaming in every day."

He could already imagine little King Street growing up, new buildings with shops and coffee houses like the ones in London, open land north of Lot Street becoming built up with new houses.

On one particularly beautiful day, John hired two horses from a nearby stable, and since it had been dry and the roads were good, we headed up Yonge Street and out into the country.

At the top of the hill, we turned around and looked at the little town spread out beneath us. We could already pick out landmarks, the steeples of churches and Fort York at the far edge of the town. Beyond the town, the sparkling lake was dotted with white sailing ships and plumes of smoke rising from the busy steamboats.

"Look over there," said John, pointing west. "There is so

much land, mostly forest. This is just the beginning. One day, we're going to have land of our own. You'll see."

Then he reached over and took my hand. "It will be good here, Jemima. A new life. Good for us."

We rode on, out past the sparse farms and into the dark forests.

John's words hung in the cool, crisp air. There it was. The thing that was unspoken.

But there, always there.

Fanny and Sidney were still with us. Alfie was recovering and growing stronger every day. A baby had died in Canada, but now Fanny was with child again.

Sarah Tuton, my only friend in York, was going to have a child in the spring. "My little Canadian," she would say, gently stroking her growing belly.

But for us, there was only the waiting. Words unspoken. Disappointment. Months passed, and then years. I was thirty years old. We had been married for five years, and still there was no child.

It had been a lovely warm day, but it cooled quickly as the sun began to set and we turned back and returned to town.

After that, we took advantage of those beautiful days by going out riding as often as we could. One morning we rode out along the beach, out beyond the end of the town and past Fort York. We were ambling along, chatting as we rode, when suddenly, feeling like a mischievous young girl again, I leaned over to John, laughing, and cried out, "Catch me, if you can." Urging my horse on, I sped ahead with John chasing after me. My bonnet flew off my head and fell to the sand. My hair became undone and I felt the wind rushing through it as it tumbled down my back.

Sunlight danced on the lake beside us: before us and all

around beyond the shore, there was nothing but forest and the cloudless, blue autumn sky. I felt so free, so filled with joy, so at peace.

I raced along, laughing, hearing John racing behind me. At last he caught up, laughing and slowing down the pace.

"All right. You win!" he called out. Coming up close, he leaned over and kissed me. "A reward for the winner."

We turned and walked the horses slowly back to town, both of us not wanting the moment to end.

I have a large bruise on my arm. I don't know where it came from, perhaps I fell. It seems to have happened to me before, but I don't remember. "Be careful, Aunt," Ellen says this morning. "You don't want to fall again."

I just want to go outside for a walk as I have always done. It is one of those perfect early fall days, the sky, a bright, aching blue. Beyond the trees, the lake is sparkling in the distance. Ellen walks beside me, taking my arm, as if I were an old lady. I try to shrug her off, but she is persistent. The garden needs tending. I try to bend down to pull a weed here, clip a dead flower there, but what used to be so easy, is so difficult now. I shake my head sadly and walk on.

When we come home, I take advantage of Ellen's worry and pretend that I am more tired than I really am. I go upstairs to rest, knowing that no one will bother me for a while.

I have time to write in peace.

Getting Started

The cooler weather filled John with energy and he quickly began to make inquiries and look for work. York was a small town then, and there was much to be done, but John needed to find someone to help him find his way. John and Sidney had a friend named John Dibbs, who had emigrated the year before. They decided to go to the nearby town of Hamilton to see if he might be of help. That visit was a turning point for us.

When John and Sidney returned home, they burst through the door, brimming with excitement. As soon as I brought them some tea they began to describe their adventures.

"You cannot believe our good luck," John began. "While we were visiting Mr. Dibbs, who should happen to call but another gentleman, an acquaintance of his. When I was introduced to him as an architect, he said, 'Well, sir. This is most fortunate. I have just received a letter that will be of the utmost help to you. None other than the Honourable Peter Robinson, the Speaker of the Legislative Council himself, has asked me to send to him the first architect who should arrive in Hamilton. It seems that you, sir, are that man.' Before leaving, he was kind enough to write me a letter of introduction to Mr. Robinson."

John then described how he, Sidney and Mr. Dibbs had intended to go to Goderich to try to settle Sidney's affairs, but they got only as far as a village called, importantly, Paris. "Nothing more," he added, "than a crossroads. Two houses, a tavern and a farm belonging to a Mr. Caprone. But again, luck was surely with us."

They called on this Mr. Caprone, and the visit ended with John agreeing to survey and lay out the land for a village. For his services, he would take a town lot of five acres. This was to be the first piece of land we would ever own!

We had arrived a few short weeks before, were barely settled in our new home, and already we would soon be the owners of five acres of land in a new town in the colony!

Ever impulsive, John was ready to go and present himself to Mr. Robinson immediately. Again, luck was with us and another new friend of his advised him to prepare some drawings to show his abilities as a draughtsman.

The garret where we were going to spend the winter had a skylight which at first seemed to be a good thing. John set up his easel under it to take advantage of what little light there was and began with great energy to prepare his drawings. He made designs for everything he could think of that would be needed in this new town. Quickly, he made plans for log cabins, frame and brick buildings, churches, villas hotels and rows of stores. Drawings of the lake, paintings of the gorgeous autumn colours, and vivid street scenes soon began to pile up in our small home.

Then in November, the rains came and the roof began to leak. In the little town, the unpaved streets became thick with mud and whole days passed when we were unable to venture outside. John was working with a frenzy, seldom leaving his work.

And then, it began to snow. At first, we were quite thrilled with it. The little streets outside looked beautiful with a layer of crisp white crystals that covered all the rubbish and glistened in the pale winter sun. We tried to ignore the fact that the snow sometimes seeped in through the crack in the roof, making our already chilly room even colder.

In no way, were we prepared for winter in Canada. All too soon, we realized that it was going to be far worse than anything we could have imagined. It had sometimes snowed at home, in England, but it was usually light and quite pretty and we just stayed home until it melted. It never occurred to us to buy warm boots or extra clothes for the cold. In truth, we would have been completely house-bound if Jennie hadn't appeared at the door one gloomy day in November. "Ma sent me over to take you and Mrs. Tuton shopping for winter," she announced in a very business-like manner.

"Well, thank you, dear. But I think we'll be just fine," I had answered.

"You won't be able to go out in those," she said, pointing to the stylish leather boots I wore to go about my errands. "Here, Ma made you a list. She says, you English ladies won't have any idea what our winters will be like."

So Jennie convinced me that we definitely needed her help and off we went to go shopping. Jennie helped us to pick warm, high winter boots lined with fur, warm flannel petticoats, and thick woolen jackets. There would be many times that winter when we would be so grateful to the Greys for all the help they gave us.

The snow started in early December and never melted. Each time it snowed, the banks that lined the street grew higher and the roads more difficult to navigate. Still, we were amazed to discover that people in Toronto had a wonderful ability to enjoy winter. There were beautiful days when the snow stopped, the sun came out and the sky over the city was an icy, piercing blue. Bundled up in warm clothing, young children tumbled out of their houses to play in the snow. On bright afternoons, King Street was busy with young ladies riding up and down in horse-drawn sleighs. Warm under huge fur rugs, they giggled and laughed and waved merrily to their friends. Soon Lake Ontario froze solid and we were so taken with the picturesque scene of all the people skating and sleighing on the lake, that John brought paper and made some sketches for a lovely painting he made of the scene. We were beginning to feel that winter in York might really be quite pleasant, but our neighbours just shook their heads. "The winter's not yet begun," they warned. "Just wait till the first real storm."

That first storm came with no warning, beginning early in the morning. All day, it fell constantly in great, big heavy flakes. Then the wind came up, furiously tossing the snow so that it swirled as it fell, making the drifts look almost like sheer curtains being tossed about.

I sat at the kitchen window, huddled in a bundle of shawls and blankets, looking down at King Street, which was already covered by an earlier snowfall and was soon impassable. Sleighs disappeared. There was no one about save for the odd horseman battling the storm, crouched close to his mount's neck. Sometimes, some poor straggler would struggle by on foot, fighting against the wind as if it were a living thing.

Later, we would learn how to live through the Canadian winter, to put down food in the summer and fall, so that it would last through the cold, to make sure we were ready to manage through days when we would be "snowed in," as they called it. But we were ignorant that first winter. I had bought only a small amount of food in the market—it was already too difficult to carry heavy baskets through the snow. I would soon learn to pay young boys to deliver our purchases to our home.

Later in the day, the snow turned to icy rain and the huge

mounds of snow were soon covered by a thin coating of ice.

It continued to snow all through the night.

By the next morning, the city was an empty, deadened place. The wind had blown huge snow drifts against the doors, the street outside looked like an empty barren field. Inside, it was so cold that there was ice on the inside of the window panes, and the water in a glass that I had left on the table in the kitchen was frozen solid.

Later in the day, we saw a few brave souls venture out down the street on snowshoes. Schools were closed and the children came out to play. A neighbour came by to check on us and see how we were managing. "The market will be closed," he said. "It will be a while till the farmers can get into town, and a few days until the vendors can even get over to open up."

The next day there was a knock at the door. The young boy who worked at Grey's Inn presented us with a large basket of food, the aroma of the freshly baked bread filling the room as soon as he came in from the cold.

"Mrs. Grey worried that you wouldn't be ready for this." He was a young lad and he puffed himself up quite importantly. "Jennie said to tell you she was sorry that she couldn't come out herself. Too much snow and ice. But *I* can manage it."

I tried to keep my spirits up, tried to make myself think of this as an adventure, a difficult time which would soon be over. But one freezing day, as the snow blocked out even the faintest light from the skylight and bitter winds blew in through cracks in the wall, I looked down at the chilblains on my red, frozen hands and began to cry. I sobbed and sobbed until I couldn't stop. John, huddled under shawls and blankets at his easel, came and held me close, wrapping me up in yet another layer of warmth.

"It'll soon be over, you'll see," he murmured. "Jemima, I promise you. One day I'll build you the most beautiful house you've ever seen, up on a hill somewhere. All this, will be behind us."

At night, we huddled in our bed, with practically everything we owned heaped over us in an effort to keep warm. Sometimes snow seeped in through cracks in the roof and the wind howled around us. On one particularly terrible night in the middle of a storm, practically shaking with the cold, I remember saying to John, "If only Mother could see us now." The utter absurdity of the scene seemed to strike us both; the piles of clothing on top of us, wind rattling the eaves, snowflakes falling on our faces. We started to laugh and laugh until we couldn't stop. We were both imagining our mothers, in their neat little English houses, horrified at the way we were living.

We clung to each other as the laughter subsided; we were poor and cold; but we had never been so close.

I was not young when we married. I had none of a young girl's giddiness and perhaps too much self-consciousness. I always thought of myself as plain, nothing like Fanny who was always the pretty one. At first, I know that I was shy with John, in that most private part of our lives. At the beginning, I was terribly embarrassed. As time passed, I grew more comfortable, but I was never at ease. There was always a slight distance between us.

We drew farther apart during those months on the ship. We slept on hard bunks, in a tiny cabin that grew more and more suffocating all the time and faced endless bouts of sickness—none of that led to any desire for closeness of any kind.

But there, in that ridiculous attic, in the freezing cold of our first Canadian winter, something thawed between us. One night, as I shivered under all my clothes and we clung to each other to keep warm, John whispered in my ear, "My little Jemima, there is only one way to be really warm." His teeth chattered as he spoke. We both started to laugh until we couldn't stop. After that night, we only had to look at each other and say coyly, "It's really awfully cold" to send us happily into each other's arms

Throughout the winter, John continued to work, sometimes shaking so much in the cold it was difficult to hold a pen. There was little for me to do. We had a kitchen with a stove where it was warm, but it had little light and I often found myself huddling upstairs under the window reading as John worked.

One afternoon, John looked up at me and asked what I was reading. I said it was a novel I had bought in the little bookshop on King Street, two years out of date in London, but very popular in York.

"Perhaps you might try reading aloud to me, Jemma," he said. "It might help to keep my mind off the cold."

And so, we spent our days together huddled in the cold and me reading until I had finished the new books I had purchased and all the old ones I had brought with us from England. A new rhythm developed in our days. If the weather was fine and the streets passable, I would slip out to the shops and come home to prepare our supper. And then, I went upstairs to read to John.

The stack of sketches had grown. Now came the task of turning them into finished drawings to share with potential clients.

Somehow, we got through that winter. Thank goodness we were young and had that energy and optimism of youth that helps to overcome obstacles, however difficult. In March, we were finally able to move into our apartment in the Tuton's building. Now we had a proper space for John's work and we were able to lay out a studio that even had space for me. It was a long time since I had done any drawing and after that long dark winter, I was so eager to make a fresh start. Before the winter set in, I had filled several notebooks with sketches of our walks in the country, and now I began to turn them into drawings. Every day, I hurried to finish my homework and found time in the afternoons to paint while John did his work. One afternoon, I had just settled down at my easel when John came over to have a look at what I was doing.

Puffing on his pipe, John stepped back and regarded my work, "You're really just as good an artist as I am. Your father taught you well," he said.

I just laughed, but John stood there, very quiet, thinking.

"Jemima, do you remember what you said when we were thinking of coming here—that you could help me?"

I did remember the conversation, but I had never really thought anything would come of it. Now I could see John warming to the idea, thinking out loud.

"What if—well, what I mean is—if we were to work together, you could help me finish some of these. You could do what you did for your father—complete the drawings—and I would be ready for my meeting with Colborne so much sooner."

"I don't know," I began, about to brush off the idea.

But John was already pacing about the room as he always did when he was excited about something.

"I'll do the preliminary sketches, you see. And then we'll talk about them, share ideas, make changes and then you'll take over."

John's excitement was catching. I could see him planning ahead.

"It will be so much more efficient, you know. You'll put the finishing touches on the drawings and I'll be able to move on to something new. We'll have our drawings ready in no time.

A pattern soon developed. We worked so well together – almost able to read one another's thoughts, draw, and paint as if we were one artist.

I felt as if we were no longer just man and wife, but something had shifted. We were now two halves of a whole— one artist moving onto heights one person alone could not reach.

John felt it too. There was a new energy about him. He hummed as he worked, rapidly moving from idea to idea, until at last, all was ready.

That terrible winter was behind us. We were ready to find out what that little muddy city of York had to offer us.

Success

March, 1833

W hen spring came, everything began to change.
I never did get used to spring in Toronto, or really the lack of it. At first, we expected it to be like England, a long, slow awakening starting in March, flowers beginning to bloom as the days warmed. But the winter dragged on through March. Piercing cold, blizzards, warm spells that turned the road to icy mud only to freeze again.

April was not much better. The snow melted leaving behind all that lay hidden all winter – animal leavings, rotten garbage, dead leaves and grasses. But mostly the cold continued.

Sometimes there was a tantalizing taste of sun and warm weather. Then the next day plunged us back into the cold. Then suddenly, it was May. Everything sprung into bloom in a rush, as if even the flowers knew that, here, the hot days wouldn't last and they would have to hurry before it would be winter again. And so it went, almost overnight, from winter to those horrible hot sticky summer days. By mid-May we were often complaining of the heat and wishing to find some way of escaping from it.

But in that first year, spring really was the beginning for us. Our little garret looked more like an artist's studio, with paper strewn everywhere, sketches, discarded drawings, all sorts of bits and pieces. We kept the final copies carefully on our one table in the kitchen and ate our meals perched on little chairs far away from the work. When everything was complete, together we prepared John's presentation and the letter of introduction he had received on that visit to Hamilton. I insisted that he visit the barber, while I brushed his best jacket and polished his boots. Off he went, at last, freshly shaven, with his portfolio under his arm and his letter of introduction to meet the Honourable Peter Robinson. I paced around our little room. Finally, I heard him bounding up the stairs and went rushing to open the door.

Silence.

I gradually realized John was angry—so angry; he was almost shaking, unable to say anything at all.

"He was ENGAGED!" he shouted at last. "Can you imagine, as if this was some kind of a social call. I waited for a while, but it seemed to be of no use. I finally left my drawings and the letter and said that I would come back next week."

We were so filled with disappointment, but there was nothing to do but wait out the week.

We went visiting, took long walks and dreamed about the future.

At last, the time passed and John returned to see Mr. Robinson.

Hours passed and I was waiting anxiously at the door as I heard John on the stairs.

"Jemma! Jemma!" he cried, "We've done it! Mr. Robinson thought so highly of my drawings that he has written a letter to Colonel Rowan, that's the Governor's private secretary. He has asked him to lay the drawings on the Governor's very own drawing room table. Just think, they'll be waiting for him when he sits down to his dinner!"

After he calmed down a little, John began to tell me what

away. When my errands were finished, I often asked her to come back with me for tea. Several times, when we were really sinking into the depths of despair, especially after Fanny went back to Goderich, and the bitter cold seemed unending, Jennie appeared with an invitation to join her family at the inn for supper. And sometime, during those visits, she began to call me "Mrs. H." I have to admit, I was quite taken aback at first. It seemed quite saucy and almost a bit rude to be addressed in this way, by this young snip of a girl. Up till then only John himself sometimes called me Mrs. H, especially when we were working together— it seemed almost too intimate to hear it from her. But this was the way here, in this new colony. Some people said it was the influence of the Americans with their casual ways and some said, it was just the lack of anything that could be called manners. But with Jennie, there was always a smile, a burst of energy when she would appear, and I soon began to look forward to her visits on those dreary days. What might have seemed to others to be much too familiar, I found quite charming.

Jennie was, at fourteen, the youngest of a large family, most of her brothers and sisters quite a bit older than she, grown up and on their own. So it fell to Jennie, who had only a few years of formal schooling to help her mother at the inn. It must have been a hard and a bit of a lonely life for her. It seemed that whenever her work was done, she was always looking for a reason to come by for a visit.

"You've not got much furniture," she sniffed, looking around.

"That will come," I laughed. "John is working on it this very minute."

In the midst of teaching his new students and working on the design for the Block, John somehow found the time to make furniture for us. I had been incredulous when he first suggested this.

town of York. He was very pleased when The Lord Bishop Stewart of Quebec, asked him to draw plans for some small churches and have them lithographed with their specifications.

What should have been our sitting room turned into an office. We set up our drawing boards and began to develop a routine for our work. John quickly made rough sketches and did the first drafts of his plans. With so much work coming in, he was usually working on several projects at the same time. For the clients, he produced coloured drawings of the buildings, and I usually worked on those, finishing off what he had just roughed in. We worked seamlessly together, chatting as we worked. We followed the same pattern when it came to the specifications, John did the preliminary work and I worked on the final copies that were ready for the builders.

At first, John kept the accounts, trying to catch up with making entries into a large ledger late at night when he had finished everything else he was doing. Unanswered letters piled up on the desk, bills and scrawled reminders were mixed in with sketches and plans. Little by little, I took over this task too, as I began to try to impose some order on all the papers, drawings, sketches, plans, and paintings that were threatening to completely engulf our small home. John put up a bit of protest, as if his feelings were a little ruffled, but I think he was really quite relieved to turn a lot of the work over to me. Soon, I added keeping the books for our business to all the other work I was doing.

One afternoon, when I had finished my daily tasks and our dinner was simmering on the stove, I sat down at my new table to do some work on the books. There was a light knock on the door and Jennie let herself in.

Peering over my shoulder with her usual curiosity, she nodded approvingly. "So, you're just like Ma. She does all the books for the inn, you know."

"Does she really?" I asked with some surprise. I remembered meeting Jennie's mother that day when we first arrived and knew that she was involved in running the inn, but I had no idea that she was so involved in the business side of it.

"Oh, yes. Pa always says he would be lost without her. He is very good at running the inn and keeping everything in order. But he always says numbers just go right out of his head."

The work continued to pour in and we began to make plans to move into a new house in the Chewett Block as soon as it was completed. We were very busy, but we decided that since our apartment was so small, I would continue to look after our home and help with all the business as well without the help of a maid.

I set up a schedule with housework in the morning, and business in the afternoon. One morning I was busy doing the washing in a tub in one corner of the large kitchen. There was a knock on the door and thinking it was probably Jennie, I called out and told the caller to come in. The door opened and a tall man whom I had never met entered the room, taking off his hat and looking a little flustered. He introduced himself as the Bishop Stewart and said that he had come to "pay his respects to me" after meeting with John earlier in the morning.

I jumped up, wiping my wet hands on my apron and hastened to greet him.

With a warm smile, he shook my hand and then made the most surprising remark. "I see that your small hands have never been used to this kind of work at home in England."

I really didn't know what to say but I'm sure I must have blushed and I remember feeling quite embarrassed. We exchanged some pleasantries and then the bishop went on his way, saying that he could see that I had a lot of work to do.

Several days later, John came home all smiles. "Well," he said. "You certainly made an impression on the bishop."

"How could I have done that? I was in the middle of the washing when he came."

"That's just it." John rummaged around in his pocket and took out a somewhat crumpled piece of paper. "This is what he said, I wrote it down as soon as he left."

And reading off the paper, John quoted the bishop. "If ladies, when they came to Canada, would unbend as Mrs. Howard has done and perform such work whenever it was necessary, Canada would have a better name than she had."

Well, I was speechless. Not just at the words of the bishop, but at the way John had written them down and quoted them so proudly. How often, in times to come, I would remember those words, John's smile and look, almost of wonder on his face. How truly happy we were in that first tumultuous year.

And yet. Work was coming in almost faster than we could handle it and John was beginning to make a name for himself. We were making new friends, visiting one another, having dinners, and going off on adventures. We began to explore the bush outside the small town, venturing sometimes quite far out into the wilds. John loved to shoot and often went out with friends. In May, we took the steamer, *Canada,* to Niagara and stayed with the Ducats, the friends we had made on our journey to Canada. The Falls were, as John said. "Grand beyond description." We both made sketches of them and then turned those sketches into lovely watercolours.

And yet. The absence was always there. Fanny and Sidney moved back to Goderich and word came that soon Fanny had given birth, a little girl they called Ellen. Sarah Tuton had her "little Canadian," a beautiful little girl named Rosa. I had helped Sarah find a midwife and was with her when the baby was born. But for me, there was only hope... and disappointment.

We had been married for six years.

Politics

1834

"**M**rs. H! Mrs. H!" Jennie came clattering up the stairs and swept in without even knocking. "Mr. Mackenzie is going to make a speech. There's a big crowd at the market. You must come with me and hear him."

"Oh, Jennie. I don't think—"

"I know. You and Mr. H. would be Tories, but please, do come."

Jennie's enthusiasm was so infectious, I finally gave in. I had to admit, I was curious. Politics was everywhere that first summer in York and certainly Jennie's constant chatter about it had made me curious. Apparently, it was all the talk at their inn, and she loved to repeat all the stories she had heard.

At home, in England, we read the gazettes and heard about the doings in Parliament, but it seemed very distant. For the most part, we just went about our daily business and what ever happened in the government didn't seem to touch ordinary people. Here, in little York, it was very different.

One day, Jennie had appeared with a copy of Mr. Mackenzie's newspaper, The Colonial Advocate. She was clearly anxious to talk about the news, so I put the kettle on, made some tea for us and settled down to hear what she had to say.

"He is really angry this time," she said, jabbing her finger on the page where the editorial was printed.

"Look at this," she said. "He calls it the family tree. For the Family Compact."

Parroting what she had no doubt heard at the inn, Jennie explained that Mackenzie wrote about the small group of men who governed the colony. "They're all related, you know," she added, returning her attention to the drawing of the tree.

"They're all on the Legislative Council and they get to make all the laws."

"What about Mackenzie?" I asked.

"He's a Reformer. Like my Pa. People like us, little people, farmers, shopkeepers. They just want to have some say in things."

Jennie left the paper with me and, intrigued, I read more after she had gone.

"What on earth is this doing here?" asked John. The paper was still open on the table when he came home.

"Jennie left it here," I explained.

"I hope she's not filling your head with all this nonsense. They say Mackenzie's a madman. Wants to turn Upper Canada into a little America, with all those radical ideas of his. He's been kicked out of the Assembly three times already, but those farmers keep electing him back in."

John noticed the drawing of the family tree, and like Jennie, he jabbed his finger on the names listed here. "You'd do well to remember, my dear, a number of these men are our clients, And I'd like to have the others come calling as well."

We had been so busy just getting settled, I had never really given any thought to who was actually governing our little colony, but now I was quite intrigued. "What have you heard about them?" I asked.

"Look here," John answered, pointing to the top name on the list. "There's your Bishop Strachan and it seems that some of these folks were his own pupils when he was just a teacher."

"Who do you mean?"

"Like John Robinson, the Chief Justice."

"Any relation to our Peter?"

"His brother."

"And then there's Henry Boulton, the Attorney General. Your Mackenzie goes on about how they are all connected, sit on all the same and generally run things for themselves."

I put the paper away that day, and didn't really give politics another thought until that morning when Jennie came to draw me out to see William Lyon Mackenzie in the flesh.

Filled with misgivings, I let her drag me along to the meeting. All around us, people strode along King Street, heading east toward the market. I saw mothers hustling along their small children, workmen in stained work clothes and maids who had somehow managed some time off or who had stolen the time when their employers no doubt thought they going on some errand.

That I did not see anyone I knew was hardly surprising. It was too late to turn back, and the street behind us was so clogged, it would have been impossible to get through. I just hoped that no one recognized me.

Finally, we reached the market. The square was already packed, a swarming mass, townspeople now joined by farmers who had come to town for market day, dockworkers up from the wharfs, labourers from the mills and factories along the Don river. With the rushing about, the calling and laughter and shouting, it was almost like a village fair.

There was an undercurrent, a nervous excitement,

Everyone had come to hear Mr. Mackenzie, or "Little Mac,"as some of them lovingly called him.

Everyone seemed to be on his side.

Everyone, but me.

A sort of stage had been built up and a group of men stood at the back, waiting expectantly.

Then suddenly, we heard cheering. The men stood aside, and a small man bounded onto the stage. He was the oddest person I had ever seen. He was quite short, much smaller than the men who stood behind him with a very large head, quite out of proportion for his body. This head was topped with very odd looking red hair. Even from where we were standing, I could see clearly that it was a bright, floppy wig.

When he began to speak, it was with a thick Scottish accent which his years in Canada had clearly not softened. It was hard to hear what he was saying, but his audience seemed to already know the main ideas. The speech was punctuated with cheers, calls of agreement, and applause. I could make out the words which we would hear so often in the next few years, Family Compact, Clergy Reserves, equal representation. As he warmed up, he began to spit out names, Bishop Strachan, and Alan MacNab. The names were met with loud boos and hoots and hisses from the audience. As Mackenzie got more and more agitated, his wig flopped crazily on his large head and his eyes blazed wildly.

William Lyon Mackenzie was to play a great role in our own lives and in the town of York. I never forgot my first sight of him.

Jennie never ceased to amaze me. It wasn't just politics that caught her attention. Everything about life in our little town seemed to fascinate her. Newsworthy events, delicious bits of gossip and outrageous stories attracted her equally. Whenever she appeared at my doorstep, pigtails flying and sometimes a smudge on her nose from the tasks she had just been helping her mother with, I knew that I was in for entertainment, maybe a surprise. But nothing quite equalled the story she told me one morning as we wandered along Front Street.

I had just pointed out the cottage John had built for the prominent doctor Christopher Widmer when Jennie turned to me, the corners of her lips turning up in an almost sly smile.

"You know what they say about Dr. Widmer?" she asked, her blue eyes sparkling.

I, truthfully, had no idea.

"They say," she leaned over to me and whispered, "He is a special favourite with the ladies."

"Oh Jennie!" I responded, quite shocked to hear this description from so young a girl. "He's married, isn't he?"

"Yes, and for the second time. And poor Edith barely buried a year!"

"Jennie, really!" I cried out.

"Well, Mrs. H. It's not secret. They had a wee bairn, came early, as they say."

I was very much taken aback by her words. Did she, I wondered, as young as she was, did she even understand exactly what she was saying. "Jennie, how do you know all this?"

"Ah, Mrs. H. I love to listen to it all, makes my day pass more quickly like. Nobody notices me, the girl polishing the glasses or wiping off the table. They all just go on like I weren't there. So I hear it all, the men talkin' all that political blather. Both sides come to us, you know. And the women, all so polite and dressed up and all they do is talk about other people. And me, I just listen. Sometimes, I think it's better than all the books you lend me."

At that moment, it seemed that even Jennie had realized she

had gone a little too far. "Oh, not that I'm not grateful. Mrs. H. I love to read those books."

"Of course, dear. I understand. But, Jennie," I continued. "Perhaps you should be a little careful about what you say. You could find yourself in quite a lot of trouble if you repeat these things to the wrong people"

"Oh, I would never tell anyone but you, Mrs. H. I know it won't go any further."

I needn't have worried about Jennie's indiscretion. I soon learned that stories about Christopher Widmer were apparently the talk of the town. Sarah Tuton heard the stories from one of her new neighbours. Another new acquaintance of mine, on hearing that the doctor was one of our first clients, had even more lurid stories to tell. Not only was Widmer the most important doctor in town, but he seemed to have his hand in everything. Oddly, for a town so given to gossip, Widmer was generally regarded as a fine man and even the most upright people seemed to turn a blind eye to the stories of his private life.

In 1834, there was something much more important than local gossip in the air. You would overhear conversations in the shops and in the market. The local newspapers were filled with it. The main question on everybody's lips was talk of legislation to turn the town of York into a city. Everyone seemed to have a different opinion about what this was all about. Some said it was the moment whose time had come; little York was clearly on the way to becoming an important place with new emigrants streaming in all the time. For others, it was all a plot on the part of the members of the Family Compact to get rid of the Reformers and run the new city the way they wanted. On and on the comments went. I overheard someone say, "It's a trick by those devilish Reformers who want to turn Upper Canada into a little America." Taxes were already a large concern, and many were saying, "As soon as they've got a new city, they'll raise more taxes to pay for it."

Everyone agreed that the town of York was badly managed. We all complained about the raw sewage in the streets, the lack of sidewalks anywhere, the intersection of Yonge and King, the main crossing in the town where you sank to your ankles or even your knees in mud if you had to get through on a rainy day. We had been fortunate to have arrived in the town just as the cholera epidemic that had followed us across the ocean seemed to be abating. But there was always the worry that it would strike again and that the town would again be unable to deal with it. Something clearly needed to be done, and although he was very much opposed to Mackenzie and his Reformers, John was hoping for change in the town.

The change came, at last, in March, with much fanfare and again, much controversy and argument. York was indeed going to become a city, but it would no longer be York. The name of the new city would be Toronto, that strange Indian name that Jennie had mentioned when she showed us around the town on our first day. No one was quite sure of the reason for the change. The settlement had been named York by Governor Simcoe in honour of the Duke of York at the time. By now, however, it was becoming known everywhere as Muddy York, or sometimes little York, to distinguish it from the bustling American city in New York State.

Whatever the reason, there was much celebration, parties and marching in the streets. An election followed and to the surprise of everyone, and certainly shock to some, the Reform candidates received a large number of votes and made up the majority in the new city council. At the very first meeting, they chose the new mayor of the new city—William Lyon Mackenzie! Christopher Widmer became one of the first aldermen of the new city.

And even more, to everyone's surprise, Mackenzie began at once to get things done. One of the very first things the new council did was decide to raise taxes to put down a new sidewalk on King Street. When a group of citizens protested, Mackenzie called a meeting to discuss the decision. The meeting turned into such a riot that it had to be adjourned. The next night, another meeting was held in a room above the meat market. It was there that a horrible accident happened that almost finished the project before it got started. The room was over-crowded and, as the meeting wore on, opponents of the proposal began to rhythmically stamp their feet in anger. The floor—never meant to carry such weight—collapsed and sent the people hurtling down into the butcher shop below. Eight people died, some by the fall and some horribly, by being impaled on the butcher's hooks below.

Mackenzie and the council were determined. The new taxes raised, the plan was made and William Lyon Mackenzie hired my John to be the City Surveyor and to be the one to lay down the new sidewalk.

I couldn't help asking, "Well now what do you think of Mr. Mackenzie?" after John had accepted the job.

"Doesn't mean I like the man," John muttered. "I don't have to agree with him to build his sidewalks, do I?"

"You have to admit, though, that this is a rather odd situation," I observed. "It's Sir John who gives you the very first job in Canada and certainly helps us on our way. And now, you're working for his enemy as well."

"A servant of two masters, you might say."

"It would seem so."

John, who had been working at his plans as we chatted, looked up from his work, and leaned back. "Nothing is ever quite as clear as we might think. People might say that Colborne and Mac are enemies. But every time Mac got elected to the Assembly, the Tories threw him out. It was Sir John who had finally had enough of their shenanigans and found a way to get around them."

I jumped in. "And, if you read Jennie's paper," which is what we called *The Colonial Advocate*, " It's really this Family Compact that he is so angry about, isn't it? He's not against the King, is he?"

"No, he's not," John agreed. "But, he's a wild man. I hope being the Mayor will keep him busy. Otherwise, you never know where his craziness might lead."

If we were busy before, now our little office was a mad house. There were plans everywhere. While John was busy planning the new sidewalk, I tried to keep up with all the other plans for our clients and to keep some order for our work. John finished the plans, supervised the work and, in a short time, the first wooden sidewalk in little Toronto was complete.

The work was finished in July and since it was still light late into the evening, John and I went for a walk along the new sidewalks. It seemed as if half the town was out. Our heels clicked on the newly laid planks as we walked proudly along, smiling, and eavesdropping on conversations as we went.

Over and over again, we heard people commenting.

"This is lovely. We're beginning to feel almost like a real town."

"It's about time!"

"And when are they going to do something about them roads? You can still sink up to your knees in the mud!"

A group of giggling young girls came clattering by, enjoying the sound of their boots on the wood.

Like them, I started to giggle. John looked at me with

surprise. Taking his arm, I leaned over and whispered in his ear. "I want to tell everyone! I want to shout, *John Howard made this! Where would you be without him?*"

"Well," he answered, actually blushing a bit, "You have to thank little Mac as well. He really had to work to push this through."

Then suddenly, he began to laugh too.

"What is it?"

"I just had a thought. We're really Toronto now. We're no longer Muddy York, not in truth nor in name."

He gestured grandly to King Street. The new sidewalks were crowded and the street itself was filled with horses, carts, carriages, stray animals wandering about, people darting back and forth across the road. Just then, a large carriage came roaring down the road, scattering everyone in its way and churning up clouds of dust in its wake. When it passed us by, it left us covered in it.

We looked at each other and started laughing again.

"Well, we still have a long way to go," said John as we turned back to home.

Spring that year was exciting for us. In March, we were finally able to leave our first apartment with its memories of that first terrible winter and move into our first real home—a two story house in the Chewett Block—that was one of the very first buildings that John designed in Toronto.

Now we were able to really settle in. John ordered a stove for the best room so that from now on, we wouldn't have to suffer again in those cold Ontario winters. It was a bright, airy room with large windows that looked out onto busy King Street. When he had time, John continued to make things for our home, including a beautiful bookcase that had two doors with beading on the glass and many other useful things. We also hired a cabinet maker to make a dining room table and chairs, an easel and two drawing boards. Our work was expanding and John was also able to rent a proper office in the same building and to have, at last, a large table with drawers. Here there was enough space for both of us to work.

We were now able to have a maid, so I was freed from the household tasks that had occupied me when we arrived and I was able to give myself completely to working on our projects with John. The business of hiring either a maid or a young man to help with the heavy work around the house turned out to be one of the greatest surprises we encountered in adjusting to our new life in Canada. The first girl we hired was called Mary. Within a week, before she had even begun to settle in, she announced that she was leaving. We were astounded.

The next morning, I went over to Sarah's to tell her what had happened and ask for some advice.

"What did we do?" I asked her. "Mary just left without any explanation."

Sarah, who had hired a maid shortly after Rosa was born, did not seem surprised at all. "Oh, it's just the way things are here," she explained. "It's not like it was at home where servants stay with you forever unless something terrible happens. Here, they come and go as they please. If they like you, they'll stay for a while until something better comes up. If not, off they go."

Later, one of our neighbours told me that this habit had come with the Yankees who came to settle in Upper Canada after the American Revolution. It was an explanation we were to hear for many situations as we got settled. It was certainly disconcerting, but after a while, we got used to the constant comings and goings and never expected anyone to stay for very long.

Ups and Downs

Building the Chewett Block and laying the sidewalks were our first successes, but nothing was quite as exciting as the competition for the design of the new buildings for the Market Block, the busy area at King and Church Streets. At the time, the buildings were all made of wood and fire was always a great worry, with all the hustle of farmers bringing their produce to market, shoppers crowding into the area and vendors selling their wares in shops and stalls. Now the city wanted to replace the block with new brick buildings and a committee was set up to develop a plan for the project. Of course, John had already designed and built a similar project—the Chewett Block where we were living—so it was not surprising that he heard about the planned design competition from Alderman John Craig, one of the members of the Market Block Committee. They announced the competition officially in October and John had just six weeks to prepare and submit his plan.

What a time it was! For thirty-nine days, John worked tirelessly, sometimes spending almost ten hours a day on his plans. As the date for submission drew nearer, he was often up until midnight, hunched over his work table, working by sputtering candle light. While he gave the Market Block all his attention, it was up to me to look after all the rest of our work and

73

I also helped him put the finishing touches on the final drawings.

Finally, on the first of December, John submitted his proposal and the next day he made a one and a half-hour presentation to the mayor, describing his plan in great detail.

The very next day, John's presentation was accepted and he received a premium of thirty pounds for his work.

Even with all the work we had to do, we were also beginning to enjoy our life in the new city. We had met new friends and now that we had a real home, we could invite them to come for tea and dinner. John and I continued our explorations outside the city, sometimes going for long walks and, more often, taking long rides together. We went fishing and began to work on our little garden. Fanny came to visit and stayed a month in the summer with Alfred, now a robust, healthy little boy and her new baby, Ellen.

Commissions continued to pour in and we were always busy. Everything seemed to be going very smoothly until one day John received the oddest notice. He had been hired by Mr. Mackenzie to be the first City Surveyor and as far as we knew, everyone was pleased with his work. But somewhere, John had an enemy or perhaps it was just a matter of an over-zealous clerk with time on his hands. Whatever it was, someone discovered that although John had been a surveyor in England, he wasn't allowed to practice in Upper Canada.

I don't think I had ever seen him so angry. Waving the notice he had received, he paced up and down the office, raging.

"Who do they think they are?" he railed. "This is nothing but a backwater! Cows and pigs roam up and down the main streets. You can practically see one end of town from the other. And they tell me I can't practice here!"

I tried to calm him down, but the rage continued.

"There is so much to be done. We're in the midst of another

cholera epidemic. Some people are saying it wouldn't be so bad if we had proper sewers here. There's garbage everywhere you go—and this is what they're fussing about! My papers? It's an outrage!"

"It is," I agreed, "but there must be something we can do about it."

"Oh, there is. I have to article for six months with a Provincial Surveyor and sit their fool exams, if you can imagine such nonsense."

"Well, perhaps you might speak to Mr. Chewett about this."

"Yes," he agreed, "That's exactly what I mean to do."

It seemed that we were again in a strange situation. John had been, as he said, "The servant of two masters" between Mr. Mackenzie and Sir John Colborne. Now he was articling for Mr. Chewett, who was our landlord, and who had also been our first main client. I began to understand what Mackenzie's Family Tree was all about. In the little society in Upper Canada, everyone seemed to be connected in all sorts of ways.

The trouble with John's papers had started when Mackenzie wanted to hire him to do an up-to-date survey of the harbour and the peninsula in front of the city. So now, he was doing the same work, but he was doing it for Mr. Chewett. Shortly after all this fuss had been sorted out, I found him sitting at his desk, grumbling under his breath.

"Now, what is that matter?" I asked.

"Confound it," he responded. "I'm supposed to be the one heading this work, with underlings to help. Now, it seems I'm the underling, with no help at all."

"Help for what?"

"Well, tell me. How is one person to go about doing a survey? Who, pray tell, is going to lay the lines, take the notes, all on his own."

I was standing behind him, looking down at the rough work plans he had made.

"There is a solution, you know." I came around to the front of the desk, leaned over the work and looked at him closely.

Almost as if I had spoken my thoughts out loud, he knew what I was thinking.

He shook his head. "I... I'm not sure."

"I could do this. I know what it's about. All those years of helping Father."

"But, that was different. You were finishing the plans. You weren't out in the street with him, doing the surveys."

We let the subject drop that night, but over the next few days, as John began to think about the survey and all the other work he had undertaken, he began to come around. it was winter, by the time we were ready to begin the actual work on the project.

I remember those days so clearly, those wonderful moments of working together. The sense of adventure. One day stands out for me still, etched in my memory, almost like watching a scene in a play.

The icy fingers of the cold on that February day pierced through the many layers of clothing I had bundled around me. Out on the frozen lake, young boys chased daringly, skating far from shore. Horses pulled sleighs loaded with goods. We had learned, that in Upper Canada, winter, for all its biting cold, was the best time to travel. At least the roads were passable with a good sleigh and furs to huddle under. The flat, frozen lake became almost like a highway. On that glorious day, the sky had cleared to a bright, brittle blue with the weak winter sun shining over the ice. There was something so marvellous about being out there together on the shore, the wind pulling at my shawl and buffeting the lines as we tried to lay them down.

My cheeks were stinging with the cold and already my

fingers were growing numb, but somehow my thoughts started to drift. Was it really only two years since that boiling day when we finally landed in the rightly called "Muddy York?" When, I began to wonder, had my longing for England begun to dissipate?

And when did everything begin to change? I realized at that moment that I was beginning to love the emptiness. It was almost as if there was some kind of courage in those straight little roads leading up from the shore. I began to be fascinated by the idea of laying out those streets where there was nothing before. It felt a little like a dream; as if one day there would be a real city here, on the edge of this frozen lake. Some people scoffed at the very idea of making something of this little colony. *It has no history,* they say, *there is nothing here.* But I began to see that there was truly something wonderful about starting out anew, freed of that burden of history that hung over every inch of London, every lane, every great building, every bridge.

"Jemima! JEMIMA! You're not paying attention!" John's voice broke into my reverie.

Huddled against the wind, I hunched over my drawing board and wrote down John's figures as he called them out.

It took several weeks of working outside to complete the survey work and then we were able to move back into the warmth of our office to finish the task. John, meanwhile, was working on all his other commissions and beginning to study for the examination that he would take in the spring. Looking back, I think those were our happiest times, working together. I never questioned what we were doing or gave any thought to what others might think, until one strange afternoon. While John was out visiting some of his new clients, I went to take tea with Sarah Tuton. Susan Ducat was there as well, visiting from Niagara.

The Tutons had become quite settled in their new home. Sarah had made new curtains for the windows and the rough oak floors were covered with carpets they had brought from England. As one of the few apothecaries in the city, Richard Tuton was doing very well and they were now able to afford to have a maid. She served us tea using the lovely china Sarah had brought from England. After the maid left the room, I saw Sarah look over at Susan and nod slightly.

Sarah sat up somewhat stiffly in her chair and cleared her throat.

"My dear Jemima," she began formally. "I hope you won't think I'm being rude, but there is something, I—" She looked at Susan. "—We—wanted to mention to you."

I looked at my friends, surprised. I couldn't imagine what they might have in mind.

Sarah continued. "It's this—" She seemed to struggle for a word. "It's this whatever you are doing with John, on the shore."

"Oh, you mean helping with the surveys?"

"That's it. Do you think it's quite proper, dear? For a lady to be out there doing, well, doing what a man should be."

At first, I just laughed. Then I realized by the looks on my friends' faces, that they were quite serious.

"But, I'm just holding the lines. And taking notes. We often work together on things, John and I...." I felt my words fading.

"You know, Jemima," Susan chimed in. "Toronto is a very small place. People talk, you know. It just doesn't seem quite right."

I shook my head in bewilderment.

"But this is Canada," I said. "Not England. Women do things here they would never do at home. They have no choice. Why look at my own Fanny, out there in Goderich with those two little children chasing after her. She is out chopping firewood and helping on the farm. She's often alone and has even had to learn to use a rifle. Even Sidney now says she's a better shot than he is."

"But, that's different, dear. It's the country. Everyone knows how rough it is and how hard it is to get started. She has no choice."

"But neither do we. We can't afford to hire someone to help John and even if we could, I don't know that we could find someone who would have the skills needed."

"Well, we're just saying, my dear," said Elizabeth finally. "Something to think about."

And the talk turned to other things, town gossip, children, the latest news from England.

On my way home, I thought about the conversation. It was clear that my friends had discussed this before and together, had decided to talk to me. I knew that they thought that they were being helpful, but it made me angry nonetheless.

I realized that ever since that day when I started to help John with his drawings, my days had been so busy. It never occurred to me that there was anything unusual about what I was doing.

During the day, we worked on drawings together or, on good days, continued our work on the surveys. At night, when we had finished our tea, we often sat together by the fire, talking about what we had accomplished and planning our tasks for the next day.

There was something else about the conversation that reminded me of something Jennie had told me in one of our gossipy conversations.

Somehow the topic of Dr. Widmer had come up again and Jennie began to tell me about the doctor's first wife.

"She was a very fine lady, you know. Everybody knew she didn't much like his ways," she said, giving me a very knowing look. And then, she added, "She was a bit like you."

I almost held my breath, wondering what was to come next.

"She liked to go riding. You would see her all around town riding on that beautiful horse she had."

"Well, why does that make her like me?"

"You and Mr. H. go riding too. I've seen the two of you going off into the country. There're not too many ladies like you who do that here."

I had never thought about it before, but it was true. You saw them, the ladies being driven in their carriages or in the winter, huddled under warm furs in their sleighs, often parading up and down King Street. Dressed up in their finery, they "did King Street" as it was called, walking with their husbands or with friends or strolling along the lake. But it was true. I had rarely seen them out riding.

At home, my sisters and I had all learned to ride at a young age. Father kept horses and we learned to groom them as well and spent many happy hours out riding together. Right from those first months in Canada, the times when I had gone out riding with John had always seemed so lovely, a way of getting to know our new home, an escape from all the worries and difficulties we had faced getting settled.

Did people notice this as well? Did they talk behind my back, saying, as Susan had, that this was something else that was "not quite right?"

I gave a toss of my head, as I entered our building. I saw myself in league with the country women I had talked about. They might be out in the fields working alongside their men and no one thought it was strange at all. They were simply doing what they had to do to survive. Well, I was the same. John and I, too, were alone in this new country with no one to ease our way.

Someday soon, we would be able to hire draughtsmen to help in our growing business, but for now, it was just the two of us, and talk as they might, I wasn't going to let anyone stop me.

It is a lazy afternoon. John has gone into town, everyone in the house is busy and with some time to myself, I look back over what I have been writing.

Is it possible that I have written so much? Words tumble out of my head, almost faster than I can write. I have filled two notebooks already, grabbing moments to write whenever I can, when I think no one is watching. I suppose I could tell John what I am doing; he has certainly spent hours writing those journals all these years, sometimes relying on me and even Eliza to keep them up when he didn't have a moment to spare.

What is it that is driving me? Why do I feel I have to hide things from him? There is so much that has been hidden all these years: what he hid from me; what I hid from myself. Perhaps that is what I am really doing, forcing myself to face the truth at last.

Upstairs in the spare room, there is an old trunk, the last of all that luggage we brought with us so long ago. Here, I have kept all sorts of bits and pieces: the list of things we needed to bring with us to Canada, letters, train tickets, invitations, theatre programs, rough sketches, garden plans and even a copy of the program for that first Art Exhibition. I drag out the old booklet with its torn cover, and sinking down on the dusty floor beside the trunk, I skim through the yellowed pages, remembering.

Later, I will hide my notebooks at the bottom of the trunk. No one will look for them there.

The Exhibition

I t was during a blizzard on a January night when I first heard
about the exhibition. I was sitting at my desk working on a set
of plans when John, stamping his feet and shaking a coating of
snow off his shoulders, swept into our old apartment.

"Mrs. H," he began with a sweeping gesture, "Meet the new
member of the Committee of Management for the Artists and
Amateurs Society."

"And what is that exactly?" I asked, barely looking up from
my work.

"Just the most exciting venture this town has yet seen.
Something to put an end to our being just a little outpost."

Now, he had my attention.

"You'd be surprised, m'dear," he continued, "How many
important people here are quite serious amateur artists. Like
minded gentlemen. Just the type you and I would like to become
acquainted with. And now, we've had a meeting, set up a
committee and begun plans to promote art in our little colony.
We have Captain Bonnycastle as our President and Charles Daly,
the City Clerk, is our Secretary. And on the new Committee of
seven prominent citizens, Mr. John Howard, Esquire." He
bowed. "Our first venture, Jemima, will be to hold an Art

Exhibition in the spring."

With a flourish, John placed a paper on my desk. The new society was placing an announcement in "The Patriot" and inviting artists to join.

Full of enthusiasm, John began to pace up and down the room, rubbing his cold hands together. I've already begun to think of what I will contribute, Jemma. Some of those landscapes I've been working on. And I can use the drawings I made for Sir John. It's an opportunity, you know, to let people see some of the things I could do for them. And, of course, the paintings are for sale. I might even sell a few."

During the dark days of the winter, John directed a great deal of his energy and enthusiasm to planning the show and selecting the paintings he planned to exhibit. He enjoyed working on the committee and took his role in helping to improve Toronto quite seriously. All of this came crashing down in February. A letter had been delivered to the office one morning while I was still at home.

Holding the letter in his shaking hand, John came into the house, breathing heavily, so ashen, I thought he was about to collapse.

"What is it?" I asked, running to him.

"Someone on that committee is against me; they want to force me out!"

"What are you saying?"

"They want to know why I changed my name—as if it were any of their business."

I had learned of the story referred to in the letter when John and I first began "to walk out together" back home in England. The young man who came to my father's office and showed an interest in my paintings and the role I played in my father's business was called John Corby.

One lovely, gentle day in May we went to visit friends. On the way home, John drew me aside. "There is something I want to tell you," he began. "I don't want you to hear it from anyone else."

I'd heard that there were whispers about John, questions about his birth and a sense of disapproval from some of my relations when we began to develop an interest in one another.

I waited.

"My mother." He hesitated, as if trying to find the words, "... was young, when I was born. She wasn't married. She wasn't wild, Jemima, but..."

"I understand," I said softly.

"Samuel Corby isn't my father. He and my mother married later. He's a good man, Jemima, he gave me his name and they made a good life together. But it follows me. I wanted to tell you. It might make you feel differently about me."

"Of course not, John," I protested. "What difference could it make?"

But the darkness surrounding his birth continued to haunt John and it was during our crossing to Canada that he decided to change his name to Howard, the name of his natural father. And so it was that we arrived in our new home as John and Jemima Howard.

Now he read the letter to me, bellowing, in an almost incoherent jumble. "We—all of them!—are—I quote this slander!—desirous of knowing if you would feel inclined to offer us an explanation, or if you would prefer resigning from the Committee! Daly dares to say I could resign from their little committee and just be a member of the Society. Well, let me tell him what I think of that!"

"Oh, John. How awful! How could anyone do such a thing?"

"They are questioning my honesty, my integrity."

"But why? It makes no sense. What does who you are, your name, your background have to do with their little committee anyway?"

"It's this place, Jemima. They are a flock of old biddies, with nothing better to do."

"It's almost as if someone is after us. First the survey papers. Now this."

"Just jealousy, I think. Things have worked out so fast. Look how far we've come in two years."

"But what are we going to do?"

For the first time since he had walked into the room, John seemed to unwind a little.

He sat down at his desk, smiled and said, "Put the kettle on, Jemima, and let's have some tea. We're going to put up a good fight."

Whoever it was who had started this campaign against John had clearly not reckoned with his fighting spirit or the good name that he had established for himself in town.

Together we drafted a letter to Lieutenant Colonel William Rowan, Sir John's Colborne's own secretary. Simply and clearly John explained the reasons for changing his name and declared that his conduct could bear the strictest scrutiny. We came up with a list of names of people in England who would be willing to give character references for him. John wrote the letter and sent it off immediately.

We never actually read the letter written in response, but we heard that it was Sir John himself who had written to Charles Daly. At any rate, the matter died down, John continued as a member of the Committee and with several others began to look beyond their own circle for artists to contribute their work for the show.

John assembled a collection of his own work—paintings on various subjects and many of his designs and plans for buildings.

By June, excitement about the exhibition was growing and we were beginning to forget the unpleasantness surrounding Daly's letter, when another letter from him was delivered to our home, this time addressed to me. At first, I was terrified. Surely they weren't still plaguing John!

But this time, it was something quite different—as if nothing had happened. It was as if the committee had completely forgotten the incredibly insulting way that they had treated John. Now, suddenly, they were inviting me to submit my paintings to the exhibition! I was dumbfounded. How did they even know I was something of an artist? John was out when the letter arrived, but I confronted him with it as soon as he came back.

"How did they know about me? Did you tell them?" I asked.

He answered with a little smile. "Well, perhaps I did. I do hope you'll make a contribution, Jemma. This is going to be a very important event."

It was a bit of scramble for me to choose some work for the exhibition. Between the move to the new house and all the work in the office, I hadn't done any new painting for a long time. I did, however, choose four pieces that I was quite happy with, three paintings I had made from sketches done when John and I went out shooting in the country together and a large piece I called "The Dying Soldier," which was based on other works I had seen on that theme in exhibitions at home. I was more than a little dismayed when John told me that the committee had decided that my name would not be included with the paintings. There would just be a little note "By a Lady." as if being an artist was not quite proper for a woman in our stiff little town.

The exhibition was to be held in three rooms in the

Parliament; invitations were sent out, posters put up about town and advertisements placed in all the papers. We hoped that there would be great excitement about the show and that it would be the first of what would become an annual event.

The rest of the winter and early spring had been an incredibly busy time for us, what with the plans for the exhibition, all the new commissions coming in and the moving and getting settled in our new home. I had seen little of Jennie for a long time. Even though I was so busy, I missed her company and her funny, spunky ways. I decided to send her an invitation to attend the opening of the exhibition with me. Almost as soon as it must have arrived at the Inn, I heard her knocking at our door.

Jennie was certainly growing up, no longer the somewhat gangly little girl with the fly-away pigtails. She was, however, as enthusiastic as ever. With barely more than a quick hello, she waved the invitation at me.

"I never got any mail before, Mrs. H. This must be something pretty important."

"It's an exhibition—of paintings."

"An exhibition? What is that?"

"It's—well, you see—Mr. Howard and some other people in the city are what you might call amateur painters. They draw and paint when they have some time. So a group of them decided to put their work together in a large room at the Parliament Buildings and then other people could come and see what they have done."

"But why?"

Her question caught me unawares. It was easy to forget that it was really only a short time since mere survival in this small colony had been a challenge. Indeed, for many—like my own sister, who settled in the country—life was still very difficult.

Something like an art exhibition was unheard of. The men who started the Artists Society believed that it was time for the people to turn to thoughts "of higher things."

I tried to explain. "People like to look at pictures. You can see places you have only read about, scenes from stories. It gives you something to think about."

"We have pictures on the wall at the Inn. Pa bought them in the market. He said it was some artist who had come to town. Do you mean something like that?"

"Well, yes. But there will be many different paintings. About different things. We used to go to exhibitions like this back home. Sometimes in London, you could go to see the work of famous artists, but there are also shows like ours here which have things local people have done."

"I've never heard of anything like that here. Must just be for society, those Family Compact types."

Politics was never very far from Jennie's thoughts, but she did have a point here, since the patrons of the new Artists Society were none other than Sir John and Bishop Strachan.

"Come with me. I think you'll enjoy it."

On July the first, the day of the opening, Jennie arrived quite early. When I opened the door to her knock, I almost didn't recognize her. Gone was the little girl in pigtails. Instead, she, or probably her mother, had put her hair up and she was wearing a very grown-up dress with long skirts. She was sixteen and turning into a beautiful young woman. Once inside the house, she twirled excitedly to show me her new outfit.

"Ma says I've got to look proper if I'm going out with society folks."

"Oh, we're not society," I said, laughingly.

"Ma also says I'm to thank you. She says with the books you give me and now going to this show, I'm getting a real education."

I had to admit I never really thought of it that way. I loved passing my books on to Jennie and then often talking to her about them when she had finished reading. I would never have told anyone, but I found chatting with her and listening to all her ideas and stories much more interesting than talking to my friends like Elizabeth and even Sarah, who were preoccupied with their families and their houses and never gave much of a thought about anything else. Going to the exhibition with Jennie would be to see the artwork and people through fresh new eyes.

It was so very hot that we walked slowly down the street toward the Parliament Building, where the exhibition was to take place. Jennie was almost trembling with excitement as we mounted the steps and entered the first of the three exhibition rooms.

"Whoever thought I'd be going to Parliament,"she said, giving me a little poke in the ribs.

I thought there would be a quite a crowd of people there on the first day, but the first room was surprisingly empty. John, who had been working busily with two or three other committee members to hang the paintings, had already been to the show to greet Sir John at the formal opening and had now returned to the office. An art show was a new thing for Toronto and I thought perhaps it would take awhile for people to begin to take an interest in it.

Wide-eyed, Jennie kept very close to me as we began to look around at the paintings which covered all four walls of the imposing room. It was hard to know what to look at first, but we soon found that we were drawn to the same things. Landscapes of places we knew leaped out at us: Niagara Falls, the Parliament Building itself, and other familiar buildings. I pointed out some paintings with scenes of England and explained that some must have been drawn from memory while others were based on well-known paintings by great artists. John had told me to be sure to have a look at the work of a young artist named Paul Kane who he said was very promising.

"Oh, look, Mrs. H. Here's something by Mr. H. I've seen that before." Jennie was pointing to John's painting of the Toronto waterfront which we had hung in our parlour.

Then Jennie saw my painting, "The Dying Soldier".

"Mrs. H., You didn't tell me you were here too! I watched you paint this." She peered closely at the name card on the wall beside the painting. "But, it doesn't have your name on it, it just says "A Lady." That's not right. They should tell everyone you did this."

"That's very kind of you, Jennie. But that's the way they do things. Never mind."

We moved on to the other rooms, intrigued by the variety of subjects, different styles and the large number of works John and his committee had collected. The heat was oppressive and although we had started out with great anticipation, we soon felt our energy flagging. Leaving the building, Jennie thanked me for bringing her to the show and went off home, while, like John, I returned to the office to catch up on the day's work.

The exhibition which had started off with such hope was not a great success. Some said it was the heat and the cholera epidemic which was sweeping the city which had discouraged people from attending. But others felt that little Toronto was just not ready for such a venture. Although it was supposed to be an annual event, it would be many years before John and another group of artists would attempt to present another art show in Toronto.

Hope

1835

I should have been happy. We had come so far in a few years. Commissions were pouring in and we enjoyed working together on all our projects. We had our own house with a lovely garden and were beginning to furnish it with things that John made himself and new pieces we bought from other craftsmen. We often went hunting and riding together and were even thinking of buying two horses of our own. We had made new friends and enjoyed visiting one another and planning outings together.

It was all lovely, but inside, although I seldom let myself dwell on it, I knew, in some ways, it was a busyness to hide the emptiness that was always there. Sometimes when I was alone, I would walk through the empty, unused rooms upstairs, and try to imagine what it would be like if they were filled with the children we had dreamed of.

Sometimes in the cold of winter, I would sit at the windows overlooking busy King Street, watching small boys chasing one another through the snow, throwing snowballs and sometimes catching an unwary walker by surprise.

I was getting older.

Fanny had given birth to another baby, a little girl they

still warm from the oven and a pot of freshly made jam. I made tea and we sat in our little garden where flowers were blooming for the first time. There was a grin on her face and I knew she was fairly bursting with something to tell me.

"Well, Jennie. What is it? What is all this about?"

"Oh, Mrs. H," she answered, coyly. "I don't know what you mean."

"My young lady, you look like the cat that has lapped up all the cream. Tell me."

Her face turned bright red, but her eyes were dancing.

"Mrs. H," she leaned over, almost whispering. "I have a young man."

"Oh, Jenny. How lovely. Tell me all about him."

"Well," she began. "Pa is getting on, y'know. And Ma finally got him to agree that he couldn't do everything the way he used to. So they hired a young man to help out."

"And?"

"And, well, that's him. He's called Peter, and he's eighteen, and, well, it seems like he's always been there. All the customers like him. He's like my Pa. He knows just what to say to them, and when to tell some of the loud ones they've had enough. And he's young and strong, so Pa doesn't have to work so hard."

"And you?"

"Oh, Mrs. H. We have such good times! We talk a blue streak and he makes me laugh. And even when the inn is filled and we're both so busy, it's like we're together."

"Jennie, this is lovely. But you're very young. You'll have lots of young men."

"No," she said, growing suddenly serious. "This is the one, Mrs. H. And I think he thinks so too. We haven't talked about anything formal yet. But you just know, don't you?"

So there was my little Jennie, growing up so fast. She had

clearly made up her mind and a young lad named Peter would clearly be a part of all our lives.

It seemed as if when I was ill, there was almost a conspiracy to somehow keep me from thinking about anything that might upset me. John brought only funny stories about what had happened in his day, but never mentioned anything serious about our business. We were in the habit of reviewing our work together each night, sitting in the garden in the summer or by the fire when it was cold, sipping our tea with John smoking his pipe. I was missing those chats, but anytime I asked him questions about work, John steered the conversation to lighter things.

Jennie, when she came to visit, fairly talked my ear off, but, and this was most unusual for her, steered completely clear of the political gossip she loved.

As for Sarah, and all my other friends, it was all news of parties and weddings, the latest gossip, the children and the weather

As I began to recover, John seemed wary of my returning to work with him. It was as if Dr. Widmer's words made him feel guilty about my working so hard. But soon it was very clear that without me, the office was in disarray and huge amounts of work had piled up. Gradually we eased into our old routine. We soon were so busy that I had little time to reflect on the trials we had faced.

Going about town, meeting with our friends and catching up on the newspapers, I soon discovered that a great deal had been going on while everyone had been so determined to keep me wrapped in a little cocoon.

We had thought that when Mackenzie became mayor, the Reformers would be happy and there would be an end to all the strife. But nothing had really changed. John had been quite optimistic when the mayor hired him to lay out the sidewalks and thought this would be a new start for Toronto. But by October, Mackenzie was back in the Assembly. John was furious about it. "That scoundrel," he had ranted. "He's no sooner sitting in the Mayor's Chair—than he's off to lead the Reformers again."

The Reformers drew up a Report of Grievances against the Executive Council that Mackenzie himself sailed off to England to present in person to the Colonial Secretary. For us, one sad result of this was that Sir John Colborne, who had been so good to us, was dismissed and sent back to England, to be replaced by a new Lieutenant-Governor, named Sir Frances Bond Head, a man no one knew anything about.

Far from bringing peace to Upper Canada, Bond Head's arrival would soon bring our colony to the point of rebellion. But we had little time to concern ourselves with politics, for we were about to embark on a new adventure that would soon become the centre of our lives.

Howard's Folly

1836

Almost out of the blue, one evening as we were having our tea beside the fire, John said, "I have a hankering after farming."

I was knitting and almost dropped a stitch.

"You what?"

"Ever since I went to visit Smith's farm out by the Humber last summer, —I've been thinking on it. There's beautiful land to be had there and so many things we could do with it."

"But farming, John? I can't see myself as the farmer's wife. We know nothing about farming."

"I'm serious about this, Jemima. I'm going to write to Sidney, maybe he'll come in with me and run the farm. It would be better for him than all that way out in Goderich."

It is so strange how conversations stay with you. We had just moved into our new home in Chewett's Block and were busy getting settled and keeping up with all the commissions that were coming in. The last thing on my mind was another new project and I thought no more about it at the time. But for John, it was an idea that never let him alone.

Perhaps, I should not have been surprised. Ever since our

arrival in muddy, little York, dreams of land had never been far from our thoughts. Nothing had come of the first little five-acre plot in Paris, but John wasn't discouraged. He tried to interest Sidney in a plan to buy a farm together, but nothing came of it. John was always thinking about land; listening avidly when the subject came up in conversation and studying the advertisements and notices for land sales. I realized he was more serious when he started riding out to the lands around the Humber River to see what was available. If I thought at all, about where we would live in the future, I think I always saw us living in town, in a house that we would build, one day, for ourselves. In truth, I thought it was all talk until, that April day when he took me to see, for the first time, that land which would become ours.

We rode together out along King Street until we reached the Garrison Creek. John was so excited, almost like a little boy, urging his horse along, looking back at me with a slight frown if I seemed to hang back.

Beyond the creek in the Reserve lands, the forest was very thick, and I wondered where we were going. But John, having already come to see the land many times, clearly knew his way about. He rode confidently along the trail until the path narrowed and we could ride no further. We dismounted and walked our horses deeper into the forest.

We were far from the city, walking on lovely rolling land with clear-running, babbling creeks running through it. At last we reached a small clearing on a height of land. We stopped walking. John put his arm around my shoulder and drew me close.

"It's hard to imagine it now," he said, "but this is going to be our farm."

With a sweeping gesture, he indicated to me the parcels of land he had been looking at.

It was clear that he had already been doing a great deal of

planning before he began to share his thoughts with me.

"This land will be good for sheep farming," he added.

"Sheep farming!" I shrieked. "Us! What do we know about sheep farming?"

I had a sudden vision of the two of us, city folk in all our city finery running out in the fields, chasing sheep. Unable to help myself, I burst out laughing. John looked quite hurt.

"Well, now. Not us. But we'll own the land and hire the men to do the farming."

That was a little better.

John put his arm around me, and turned south to where we could just catch a glimpse of the lake through the trees.

"And here, this is where we'll build that house I promised you."

After that day, things began to move very quickly. In May, John bought one hundred and sixty acres of land fronting on the Humber River, from the edge of Lake Ontario all the way north to Bloor Street. Within weeks we were bringing our friends on expeditions out to see what we had done. At the end of May, we planned a big picnic to celebrate.

It was quite a procession, some rode horses, others travelled in small carts. We carried baskets of food and drink, carpets and pillows to sit on, rifles for shooting game. At the edge of the forest, we had to leave the carts behind and carry everything into the clearing. The children played happily all day. We ate and drank, played cards, and went out exploring. The shooting party went out and came back with trophies of their success.

It was later in the day when everyone was resting before the journey home, that I found myself looking at the lush forest around us. How strange it was to realize that there was nothing around us for miles, and that we actually owned all this. So much land. If you could walk straight through the forest from the lake, our land would run all the way to the first concession, over two miles. We had been in Canada only four years; and we were the owners of all this land.

Almost as an echo to my thoughts, Sarah, who was sitting beside me, said softly,

"You're not actually going to live here, are you?"

"Not now," I answered. "Perhaps someday, in the future."

"It's lovely, but it's so far from town, and so hard to get here. You're much braver than I am to take on something like this."

Was it brave, I wondered, *or folly?* Only time would tell.

Almost as soon as we got home, John, in a flurry of activity, cleared all his drafts and drawings off his work table and sat down with a large, fresh sheet of paper and began to draw. He was so excited that he hadn't even stopped to take off the clothes that were so dusty from our journey home.

"What on earth are you doing?" I asked, leaning over his shoulder.

"This, m'dear is going to be what I am calling Howard's Folly."

His words strangely echoed my thoughts earlier in the day.

He must have been thinking about this all day, while we were out riding, picnicking, talking with our friends. Planning, imagining what he would draw. For here, on the drawing paper was a sketch for a house, unusual, white and airy, unlike anything I had seen in Toronto.

Several days later, the drawings had turned into a little model that sat in the middle of the table. It was to be a small house, one storey, in the Regency style that had been popular in London before we left.

"It's going to be on the piece of land I showed you, over-looking the lake. As soon as we get the land cleared, we're going to start building."

"And you'll be quite the country squire, won't you?" I said with a laugh.

There was no stopping him. In spite of all the work we had coming in, John always had time to work on his plans. He hired some men to clear the land, worked on his design for the house and proudly invited our friends to see the model.

Just after breakfast, one bright morning in June, he looked up and said, "Well, Jemima, it looks like a good day for planting." He had clearly been planning this outing and off we went with John carrying a hoe and shovel and a packet of seeds.

It was nothing short of amazing to see how much work had been done in a short time. The path into the forest had been widened and it was now possible to ride far into the woods. A large field had been cleared and we were ready for planting.

We worked hard together all morning and by noon, we had planted our first crop of potatoes. I must have looked a sight, my once-white shirtwaist clinging to my back, my skirt covered with clumps of soil and my hair hanging damply around my face. But we were laughing. Two short months ago, I had scoffed at the idea of being a farmer's wife and now, here we were with our first planted field.

"Well, Mr. H," I said, trying to brush the dirt off my skirt, "you might make me a farmer yet."

As we rode back into the city, leaving the farm behind, I found myself thinking of Fanny.

How different it was for her, living as she did on a farm far from the nearest town. Having a successful harvest meant plenty versus going hungry all winter. I thought of her, and women like her, having children alone, especially in the winter when travel was so dangerous, giving birth with only a neighbour to help her. Yet she always seemed to be happy, never complained or showed any anger when yet another one of Sidney's ventures turned out to be a failure.

As for us, we had our warm house in the city, the markets close by and good friends to keep us company. At the time, I thought having a house and a farm in the country would be something of a hobby.

In that busy year, John designed and built houses and cottages for a number of clients and continued to do work for the city as well, making plans and specifications for a King Street sewer and for cleaning and repairing streets. We were very excited when he received a premium of forty-five pounds when his plan of the Court House and Gaol were approved.

Somehow, we found time to buy two horses of our own and in addition to going out to see how the clearing of the land was progressing we went riding together and went out with friends. There was a small theatre in town and visiting troupes of actors and performers often performed.

There was, however, a sense of unrest that was felt everywhere in the city that was difficult to ignore. We kept hearing of meetings where the speeches of Mackenzie and his followers became wilder and more threatening all the time. In the market, on street corners I would overhear arguments, or worse, notice that, sometimes, people stopped speaking when I passed by.

Far from solving the struggle between the Tories and the Reformers, the new Lieutenant-Governor seemed to have made things worse. In the Assembly, the Reformers voted to cut off salaries and pensions to all lesser government workers. We heard that they had sent a letter to Sir Francis denouncing his arbitrary acts and manner. Sir Francis, in turn, refused to sign bills for a program of building roads and schools. I would have thought that we would not be affected by decisions like this. They seemed far away from everyday life. But work slowed down everywhere. Many people were out of work and we heard that large numbers were leaving the colony and seeking work in The States. People who were planning building projects began to have second thoughts and there was a general malaise everywhere.

"This is why we left England," said John with disgust, closing the newspaper he had been reading. "We came to escape a depression at home, and now one is dragging us down here. And I worry that this is just the beginning."

The stalemate between the Assembly and the Council continued until the spring, when Sir Francis dissolved the Assembly and called a General Election. Tempers ran high for everyone and it seemed almost impossible not to end up "talking politics" no matter how we tried.

One evening, our friends Henry and Elizabeth Rowsell held a dinner party and what started out as quite a civilized discussion ended with raised voices and anger.

Henry and Elizabeth, seated at opposite ends of the table, tried to keep the conversation light, turning to news from England or the latest shipment of books that had arrived at Henry's bookshop. He was just about to tell us about them, when we heard a loud voice which seemed to boom over the rest of the conversation.

Several guests had been having a quiet conversation which suddenly erupted.

"They should just take them out and hang the lot of them. Starting with that traitor, Mackenzie."

"That would certainly send that mad wig of his flying," someone added, trying to make a bit of a joke.

But the speaker, a man I had not met before, just raged on. "They should have drowned him and not his printing presses years back. We'd all be better for it."

"I don't think Bond Head has helped the situation. I heard he was sent here to calm things down and all he's done is pour oil on the flames." It was the same speaker who had tried to make the little joke which had failed.

"Wish we had Sir John back," said Elizabeth, almost wistfully. "Things were much calmer when he was here."

"Well, he's here alright. Down in Quebec leading the army. I've heard this rebellion talk is getting very serious down there."

"They should have listened to Dr. Baldwin when they had the chance," another guest added. "The moderates have given up and he's gone to live in his big house away from politics."

"Nonsense, give these people an inch and they'll have us living in a republic."

"But, they have a point; you must give them that. When you look at some of those grievances..."

"Which side are you on, man?"

At that moment, flustered, Elizabeth rose. "My dears, she said to us, "perhaps it's time for us to leave the gentlemen," and we ladies followed. As we drank our tea in the drawing room, we could still hear the loud voices arguing.

"I don't understand what happened," I said to John as we walked home. "We're all on the same side, aren't we?"

"Everyone's on edge," he answered. "Best not to talk about it at all."

I am finding it harder to go on. When I immerse myself in the past, it is as if I am there. Everything is so vivid, it is almost as if it is happening all over again. I can hear the voices, feel the excitement, the joy of the moment.

But when I stop writing, everything is different. I know that

I am forgetting things. Sometimes, in the middle of a sentence, I reach for a word and it isn't there. I know that I cover up, find ways to fill the void and keep on chattering. In the middle of a task, I put something down and then forget what I was doing. Reading is becoming difficult. I read words on a page, but sometimes I can't remember what I am reading about. Knitting is becoming impossible. Sometimes I look down at my hands and I am not sure what they are supposed to be doing.

I can still laugh about it, when someone notices. "Oh dear, I must be getting old," is a good way of covering up an awkward moment. We have a laugh and carry on.

Inside I am seething. Filled with shame.

I make mistakes. Simple tasks are somehow growing beyond me. There is something that I struggle to understand. I want to keep writing, to say all the things that have remained unspoken for so long. I'm afraid that I will run out of time.

The Coming Storm

Henry Rowsell never got a chance, that night, to tell us about the new books which had arrived, but the very next day several of us went over to his bookshop to have a look. Rowsell's had an excellent lending library, but I still liked to buy at least one of the new books whenever they came in from London or New York.

It was only later in the day, when I was putting my new purchases in our bookcase that I realized that it had been ages since I had seen Jennie. I had been in the habit of passing on a book or two to her whenever I bought something new. I knew that Jennie had been taking on new tasks at the inn, but still, it seemed a little strange that she hadn't found any time to come by. I decided to go round and deliver a book to her.

I didn't see Jennie when I entered the inn, but her mother was sitting at the counter, pouring over her account books, just as Jennie had described her. She got up when she saw me and came to greet me.

"Mrs. Howard. Good morning. We haven't seen you for a long time." Her manner seemed a little cool.

"Good morning, Mrs. Grey. How are you?"

"Ah, we're all doing very well, thank you," she said, taking my outstretched hand. And then, quite abruptly, she said, "I'll go and get Jennie for you."

She disappeared upstairs and a few minutes later, Jennie came clattering down.

She stood at the bottom of the stairs, started to speak, then stopped. confused. Not at all the young girl I knew.

"I... I haven't come by," she began. "I didn't know if you would want to see me."

"Why ever not?"

"Well, y'know. Us being on opposite sides and all that."

I was really quite taken aback. "But we're not— All these goings on. They don't really concern us."

"Ah, but, Mrs. H. They do. Pa and my Peter..."

"Your Peter," I interrupted.

And suddenly, there was the old Jennie, an impish grin on her face.

"I guess there is so much I haven't had a chance to tell you. Peter and me, we're engaged." And there on her finger was a lovely little silver ring which she proudly showed me. "Peter is a real gentleman, y'know. He came and asked my Pa, real proper."

"That's lovely news," I said, coming over to give Jennie a hug. "When are you getting married?"

"Oh, not for a while. Not till all this settles down. And Peter, he wants to work and put money aside for us to get off to a good start."

"He sounds like a very sensible young man,"

"That he is. And I'm working too—at the inn. Ma says, I'm not just a little girl helping anymore. So I have a real job." Jennie leaned over and added confidentially, "I'm getting paid too. I think, y'know, they can't give me a dowry, like rich folk. So this is their way of helping us."

"And very wise, too," I said. "But what is it you were

saying about Peter and your father?"

"That's what I meant, Mrs. H. That we're on different sides. Peter and my Pa, well, if there is fighting, they mean to be there."

I was caught, speechless. For me, up till now, it had all been talk. But here were people I knew, people I cared about talking about fighting.

"But surely, nothing like that is going to happen."

"People are angry, Mrs. H. Poor people. Nothing changes. Times are bad and that Governor blames the farmers and working men. And all those Family Compact people, they just give each other jobs—and they get paid for them too. That's what Mr. Mackenzie has been saying for years. And they keep all the good land for themselves. They take all the money, and what do we get. Nothing. No roads. No schools. They promise things, but nothing happens. We just want to have a say in things."

Jennie's passion astounded me. This version of her, this serious young woman was almost a stranger to me, but her words deeply touched me.

"But, your family— You are..."

"Oh, we're alright. Pa says, *No matter, how bad things are, men will always find money for drink.* We know what that means, Mrs. H. That they'll drink up the money and their children will go hungry. But if they don't come to us, they'll just go somewhere else. Pa says, that's why he's always been for reform. Maybe if things were better, they wouldn't have to turn to drink so much."

I nodded in sympathy, letting Jennie's words sink in. Grey's Inn had always been known as a respectable place. That was why it was recommended to us when we had first arrived in the city. But drinking was a terrible problem in Toronto. There was a tavern on every corner and many men and their families had been ruined by it. All too often we would hear of men who, having had too much to drink would go out into a storm or the freezing cold and die in the street.

I really didn't know what to say. But I reached out to Jennie and took her hands in mine.

"Ah, Jennie. I don't want this to come between us."

"I don't either. When we have our wedding, will you come?"

"Of course, I will. In fact, if you don't send me a proper invitation, I will just steal into the back of the church. I can't wait to see you as a bride."

I gave Jennie the books I had brought her and went on my way. But our conversation continued to trouble me. The threat of some great upheaval had suddenly come much closer.

The Rebellion

1837

For the most part, in that memorable year which began quite calmly, we went about our daily lives, busy as always. John hired men to clear our land by the Humber and had a cottage built there for a tenant. At night, we worked together on the plans for the new house, making sketches of the rooms and beginning to think of what we would need to set up house there.

And all the time, the unrest in the province continued. The election results had not solved anything, and now, a depression in the United States and bad harvests at home were creating even more hardships.

Rumours swirled everywhere, some real, some false, each one a spark that could set a fire ablaze. Mackenzie and his followers were talking of outright rebellion. In Lower Canada, the situation had grown so serious, that we heard that Sir John Colborne, who was now the Commander-in-Chief of British North America, was deploying his troops to put down a rebellion led by someone called Louis Joseph Papineau who was leading the Patriots against the government. In October, everyone was quite shocked to hear that in spite of rumours of trouble in our province, Sir Francis Bond Head had sent the troops from Fort

York and Fort Henry in Kingston to aid Colborne's forces. When word got around that they left behind several thousand rifles and a supply of ammunition that was stored at City Hall with only two lone guards to keep order, people became even more uneasy.

The rumours grew more threatening. Mackenzie was meeting to plan an attack. Farmers and workmen had armed themselves with whatever they could manage—rifles, pitchforks, even pikes which they were sharpening as weapon. People saw them doing military drills. Sir Francis continued to pay no attention either to the rumours or the urgent pleas of Colonel James Fitzgibbon to make preparations in case of an attack.

One night, quite late, there was a knock at our door. John went to answer it, and I heard low voices, quick responses with a sense of urgency.

John came back upstairs, rubbing his hands together.

"Who was that?"

"James Fitzgibbon. Now *there's* a man who knows what he's doing."

"What is going on?"

"That other fool, Bond Head won't take any action, so Fitzgibbon is taking matters into his own hands."

"What do you mean?"

"Well, let's just say, he's asking around, lining up some of us to be prepared if need be. Fire arms at the ready, and all that."

I felt a chill sweep over me. This rebellion was no longer just talk. Years ago we had left behind riots in England. Now it seemed the unrest had followed us here and was about to explode. And it wasn't just John. On the other side Jennie's father and her young sweetheart had volunteered to fight. Could it be that they were all in danger? That they might soon be shooting at one another?

Fitzgibbon also wanted the mayor to arrange for the great

bell of Upper Canada College to be rung as a warning should an uprising take place. Again, Sir Francis ignored his pleas.

Meanwhile the rumblings about rebellion began to swell. We heard numbers: five thousand armed men were getting ready to attack Toronto. The Governor urged everyone to remain calm and go about their daily business. What business? we wondered, grateful that John had his teaching at the College for that is what really kept us going.

On Saturday, December the second, there was a heated meeting of the Executive Council. Just weeks before Chief Justice Robinson had accused James Fitzgibbon of alarming people when he tried to warn them about Mackenzie's plan. But now we heard that when Fitzgibbon burst into the meeting with news about an imminent attack, they finally began to listen. Fitzgibbon was given permission to organize militia regiments, Mackenzie was accused of treason and a warrant was issued for his arrest.

The city erupted in gossip. We heard that someone had found a letter with Mackenzie's plans in it. There was talk of City Hall issuing guns to Orangemen.

Over and over we heard the same words. "Little Mac's for it now. High treason, that's what it is."

For the next few days, there was a strange quiet over the city. We waited, suspended, not knowing what was going to happen.

On Tuesday morning, John set off to go to the College as usual, saying as he left, that life had to go on. A short time later, he came rushing back home.

"I met some of the young lads, on the way," he cried out. "The school is closed. Somehow we slept through the alarm bells, but I think it's really starting." John saddled up the pony and went off to see what was happening in the city.

"It's as if the city is paralyzed," he said, when he came home later. "The shops are all shut, the market closed, and men are roaming the streets, armed, waiting for an attack, waiting for someone to tell them what to do."

John went racing upstairs to the storeroom where he kept his guns locked away.

"What on earth are you doing?" I called after him.

"Going off to see what I can do to help. That was the plan, remember? That visitor in the night."

He rushed around, putting his papers in order and stashing them carefully away.

"I think, Jemma, you might go and stay with the Tutons, just to have company—be on the safe side, you know."

"No, I'll be fine here. I have Mary Ann and young James. I won't be alone and I want to be here when you come home."

John kissed me, and armed with his rifle, went off with a friend to arrange what he called "a skirmishing expedition." I had no idea what that was, but it sounded ominous.

Restless, I paced about the house, trying to read or do a little work, but it was impossible to think about anything but the coming fighting and the danger John might be facing.

Outside, that strange quiet still hung over the city. Shop windows had been boarded up, schools and businesses were closed and the bells continued to ring. Watching out my window over King Street I could see men of all ages, some with rifles on their shoulders, hurrying down to the Market Square. Young boys strutted along with them, trying to look important, as if they were part of the force. I sent young James down to the square to see what was happening and he came home to report that a cannon had been set up and rifles were being handed out to those who joined the militia. He heard that the inns and taverns were still open and doing a lively business with all the men waiting around for something to do. Was Jennie's father still there, or had he and Peter actually gone off to join the rebels?

And there was more. James said people were grumbling about the latest news. Realizing at last the seriousness of the situation, Sir Francis had moved from Government House to City Hall, where he set up his headquarters on the second floor. He had sent his wife and the families of other government officials for safety to a ship anchored in the harbour, so it could sail to the United States if necessary. It was all very well for them, I thought, but what about the rest of us left to face the unknown.

John came home later that night and told me that Mackenzie's forces had assembled at Montgomery's Tavern about five miles north of the town on Yonge Street. He heard that they had set fire to the house of Sheriff Jarvis, which John had just finished renovating. The next morning we learned that this was just a rumour. Dr. Horne, the head teller of the Bank of Upper Canada, lived in a house on Yonge, just north of the tollgate at Bloor Street. After driving Mrs. Horne and her children out into the snow, Mackenzie had set fire to this house instead, thinking it belonged to Jarvis. The violence seemed to be coming closer and closer to us.

John put aside his rifle, took up his double gun and a brace of pistols and went off again into the night.

The next morning, I could no longer stand to be cooped up alone inside. I went to visit one of my neighbours whose husband had also gone out to join the militia. We sat together, drank innumerable cups of tea and kept each other company as the day dragged by. John did not come home that night at all, but he did send word that all was calm and that he and the group of men he had assembled were guarding the Bank of Upper Canada for the night.

All was still quiet on Thursday morning, when all of a

sudden, we heard shouting coming from a distance. At first we were terrified that it was the rebels really coming into the city.

Again, I sent James out to find out what was happening. Not long after, the door burst open and he came charging into the house.

"It's the militia," he cried, "They're marching up Yonge Street, chasing after those rascals. Listen, you can hear the cheering."

It was true. On that cold, bright morning we could hear the cheering coming all the way across the city as the militia began to move up north. Bands were playing and we heard singing as well, but we couldn't make out the words or the tunes. Not wanting to miss the excitement, I grabbed a warm coat and shawl, asked Mary Ann to come with me and we hurried off to Yonge Street just in time to see the tail end of the parade go by. The band music was still loud and clear and now we could hear that when the people cheered, they were calling on the militia to fight for the honour of the new young Queen. Eighteen-year-old Victoria had just become our Queen in June of that year and even from our far distance in Canada, there was great excitement about her. We clung to every bit of news we could get about her, waiting with great eagerness for the papers to arrive from London with the latest stories, even if, by that time, they were months out of date.

All up and down Yonge Street, people were leaning out of windows, waving flags and cheering. It was very cold, but people were even out standing on the rooftops, singing and shouting as the men marched by. The air was so festive, it was hard to believe that these were armed men about to confront the rebels coming down into the city.

When the last of the militia disappeared up Yonge Street, we turned and went home to wait anxious for news of what was happening. I wondered fearfully where John was and what was happening to him.

It wasn't until seven that night that John finally returned home, weary and disheveled, his face, blackened, a tear in his jacket. Once settled with tea and a strong drink, the words began to tumble out.

"What a time it was, Jemma... And all over, really in an hour. Maybe, they'll try again... No one knows what will happen now."

"Was anyone hurt?"

"Hard to say. None of our men, certainly. Don't know what happened on the other side. We took some prisoners, that's about all I know."

By nine, John had gone off to bed, almost, he said, too tired to sleep.

The next day, John was on guard around the city and on Saturday, he was made a Lieutenant in the Queen's Rangers and ordered up to the Garrison where he drilled for three days. For a brief instant, it even seemed as if John might even join the military, but he soon gave up the idea. Classes at the College were starting up again, and he wanted to go back to his teaching.

Over the next few days, the story of John's adventure came out in bits and pieces. That first day had been mainly a lot of confusion. Skirmishes here and there, a great deal of running back and forth to the Don Bridge. The next day, after guarding the Bank at night, John took command of a group of sixteen men and led them out to scour the bushes for the rebels. They found two and took them as prisoners.

"You know, I proved to be a pretty good gunner. It's all those years of hunting. Keeping the guns in order and all."

Oh yes, I thought to myself. For some strange reason, the memory of another time flitted through my mind. *I almost lost you, then, before we even started when you went off from the ship to hunt that horrid day.* But I didn't say anything.

"I'll tell you about the rest," he continued. "We had one of those rebels cornered and fourteen men firing at him. None of their bullets went within fifty yards of the man who ran off into the bush."

Proudly, John told me that he had the honour of firing first when the main body of the militia battered down Montgomery's Tavern. A cannon ball was shot right through the tavern, sending all the men who had been hiding inside racing off in all directions while the militia fired at them. The battle was over in an hour. That night, before he went back to teaching at the College. John sat down and wrote the story in his journal.

"It really was quite a grand time, you know," he said. "I want to remember every bit of it."

It was only after John was safely home that we all realized how close we had come to actual fighting. In the end, the rebellion fizzled. Mackenzie escaped over the border into the United States, leaving others to be rounded up and arrested. Word came that there were many minor injuries, but thankfully only a few people were actually killed. Sir Francis ordered Montgomery's Tavern destroyed and, of course, Dr. Horne had lost his home. Later, we heard that Mackenzie had actually gone off to set fire to Sheriff Jarvis' house as well, but that some of his more sensible men stopped him. His behaviour on those fateful days was certainly very strange, some of his own supporters described it as lunatic. In the middle of everything, when he should have been planning his attack, Mackenzie went off with a small party and robbed a stage coach which was carrying the mail into the city. With a different leader, there might have been a very different ending.

Colborne Lodge

M ackenzie's rebellion collapsed, but it would be years before the wounds and the divisions between people actually healed. I would not know for a long time whether Jennie's father and Peter had joined the rebels or whether like many people who supported Mackenzie, they decided, at the last moment, not to go out and fight. For a while, there was a distance between us, Jennie no longer dropping by as she had in the past, and I no longer sending her notes or inviting her to join us for activities.

Once the danger had passed, we faced another great challenge. The years of turmoil, the rumours and the actual rebellion had affected our work. Everywhere, business slowed down. People who had hired John to build houses were finding it hard to pay, making excuses, asking for more time and even giving up and walking away from the projects. At the same time, commissions were slow to come in. There was little work, and money was as scarce as it had been when we first arrived in Canada. To help tide us over this difficult time, we even rented out the rooms on the second floor of our house. Without John's teaching at the College, things would have been much worse for us.

In spite of all the unrest, John had always continued to work on the land we had purchased out on the Humber. He had been so eager to buy that he had borrowed the money from Mr. Chewett, who as our landlord and our client, was very understanding about our debts: still payments had to be made. The men John had hired finished clearing the first portion of the land and now a tenant was moving in to the small cottage that John had built there. At last, some money would start to come in, but it would not begin to cover what was needed for the house of our dreams.

The little white model of the house continued to sit on our dining table, almost mocking us. It even had a name now, Colborne Lodge, in honour of John Colborne, the Lieutenant-Governor, who had helped us so much when we were just starting out. It was really only a cottage and although I couldn't help but feel that the name suggested something so much grander than it really was, I could see that John loved it. What I didn't really see was the need to start building so quickly, but John was determined. The land overlooking the lake was cleared in the summer before the rebellion and work on the house started in the fall.

How carefully we planned the house together. It was going to be so different from most of the houses in Toronto, which like John's first commission, the Chewett Block, where we were living, were built of red brick in the Georgian style of the last generation. Our house would be a country house, all light and airy, with views of the lake and the forest that stretched out over the hills in all directions. There would be a verandah running all around the house, again quite unusual in the city. On our explorations outside the city, we had seen country houses and even log cabins with verandahs and we became quite intrigued by them. One summer, as we rode along a dusty road late in the

sharing in the joy of a new baby and cheering them on as they tried to find yet another way to make a life for themselves. But sometimes, I felt so much anger.

Over and over, John had tried to help Sidney, offering him a chance to buy land, to join John in a business venture, to move closer to Toronto. But Sidney was stubbornly determined to make his own way, even if meant poverty and hardship for his ever-growing family.

Why was what was so hard for me so easy for Fanny. We could have given so much to a child.

For them, another mouth to feed was such a struggle.

In January, just as we were getting settled in our new home, John planned a trip to London on business. But he arrived in Dundas, too ill to continue and had to return home. It was the same illness that constantly plagued him and often forced him to spend several days at a time in bed until he recovered. Dr. Widmer kept telling him that he was working too hard and that he ought to try to slow down, but for John, that was not possible. There was so much he wanted to do, and so much we had taken on, I sometimes thought it was like telling a hurricane to stop blowing.

Those bouts were difficult for me, not only because John was so ill, but also because I now had to look after him and the office at the same time. We were hoping to be able to hire people to help us, but that would still have to wait until better times.

Looking back, I marvel that we got through that first winter at all. As soon as John recovered, he started going into town regularly and I usually went with him, no matter how arduous the journey, but really there was still little work for us. It was not really until the next year that things started to improve. Now new work began to come in and suddenly we were working late at night on plans and specifications. There was, in fact, little time for anything else. We managed a few walks and horseback rides and saw friends for dinner or tea.

All through those dark winter nights, we dreamed about our garden. We drew plans and made long lists of what we wanted to plant; plum trees, rice, carrots and onions, all sorts of greens; peas, lettuce, broccoli, cabbage, cucumber and root vegetables, turnips parsnips, squash, Indian corn, and rutabaga. When we had just bought the land, we had planted potatoes together as a kind of celebration. But now, we were planning a real garden that would provide enough food for us to be able to live on what we grew. John built a barn with a hayloft. We had a well dug and made an ice house and we were already making changes in the house and planning for the addition.

When spring came and the travel was easier, I usually spent my days in town at the office. One morning, when things were quiet, I took some time away to do some shopping. A young woman hurrying along the street with a walk that just radiated energy caught my attention. It was Jennie. It had been so long since I had seen her, I almost didn't recognize her.

I called out. She turned and stopped. We stood there for a moment, in the middle of King Street, a little awkward, as if not knowing what to do next.

I was the one who broke the silence.

"Jennie," I cried, as I caught up to her, "it's been so long."

"Oh, Mrs. H," she said, beaming. "I have thought of you so often, but I didn't know—" She stopped, self-conscious.

"Jennie, I'm so happy to see you. You must come and have tea with me. There is so much to catch up on."

Jennie told me that she was busier than ever at the inn, but we arranged for her to meet for tea, the very next afternoon. We met in a lovely, new tearoom which had just opened.

It was hard to believe that this very self-possessed young woman had been, such a short time ago, almost a little girl with her red hair in braids. Now her hair had darkened to a lovely auburn shade and she wore it up, almost primly, wound neatly on her head. Her blue eyes still sparkled and I could see that she was almost bubbling with news.

After we exchanged pleasantries and settled down to our tea, I said finally, "Well, Jennie. You must tell me everything that has been happening to you."

"Mrs. H. It's hard to know where to begin. The most important thing is that we have set a date for our wedding. It's not going to be for a while, but we are making our plans already. The most important thing is that Peter and I are going to take over the inn!"

"But you are so young!" I exclaimed.

"That's what some people say, but my Ma says, she and Pa were just as young when they started out and look how well they have done."

"Are they giving up entirely?"

"Oh, no. They'll still be around. But they are building a little house for themselves, out in one of the new parts of the city, and when it's ready, they are going to move there, and we are going to take over their flat at the inn. They'll still be around to help, but we'll be the ones in charge. Isn't it exciting?"

Jennie explained that her older brothers had never had an interest in being innkeepers and had both gone off on their own to work together in a number of ventures in the city. They were both married and becoming quite successful.

"I was always the one who loved helping out, even when I was a little girl. Do you remember how I showed you around the town when you first arrived?"

"I've never forgotten that day."

"Well, I was always doing things like that, helping people out, chatting away until sometimes Ma had to shoo me out and listening to everything. That was always the best. You never know what people will say, especially when they've had a drink or two."

"But you always listened, and you learned so much. Most young people would never have paid attention as you do."

Jennie smiled. "And then Peter came along and my parents say it's time for them to have a bit of a rest. We're going to be a team, you know. Like my parents. Like you and Mr. H."

"It's going to be wonderful, Jennie. I can just see how successful you'll be."

We talked so easily about news in the town, bits of innocent gossip that we loved to share and more of her plans for the future that it was hard to believe that it had been many months since we had seen each other and that once things had been so uncomfortable between us. I was so glad that all of that unease was now in the past.

I poured another cup of tea for each of us and we sat for a while, just enjoying each other's company and then, all of a sudden, a more serious look crossed Jennie's face.

"Mrs. H," she said. "You know how I listen—not that I'm eavesdropping or anything."

"Of course not, dear."

"Well, two gentlemen come in sometimes. I think they have something to do with the city. They drink a bit, and they do get loud, if you know what I mean. There was no one else around, so I couldn't help overhearing. And they mentioned Mr. Howard and somebody called Young. It's happened a couple of times, and I..."

"You wonder what is going on."

"Well, yes. You probably think it's none of my business."

"That's all it is, Jennie. Business."

"Mrs. H, I didn't understand a lot of what they were saying, but it seems like he's taking things from Mr. Howard."

"Thomas Young. He's an upstart, that's all I really have to say about it. Came here from England just as we did. They called on us when they arrived, him and his wife, nice as could be, and the next thing you know, he's stealing work from us. First King's College and now we're hearing rumours about the Market Block."

"But, that's terrible."

"It is. And I don't doubt it's making John ill, being so angry about it all. But I do wonder, who were these gentlemen you heard talking about it at the Inn? I wouldn't think anyone in town would even be interested in what a pair of architects were up to."

"Ah, Mrs. H. You know this town, as you call it. People have something to say about everything."

Soon, Jennie was off and I found myself thinking about this rivalry which had developed between John and Thomas Young. Certainly, there was more than enough work in the fast growing city for both men, but it seemed to us as if Young was dogging our footsteps, deliberately pushing his way into projects which John had already made a start on.

Thomas Young

I t began with the design from King's College which would be the first university in Upper Canada. One of John's very first commissions in Toronto was the design for two entrance lodges and a fence for what would become the King's College property. How hard he worked on those drawings, spending most of his time on them for one and a half months. When his plan was accepted, we thought for sure he would be in a good position to design the College itself. He went ahead and submitted a plan for the actual building, but nothing came of it. And then, along came Mr. Young. Didn't he worm his way into getting the commission, by writing to Lieutenant-Governor Bond Head himself and suggesting that he should be the superintending architect for King's College. Plans for the College had actually been developed many years before, and from what we heard all Young did was build on those plans. He wrote to Bishop Strachan as well, promoting himself and the next thing we knew, he got the job. We heard talk of grandiose plans, of bids, of contractors being hired. But then, came the rebellion, and as with everything, the project slowed down, and eventually, it was abandoned. I can't say John and I were sorry to hear that Thomas Young had been dismissed.

Still, the conversation which Jennie overheard worried me. Who were those men and what were they saying about John and Thomas Young? More importantly, did they know something that we didn't?

I found myself thinking back to the time when John first heard about the competition for the design of the new buildings for the Market Block. After working tirelessly for over a month, John won that competition. We heard later that Thomas Young had also made a submission, but his plans were unfinished and his request for an extension of the deadline was turned down.

Like the plans for King's College, so far nothing had come of the proposal for the Market Block.

We knew that the unrest before and even after the rebellion and all the financial difficulties it caused had affected a great deal of work planned by the city. At first we weren't concerned, but as time went by, and we heard nothing about the project, we began to suspect that something was going wrong. Could it be that Young was meddling again?

It wasn't long until we found out that was exactly what had happened. The Market Block was starting up again, but we hadn't been consulted. Instead, Mr. Thomas Young had somehow managed to get himself added to the Select Committee overseeing the project and the next thing you know, didn't he get himself appointed City Surveyor to oversee the erection of the buildings of the whole Block. Later we were to hear that Thomas had written to the Mayor. He suggested the creation of the position of City Surveyor and then somehow managed to make sure that he was the one appointed to do the job. Young was the one who was going to build the Market Block. After all the work that John had done on the original plans for the project, we were left out in the cold, and that upstart got to do the job that should have been ours.

John was in a rage for days after we heard the news. He threatened to sue the city, to take Young himself to court, even to pick up stakes and move somewhere else. As I told Jennie, this rivalry and the financial worries it caused us seemed to be making John ill. I was just as angry as he was but somehow managed to remain calm. We had taken on a great deal; buying and clearing the Humber land and building our new house. John wanted to buy more land, even while we were struggling to keep up with all his plans. It would not do for both of us fly off in a rage.

Fortunately, John calmed down and soon everything began to improve. People were coming to the city again, business was picking up and projects that had been put off or even cancelled were starting up again. Suddenly we had almost more work than we could handle. We still were not able to hire anyone to help us so John and I continued to do all the work together, just as we had always done.

Over the next few years, the rivalry continued. It was John who got the commission when the city decided to build a new jail, but Young was hired to build the Courthouse Block which the city would then sell off to finance it. When St James Anglican Church was damaged in a fire, both John and Young were hired to write reports, but Young was finally chosen to complete the project. If that wasn't enough, much to our dismay, Young also got the commission to enlarge St. Andrew's Presbyterian Church. Then, the next thing we knew, Young was dismissed from the project, after going to court over lost payments, and John took over the project. And so it went, both men competing over work, and all the while, rumours about Thomas Young began to spread as so often his work ended badly. What a strange twist it was, that after all the great disappointment of losing the Market Block and seeing Young appointed City Surveyor, after only four years in the post, Thomas Young was dismissed. Finally, John was ap-

coming fall.

Knowing that we were moving, we did manage to invite our friends to come out and visit quite often during the summer and Fanny and Sidney came with the children to stay with us for a while. What a brood she had now! Alfred growing into quite the young man, and now there was Ellen, Eliza, baby Clara and yet another one coming. Fanny seemed to be able to manage it all. She doted on her children and never seemed flustered by the din and the chaos that accompanied four children running about. As always, with the first few days of the visit, I loved to listen to the children and watch them play. It was hard not to imagine what could have been for us, a house full of laughter and boisterous play. The children loved coming out to the lodge where they could have the run of the barn, the gardens and the woods around the house. At home, Fanny said they all had chores to do and there was little time for play. As much as I loved having those visits, sometimes, it all became exhausting and I began to long for the quiet I was used to.

One sunny afternoon, Fanny and I were at last able to rest and chat, sitting on the verandah as we watched the children play.

"Alfred is really growing up," I said, watching him lead his little sisters in games they invented.

"He is," Fanny agreed. "I worry about him."

"But, why? I've just been watching how patient he is with the girls. He's so bright and kind."

"That's just it, he's a bright young lad. He should be going to a good school, but there is nothing for him where we are, even if we could afford it."

I knew that Fanny had tried her best to teach the children at home and had sent them to school when she could. She had often talked about how difficult it was living so far out in the wilderness. There was a small school, but it was quite a distance from their farm and even if Alfred was old enough to make his way there alone, so often bad weather prevented his going out at all.

Fanny and I went in to prepare supper, and as we worked together in the kitchen, I kept turning our conversation around in my mind. What could we do to help Fanny? And more to the point, how could we help Alfred?

John and Sidney had gone out hunting that day and by the time they came home, successful with a brace of ducks and some rabbits which we would put to good use, I had the answer. The question was, would John agree to it, and if he did, what about Fanny and especially Sidney who seemed always to reject whatever John suggested. Before supper, I drew John aside to try out my idea.

"Fanny and I had a long talk today." I began.

"You two always do," he responded, not paying much attention.

"No, I mean, this was something serious. I want to talk to you about it."

I explained to John how Fanny was concerned about Alfred's schooling and did not know what to do about it.

"I've already thought about it," he said. "Sidney talked to me about this last time they were here. He usually tries to be quite cheerful about their, shall we say, situation. But he seemed to be sorry he couldn't do more for the boy. I gave it some thought, made some inquiries, and if they are agreeable, I think I have a solution."

Later, when the children were at last asleep, we sat by the fire, the men smoking their pipes and Fanny and I with our tea.

I let John broach the subject to the Mountcastles.

"Do you, remember Sid," he began, "when we talked a while back about young Alfie and his schooling?"

It had probably been the last thing on Sidney's mind as he sat back with his pipe and enjoying a quiet moment. He looked quite surprised.

"I think I might have a solution for you," John continued. "I can help you get him enrolled at Upper Canada College."

"But" cried Fanny. "We couldn't possibly afford that, even if they would have him. It's for the rich boys."

"That's true," John agreed. "But I've explored this a bit, asked the right people and it seems that if I make Alfie my ward, than he can attend as a day boy. And since I am a teaching master, the fees are... not a question."

There was silence. Fanny and Sidney stared at us for a moment, speechless. It was an idea so far from anything they had thought of that at first they seemed hesitant, bringing up one obstacle, then the next.

"He's so young," they said.

"He's never been away from home."

"How can we impose on you?"

"He's a country boy, How will he fit in?"

John knew Sidney well. He had already thought through the arguments that Sidney would raise and had his answers ready. By the end of the evening, the Mountcastles had agreed to the plan.

We would have Alfred come to live with us while he became a student at the College. For a while, at least, we would have a child in the house. It would be almost as if he was our own.

In the years that followed, the girls, one by one, would come to us, and I would care for them and almost feel as if they were mine. Sometimes, it seemed that they would fill, for a while, the great emptiness I always felt inside.

I don't go out much anymore. Not after the last time. I put on my bonnet and went out for a walk, just as I have always done, alone,

with my basket to pick some flowers. I remember that. And then, suddenly it seemed, I heard loud voices, hands pulling at me, dragging me along through the woods. John seemed so angry, but I don't really know why. Now, someone watches me all the time.

decision, long before a design competition was even announced, John began to develop his plans. He read everything he could about asylums and what could be done to help the people who would be living there.

We soon heard that Thomas Young was also working on a design to submit to the competition. When the deadline was announced, he asked, as usual, for an extension. The Committee turned down Young's request. John submitted his plan which was accepted and he received a premium of thirty pounds for his design. Although the project was approved, work would not actually begin for some time.

It was almost ten years since we had arrived in that little muddy town of York, ten years since that frightful winter when we huddled in the freezing attic as John made his first drawings for Sir John. Now as he embarked on his great work, we had a proper business, with a bustling office.

We were often so busy that our social life seemed to suffer. We had a small circle of friends and we saw them as often as we could for dinner and tea, but I never had time for the sewing circles and book discussions that many of the other women did. They were good-hearted women who in addition to raising their families were involved in church work and establishing societies to help the poor. With their households, their children, and their good deeds, they always seemed to be busy and kept appointment books that were filled in weeks in advance.

Although the women I knew like Sarah and Lizzie Wakefield, had all become used to the idea that I was generally busy working in our office and couldn't participate in their activities, I knew that they had never quite accepted what I did. Sometimes, I often felt as if they looked at me with something that was almost pity. Was it just my own imagination, or a perception that arose from my own deep sense of loss? I imagined them thinking I worked with John only to fill the emptiness. Perhaps there was some truth to this. If we had children like everyone else would I have continued to work as I did?

What would I have done without Jennie? Unlike all my other friends, she had about her a wonderful spontaneity. Perhaps it was because we had established our unusual friendship when she was so young, that we never felt that we had to stand on ceremony with one another. Now, at twenty-two, even though she was beginning to take on more work at the   inn we still managed to meet for a walk or a visit to a tearoom. Recently though, I felt as if I caught her looking at me thoughtfully sometimes. It was as if there was something she wanted to say. But always drew back, unusually silent, almost shy.

And then came that spectacular fall day, when Jennie and I had a conversation that would etch itself in my being forever. I had been working on the books all morning. But the sun was so bright and sky so achingly blue, that I just had to go out. Needing a companion, I went round to Grey's and pulled Jennie out to walk with me.

We went down to the lake and walked out along the shore. Bright leaves, yellow and gold and red were now beginning to fall. They scurried around us and crunched under our feet. It was still warm, but there was a touch of crispness in the air, a hint of the cold which would come all too soon.

I was feeling truly happy, much better than I had felt for a long time. Jennie, however, seemed preoccupied.

"What is it?" I asked finally, curious about her unusual silence.

"There's something I've been wanting to say," she began. "You may say, it's none of my business but..." Jennie looked away, staring out at the lake.

"What?"

Jennie drew a deep breath and stared straight ahead as we walked. "I... I know when you were ill a few years back." When she spoke it was almost as if she had underlined the word ill with her voice.

"I don't know what you mean?"

"Jemima," She had never called me by my name before. It was as if something shifted between us. She stopped and turned to me. "I know you lost a baby."

There was a silence. I didn't know what to say.

"But how?"

"Women know these things. I know that it's happened before."

We walked on in silence. Somehow, I knew there was more to come.

"Jemima. You know... my mother. Well, people talk to her, women talk to her. They come, sometimes, in the afternoon, when it is quiet at the inn. They say things to her that they can't say to others, to their husbands."

"And?"

"And she helps them."

"I don't know what you mean."

She took my arm and leaned forward to look at me closely.

"My mother thinks maybe she could help you."

"You've talked about this with her?" I was appalled.

"Only because, I have seen how you suffer, the sadness that is always around you."

"Well, say it then. What do you mean?"

"Ma knows an old woman who lives on the edge of town. She was a midwife, back in the early days here, before there were many doctors. She knows the old ways, herbs and potions, things that heal when our doctors have no answers. Women go to her ... and she helps them. Ma knows her, she could make arrangements—"

Nothing more was said that day. But Jennie's words and what was unspoken swirled around in my head. Part of me said that this was nonsense, superstition only. But like everyone in the city, I had heard stories of the old ways that new settlers had to learn in order to survive in the wilderness. Medicines that came from the trees and the wild bushes that had saved lives when all else failed. Ways to survive in the forests and farm when there was no one near to help.

It was strange. Jennie had become so much a part of my life, like a younger sister or life-long friend. Her mother, Anna, was the first person I met that day when we had arrived in York and she had done so much to help us get through that first terrible winter. But I had never really talked to her. To me, in spite of all that Jennie had told me about her unusual mother, she was just the innkeeper's wife. Agreeing to meet with her, to talk about something I thought was so hidden meant making real what I had never really admitted even to myself.

Several weeks later, I told Jennie I would like to come and talk with her mother.

One gloomy, rainy afternoon, I told John I was going to do some shopping and set off for the inn. I was filled with so many conflicting feelings—embarrassment, suspicion, curiosity. Twice, I almost turned back, but Jennie's words had planted just that slim ray of hope in my mind and finally, I arrived at the inn, relieved to find the dining room empty in the mid-afternoon just as Jennie had told me it would be.

Talking to Anna Grey over tea was surprisingly easy. I realized that I had rarely seen her sit down; she was always in motion, serving food, looking after her customers or family. Now she sat still in her chair, looking at me with a frankness I found almost startling. Looking at Anna, I could see the woman Jennie would become: her hair, once probably red, like Jennie's had darkened and was now streaked with grey; She was tall and sturdy and had a no-nonsense attitude which I could sense even when she was sitting still.

"Mrs. Howard," she began, skipping any niceties and going straight to the point, "this is a hard thing."

"It is, very hard."

"You've been so good to our Jennie. She's a good girl, y'know. And her heart goes out to you. That's why she told me about you. Not that she gossips, you understand."

"Of course."

"Running an inn, y'know. People come to you. The men get into their cups and talk to George like he was their preacher. And, I guess, word gets around. The women come for tea and talk."

"I see."

"Ya hear things. One day it's this, one day, it's that. And before you know it, well, if I can help things along, that's what the Good Lord meant me to do. But sometimes," she leaned over and dropped her voice to a whisper. "He'd be pretty shocked to know what I'm up to."

Anna leaned back and continued.

"Jennie told you, I think, about Marie. She knows the old lore, the ways of herbs and potions. Sometimes they do help people, but if not, at least they do no harm. I've sent many a woman to her over the years. If anyone can help you it would be Marie."

It was odd to talk to a woman I barely knew about something hidden so deeply. But I knew, without question, that I could trust her, that like Jennie, she truly cared for me.

"But who is this Marie? How did you meet her?"

"It was a long time ago, I had some... woman's troubles,

y'know. Someone told me about her and well, we've been good friends ever since. Years ago, she and her husband got some land far out in the wilderness and settled there. She seemed to have the gift, y'know, for helping other women. Soon she was always being called out to help birthing the babies. It must have been so hard for those women, all alone,.."

Like Fanny, I thought.

"One night during a very difficult birth an Indian woman appeared, brought both mother and child through safely and then taught Marie everything she knows."

"What is she doing here, in Toronto?"

"After her husband died, she tried living out there alone, but it was far too lonely. She came here when York was still almost just a village and set up as a midwife. You know Dr. Widmer of course?"

I nodded.

"Even he often turned to her for her knowledge and help."

After sharing more stories about Marie, Anna Grey had me convinced.

"I would like to try."

As I rose to leave, Mrs. Grey reached out and touched me lightly on my arm. "And, don't offer to pay her anything. That could be a problem for her—she's not supposed to take payment for her services."

"What can I do?"

"Bring her a gift, some food, warm clothes. A nice bottle of wine wouldn't be amiss."

And so it was arranged. Jennie would take me to meet the old woman as soon possible.

A week later, I told John that I was joining some of the ladies and would not be able to come in to the office as I usually did. Work had really mounted up and he was a little put out, but

I so seldom took time for myself there was really little he could say.

Jennie came to meet me early on that misty Fall morning, carrying a large basket covered with a brightly coloured cloth. We drew our shawls closely around us as we set off down King Street. Jenny clearly knew where she was going as she walked so purposefully along, I had to hurry to keep up with her. We walked down east, to a part of the city I had never seen. It was here that the mills and factories had been built along the river and the workers lived, crowded in small, ramshackle huts nearby. Soon she turned into a small lane that led to a shabby little settlement. There were small cabins, some lean-tos and even a few tents. Jennie made her way through the buildings and stopped in front of a small cabin that stood apart from the rest. She rapped lightly on the door and it was opened by a tiny, old woman with a wizened face and a mass of grey, frizzy hair. She was almost like something out of a fairy tale.

"Good morning, Marie. Ma sent these for you." Jennie set down her basket at the woman's feet.

"Your mother is good woman," she said.

"She says the same of you."

Jennie turned and gestured to me. "This is Mrs. Howard, the lady Ma told you about."

Marie nodded to me. "Let's go inside."

The cabin lit by only one small window was dark. Dust motes danced and a pale light penetrated through the grimy panes. There was a small bed, a table, a place to prepare food. As we entered, Marie drew me close to the window, put her hands on my shoulders and peered closely at me with her large dark eyes. It was almost as if she could see right through me. Jennie had somehow made herself disappear into the darkness of the cabin.

become quite a friend and for whom John had designed and built several houses was always well dressed. I remember his well-pressed suit, the gold watch chain and fob across his vest, his hat in his hand. He sat down beside me on my bed and took my hand in his and shook his head sadly.

"This is Marie's doing, I think."

I tried to protest, not wanting to make trouble for her.

"No, no. She's a good woman," he said, echoing Anna Grey's words. "She knows a great deal and, in the past, I often looked to her for help. But sometimes, she tries, still, to—ah—meddle where she shouldn't."

Widmer shook his head again.

"Mrs. Howard, you've been very ill."

I nodded.

"If this were to happen again, you would not survive. Do you understand me?"

I nodded again.

When the doctor left, Fanny came back and sat with me. Mary brought us more tea and cakes and I tried to eat a little, although even trying to eat demanded more effort than I could summon up. I lay back on my pillows.

Fanny reached over and took my hand.

"Do you want to talk about it?" she asked.

"What is there to say?"

"You survived, Mimie. Dr. Widmer says now he wasn't sure you would."

"But, for what, Fansi? What am I here for?"

"Oh Mimie." Fanny looked at me sadly. There were tears in her eyes.

She paused, searching for an answer. "I know you, Mimie," she began.

"Better than anyone," I said.

"I know what you are going to say," she continued. "But hear me out. Right now, you don't want me to tell you how fortunate you are, all that you have. You think that's just the easy answer. You look at me, dear, with such envy. I know you do. But you, of all people, know how hard it's been. Do you remember how you found us that awful day on Church Street when we had to sell our treasures to survive? Do you know what it is like for me? Always a baby and another one on the way. I love them, of course, but each time it gets harder..."

I shook my head wearily. "What are you trying to tell me?" I asked.

"I envy you too." she said. "Your life, your lovely house, the servants. You have a good husband. He cares for you deeply. I know, I was here when he was so afraid he might lose you. And he is growing more and more successful. While Sidney, well, you know. Do you think I wouldn't want to work as you do, in an office, doing important work?"

"But you do work, all the time."

"Of course," she said bitterly. "As a farmhand when we can't even afford to hire one. All the cooking, and the cleaning, trying to teach the children when I can find a moment. It never ends."

Fanny had never really talked about her life before. For the first time, I realized how she had been putting up a good front all this time, never complaining, going along with whatever plan Sidney came up with next. I knew that she cared for him, and didn't blame him for their troubles as many women would have done. I knew, too, what she was trying to do and how much it must have cost her, being so honest with me in order to help me.

"You should rest now," Fanny said, getting up and seeming to slip back into her cheerful, brisk self. "And besides, you have my Alfie with you. He can be quite a handful, as you know. And

Ellen loves to visit, any time you want to have her. She's a sharp one, she is."

"What do you mean?"

"I've noticed already. She likes being in your lovely house. You spoil her. Here she's got servants to wait on her instead of chores to do and children to look after."

I found myself laughing in agreement. Having the children with me would be a great help.

Fanny took away the tea things and left me alone to rest.

Alone. I lay in my bed thinking of how for such a short time I had dared to hope and now that hope was gone. I would keep those feelings locked inside me forever.

But Fanny's words had touched me deeply. In all these years, she had never shared her deepest thoughts with me. I felt a sense of shame when I thought about her losses, the little one who had died in Canada just before we arrived; another child, stillborn. And all this time, she had never said a word. It must have cost her a great deal to be so frank with me. I knew that somehow, I had to find the way to go on.

Soon life began again. Friends started to visit. Sarah Tuton came often with Rosa, bringing hearty soup, bustling around and filling me in on all the town gossip. One afternoon, however, she came alone, settling down in an armchair the maid had brought into our bedroom for the visitors. Usually quite forthright, Sarah seemed nervous, her fingers working the lace that edged the handkerchief she held. There was an awkward silence.

"What is it, Sarah?" I finally asked, fearing that she had some sad news to tell.

"I wanted to say, I know how hard this is for you." She hesitated. "I've never said anything before, but it's happened to me, many times."

"Sarah. I didn't know," I said, reaching for her hand. And

then I remembered. "Those times when you said you were just 'under the weather' and didn't want company?"

She nodded.

"I wish you had told me. I could have helped."

"What was there to do? So often, I thought there was another baby on the way, and then, suddenly, it would be all over." A wave of sadness passed over her face. "I thought we would have a big family, strapping big lads with lots of room to roam in this new country. It wasn't to be."

"How did you manage to—" I hesitated, "—to keep going on?"

Sarah sighed. "Those were hard times, hard for Richard too. But, we said, if this is what the good Lord has planned for us, then this is what it will be."

"And, of course, you have Rosa. She is such a comfort."

"Yes, she is. With Richard gone, I don't know what I would do without her."

That day, a window had opened between Sarah and me as we talked about what we had lost, but then it closed again. Although we would remain friends for many years, our secrets and our losses remained our own.

After Sarah left and I was alone, I thought about what she said. Resigned, I wished I could be like her, at peace. It was God's way, she said. Perhaps, one day, I would come to believe that as well, but then, in those dark days, there was no such solace for me.

Lizzie Wakefeld also came to visit with another friend. Neighbours came by and soon our sitting room was so filled with flowers it began to seem like a florists' shop.

And, after sending me a note to ask if she might come by, Jennie came to visit me at last, bringing as always a basket filled with delights; vegetables from the garden, a freshly baked pie, some jam and bread still warm from the oven, its rich, yeasty smell piquing my appetite for the first time in weeks.

I was up, resting on the sofa in the sitting room, when she came in, stopping at the door, almost awkwardly. Jenny was so unlike her usual, exuberant, smiling self.

"I came several times when Mrs. Mountcastle was here. She said you were sleeping so I didn't stay."

"I did sleep so much, at the beginning. I don't think I wanted to wake up."

"I wasn't sure that you would want to see me."

"Why ever not?" I asked, not understanding what she meant. "I'm always delighted to see you."

Jennie came and sat down beside me.

"I was afraid," she continued, "That you would think it was my fault, me and my Ma. That we shouldn't have meddled in..." She seemed unable to find the words she wanted to say.

"Oh, no, Jennie." I said, taking her hands in mine. "You didn't do anything wrong. You wanted to help. It's just..."

"It was God's will, in the end. As Marie said, do you remember?"

I nodded.

"Jennie, I'm not sorry... that.... we tried. I'm grateful to you and your mother, for helping me."

"My ma would like to visit, if you would like to see her too."

"I'd like that very much."

Then Jennie looked up at me, smiling, a slight blush touching her face.

"And, Jemima, I have to tell you, you have to get well soon. Peter and I have set the date for our wedding. It's to be in June, and you promised to come. Do you remember?"

"Of course, I do. What wonderful news. Just the tonic I

need. We talk about Peter all the time, but I have never met him. "As soon as I am feeling better, you'll have to bring him around."

"I know he would like that very much. Peter says I talk about you so much, it's time he met you."

Slowly, my strength began to return. When friends came by, they encouraged me to take short walks and spend more time sitting in the garden.

As for John, he was gentle and kind—and quiet. Even his step lost its usual jauntiness. At home, in the evening he worked silently on his drawings or read by the fire. He turned down invitations to go shooting and sent his regrets to his club meetings.

Sometimes, I would catch him looking at me sadly, but when he noticed me looking, he would turn away. No words were ever said. Separately, we dealt with the loss of the child, the loss, finally, of all our hopes and dreams. Sometimes, rarely, he reached out and touched me, stroking my cheek as if I were something fragile that would break.

I longed to reach out to him, but I was locked in the cage of my own misery.

I knew that John had always wanted children, that he loved watching other people's children at play, delighted in taking them sailing on the pond or showing them his inventions. Perhaps, there were other husbands and wives who might have been able to talk about their loss, but it was never to be for us.

Perhaps it was the medicine I had been given to help me sleep or perhaps it was my own mind trying to keep feeling at bay, but I felt that I had been numb for a long time. Now, alone in the garden as spring turned to summer. I felt as if, like the flowers around me, I was beginning to come back to life. Starting to awaken, I remembered fragments of what had happened, bits of conversation, the pain and the horror. Those days when I was weak and feverish were hazy as I drifted in and out of sleep, a sleep induced by strange drinks and potions I remember being given.

I remember waking to find Dr. Widmer standing beside my bed, looking down at me very sadly. Like a scene being played over and over, I remember him taking my hand.

He had said, "If this were to happen again, you would not survive. Do you understand me?"

I had nodded, but in the haze of my illness, I did not really understand.

It is strange how we women are raised to know that there were many things that are never talked about openly; not to our husbands or our sisters or even our good friends. And yet, knowledge is passed about and shared.

Often, it will be a conversation about somebody else.

It begins in a gossipy way.

"I have heard," someone will say, "that Mrs. S. was determined not to have any more children."

"Three in such a short time. I shouldn't wonder..."

"But what did she do?"

"It is said, she turned Mr. S. out of the marriage bed."

There would be a dramatic pause. An intake of breath! Perhaps, a sort of pretense of shock—the pretense that such things should not be even considered. An uncomfortable titter. Then the talk would shift to other more acceptable subjects, and the knowledge gained would be tucked away.

And so we would talk, of women's illnesses and problems with husbands, of men who beat their wives and women who betrayed their men. Stories would be told of husbands who had squandered their wives' fortunes and wives who drove their husbands to despair at their extravagant ways. It was all told through the lens of someone else's experience so that one never had to admit that anything so terrible could happen to them.

"If this were to happen again...." I kept on hearing those words.

Now I understood what Dr. Widmer was saying. I was thirty-nine, growing older to be sure, but not so old that I could not still conceive a child. If that happened, I would not survive. I knew that I couldn't even face the possibility of all that pain and suffering. I knew what needed to be done to prevent it.

I don't know how to write this. I have filled so many notebooks, but those words would not come. I know, now, I have come to this. I can no longer avoid it, the part of the story I still after all these years cannot bear to face.

It began so long ago, after I was ill, after the baby that never came. At first, I thought it was because I had been so ill that John would come to say goodnight to me—and turn away, to go back to work, to walk the dogs. I thought it was so that I could rest.

And then, I was well again. I went back to the office. Our busy days, the rounds of visits, the plans for the new house went on as if, on the surface, nothing had happened. But really, everything had changed. It seemed as if something had grown between us, almost an invisible wall, something intangible, but there, just beyond reach.

One night, after a long trying day, we sat together in the garden. It was a soft, starry night. Silent, save for a slight rustle of a breeze in the trees. It was so peaceful, we were reluctant to break the spell.

At last, John stood up, stretching. He put out his pipe.

"Come, my dear," he said. "We have a busy day coming tomorrow."

Lighting a candle, we climbed the stairs together and prepared for the night. I climbed into bed, hesitantly.

John stood for a while, on the other side of the bed, then, silently, climbed in beside me. He turned to me and held me in his arms. I wanted him to love me... and then...I saw for an instant, Dr. Widmer's face instead of John's. I heard the doctor's words. I froze. My whole body stiffened, pushing John away. His own face reappeared.

I struggled to speak. "No, John—we can't! Widmer said..." I couldn't force myself to continue.

John jolted away from me, staring at me almost as though I was a stranger.

No!

It was not like that. Over and over the scene plays out in my head. My memory play tricks with me. Sometimes, I see it this way, I struggle and thrust John away.

And sometimes, I see another scene.

John stood for a while, on the other side of the bed, then, silently, climbed in beside me.

He turned to me, looked at me sadly, reached out touched my face and leaned over to kiss me on the cheek and shook his head. Turning away, he blew out the candle and turned his back to me to go to sleep.

What is the truth? What really happened?

Did Christopher Widmer speak to John as he had to me? Did John listen to his advice?

As the years have passed, I have become less and less sure of anything. Did I make all this up? Was there something else entirely that happened between us, a scene so troubling that I willed myself to forget it? The truth is buried so deeply, I will never find it.

However it happened, from that time we lived together, but alone. A part of our life died with the child who had never been born.

No words were ever said between us. A door closed which could never be pried open.

I am lying, stretched out on the sofa in the parlour, a coverlet over me, pillows behind my back. Phoebe has brought me some tea. It seems as if I'm ill, everyone fussing over me, but I don't feel ill at all. Around me, there is a hustle, people running up and down the stairs. I hear furniture being moved. The thunk of hammering. Hushed voices.

Ellen was here. We went to for a ride in the carriage, but I can't seem to remember where we went. She kept holding my hand. I caught her looking at me sadly. We used to have long talks together, but we don't seem to talk much anymore. Now she has gone away and I don't think she even told me where she was going. I don't think she even said goodbye.

Nobody talks much to me anymore. They talk at me, they ask me things.

"How are you feeling?"

"Do you want some tea?"

They don't seem to want to talk about anything. It's almost as if they are talking to a child. And John, he doesn't talk at all. He seems to be angry with me all the time, but I don't know what I have done to make him feel that way.

We were never angry with each other. All those years together, we never quarrelled. I don't remember ever saying a harsh word. But now, he doesn't talk at all, he just sits, reading his paper, sometimes looking at me and shaking his head.

But now I am angry—all the time.

At first, it was so hard.

If I saw a woman with a baby on the street, I dissolved into tears and had to turn and walk the other way. When I tried to sleep, I was so plagued by horrible images that I wished for the medicines to take me away. Then one night, lying in my bed, hot, sweating, the sheets twisted by all the tossing and turning, I found a way to fight back. I learned to push those thoughts out of my mind. I imagined myself driving them out. I saw myself putting them in a box, tying up with string that I could even see. I picked up the box and hid it, high on a shelf in a closet that no one would use. I locked the closet door and turned away. Whenever the thoughts came, I put them in another box and hid them away as well. After a while, the thoughts disappeared.

Slowly, my strength began to return and friends came by to encourage me to begin to take short walks and spend time sitting in the garden. Although John sometimes brought work home to keep me company. I noticed that he seldom talked about the office and I had a suspicion that Dr. Widmer had probably advised him that I should not be bothered with it.

In spite of this advice, our business was so much a part of

our lives that it was difficult for John not to talk about what he was working on. As I began to get stronger, he began to share more with me and it was not long until we started taking on small tasks at home. As soon as I started to work again, I realized how much I missed it and how much it helped to take my mind off what had happened. As John's work so often took him on journeys outside Toronto, I soon began to go back to the office and it wasn't long until I had returned to the usual busy life we had known.

Early in May, we received a note inviting us to Jennie's wedding. I have forgotten so much, but that day always stands out in my mind. I remember it as though it was all happening again.

The Wedding

I have forgotten so much, but always, Jennie's wedding stands out in my mind. I remember it as though it was all happening again.

She was married on a June morning, before the blistering heat of summer, a morning of clear blue skies and a gentle breeze.

"I don't know why we were invited to this thing," John muttered, grumpily, as we made our way to the church. "It's not as if they're friends of ours."

"Jennie's my friend, John!" I answered. "I watched her grow up."

Jennie and her mother had been busy with wedding preparations for months, but she and I had made some time to meet. I invited her to tea in one of the tearooms in town—a formal event, I thought for a young bride. Fairly bubbling with excitement, she told me all about her plans.

"Are you going to wear white?" I asked.

Since the marriage of our young Queen Victoria the year before, I knew that many young brides were choosing to wear white gowns just as the young queen had. I remembered how excited we had all been about that wedding. Reading about this young, lovely woman who was marrying her prince was like something out of a fairy tale, and although we were thousands of miles away and the news was months old, my friends and I pored eagerly over the papers when they finally arrived from England. We studied the details of the wedding and tried to imagine ourselves in the crowds in London waiting to see the young couple drive by.

"Oh, no. White's not for me." said the ever-practical Jennie. "What would I do after the wedding with a white dress? I'm just having a nice, sensible dress, Not too fancy, so I can wear it to church afterwards. But I am having it made by a dressmaker," she added proudly. Then she grinned at me. "And besides, I'm a bit old to be a blushing bride."

"Nonsense. You're only twenty-three."

"Old!" She repeated. "Some of my friends have two babies already."

Jennie's wedding was held at the Methodist Church in the east end of town. John and I normally attended St. James Cathedral where we had recently acquired a pew. We had never been to a Methodist Church before and we found this simple building quite austere to our eyes. There were only a small number of guests for the wedding, Jennie's brothers and sister and Peter's family as well. We sat near the back, not wanting to intrude on the family.

How radiant Jennie looked! Even now I can see her as she was on her wedding day. Slim and elegant in her pearl-grey dress. It was modest, but flattered her trim, young figure. Jennie had white flowers wound in her hair which, as she matured, had darkened to a rich auburn.

Peter, a little uncomfortable in his new suit, gazed at her which such love and pride,

I felt my own heart swell as I watched them take their vows. Although I had never really admitted it to myself, Jennie was almost like a daughter to me. Sometimes I had imagined her as the daughter I never had. Now, as I watched her take this step, I found myself wondering if we would grow apart as she took on her new life.

I thought, too, of my life. It seemed not so long ago that we had married in St. Leonard's in faraway London. Had we ever been so young and hopeful?

Afterwards, there was a wedding breakfast at the inn. The dining room was filled with flowers and many people came to celebrate. Both Jennie and Peter were the youngest in their families; their older brothers and sisters were married and their many children ran around, gobbling food from the tables and chasing one another in and out of the inn.

Relatives from both families milled around chatting with one another and enjoying the festivities.

Of course, everyone wanted to greet and congratulate the bride and groom, but at last we were able to have a moment with Jennie. When I took her by the hands, I felt so happy for her, my eyes almost welled up with tears.

"Jemima," she exclaimed, enveloping me in a hug, "I am so pleased that you are here."

When Peter came to stand beside her, I turned to introduce him to John.

"Thank you, so much for coming, sir," he said, quite stiffly.

Slipping between us, Jennie took us both by the arms and led us up to greet her parents.

There was, for a moment, an awkwardness, a hesitation, as if both Anna Grey and I were remembering the last conversation we'd had.

"Congratulations, Mrs. Grey," I said, taking her hand. "Such a beautiful wedding."

"And, of course, you remember my husband," she said,

turning to Frank.

John and Frank shook hands, but there was a stiffness between the four of us and Frank, especially, seemed particularly uncomfortable. It was a relief when others came bustling and took the Grey's off to meet other guests.

We met Jennie's brothers, both tall, strapping young men, and their wives. We all shook hands, talked a little about the wedding and the young couple, but again, there was that sense that we had little to say to one another.

Later, there were toasts to the bride and groom, Frank made a little speech and Jennie and Peter cut their cake.

Like the white wedding gown, Queen Victoria had also made wedding cakes a new feature of stylish weddings. We had all read about her legendary cake, so huge that it took four footmen to carry it. Every paper had carried drawings of it, and every bride wanted a cake just like the Queen. Jennie's mother had made her daughter a very pretty wedding cake

And so, there it was, the wedding that I so looked forward to was over. John and I sat for a while at a small table, watching all the others enjoying the party. As much as I hated to admit it, John was right. Jennie was my friend, but I had no place in her world, just as she had no place in mine. Toronto was still a very small town, but the divisions in its little society were very clear.

Feeling more and more uncomfortable, John and I left quietly as soon as we could.

"Churches and taverns," John muttered as we walked along home from the wedding.

I had long become used to this habit John had of turning an idea around and around in his mind until it burst out, in some comment that seemed to come out of nowhere.

"Pardon?" I asked, wondering what he was thinking of this time.

"Churches and taverns," he repeated. "That's what some wag said about this city when he got here some time back in the thirties. Did you know that there were no less than seventy-nine taverns in this little town when we arrived? I can't help thinking that's exactly what today was all about. First, that church that we'd never been to and then the tavern."

"Now, John. It's an inn, we stayed there when we first arrived, have you forgotten?"

"It's an odd place, this," he continued, ignoring my comment. "And almost as many churches as there are taverns. So many churches, because, after all, everyone has to have his own. You've got the Methodists, like these folk, then there's the Baptists, the Presbyterians, the Catholics."

"And don't forget the English," I added, thinking of our own St. James.

"Not that I'm complaining. Where would we be, Mrs. H, if I weren't running around the province building all those churches? Why in the tiniest village there are as many as four churches. Just the ones in Toronto alone keep us busy, don't they?"

As we walked along, John's thoughts must have turned to the wedding, because after walking in silence, he suddenly said, "That Frank seems a nice chap, doesn't he? Quite a personable fellow. He was a little stiff with us, but I watched him with the others. I can see why the inn is a success." He turned to me, and with a wry smile continued. "Much better at it, I'm afraid, than your family was."

He was referring to the time when Sidney and Fanny attempted to run an inn near Goderich. That venture, like so many of the other things, they tried failed dismally after a short while. It used to be that John tried to be quite accepting of their efforts, but recently, having made many attempts to help which were rejected, he had become quite critical of Sidney.

We walked the rest of the way in silence, each with our own thoughts.

That night I couldn't sleep. I had so looked forward to this wedding, the ceremony, and the party afterwards. While the happy young bride and groom and the celebrations were all lovely, the very thought of our presence there made me feel uncomfortable and somewhat foolish. I realized that John had been right. The Greys weren't our friends, and our presence at the party had been awkward for everyone. Although I had never put it in so many words, I might have thought of Jennie as a daughter, but when I saw her in the midst of her own family, I realized it was a fantasy. Now Jennie was starting out in her new life and I wondered if there would be a place for me in it.

My thoughts drifted also to the people in Toronto who were our close friends. Although we hadn't set out to choose particular people to make friends with, it seemed that most of our circle were British immigrants like ourselves. Some were newly arrived, some had lived in Toronto for many years, but we all had connections in England: family we wrote to regularly, papers that we still read, politics that we followed. The men, like John were professionals or merchants. At the time of the rebellion, we had all been Tories, supporting the Queen's government.

Jennie and Peter came from families who had been in Canada longer than any of us; they were tradesman, labourers, many of them quite successful and making a good living. They had supported the Reformers and now voted for the Whigs. Clearly, there was a gap between us. Jennie and I, in our unusual friendship, had never noticed it. But that day, at the wedding, the gap was almost palpable. It was as if there was a line between us that we could never cross.

On the other side, of course, there was still that Family

Compact, although no one used the name anymore. John might design houses and do work for the Ridouts, the Jarvises and the Baldwins. We might go to the Governor-General's balls and meet them at formal occasions, but we would never be part of that society either. We might all meet in the course of the day, in the shops, or dealing with the trades. But we would never visit one another's homes or become friends. Toronto was little more than a small town to which we had brought all our English sense of class and it seemed as if for most people that would never change.

But, not all, as we would soon discover. One day, not long after the wedding, as John was going through the day's mail, he remarked, "Well, this is interesting."

"What is it,"

"It seems that your Jennie's young man—"

"Her husband," I reminded him.

"Of course, her husband. He is asking to see me to seek some advice in business. Here, have a look."

With interest, I read Peter's well-written letter. In it he explained that he was, of course, just starting out, but he was hoping to one day move beyond just being a tavern keeper. He had heard from Jennie about all our many endeavours and he was hoping that John might give him some guidance.

"Do you think you might help him?" I asked.

"Well, I was impressed by what I saw of him at the wedding. Perhaps you might invite them both to dinner and you can visit with Jennie while I take the young man aside for a chat."

I wrote a note to Jennie and we arranged a date for dinner the next week. When they arrived, both Jennie and Peter seemed ill-at-ease. Although, Jennie and I had spent much time together over the years, our friendship seemed to be something outside our usual circle of friends. Now, the young couple were entering our lives in a way that was quite new and unusual for all of us.

Conversation was somewhat stilted at dinner; all of us not quite knowing what to say or what subjects to discuss; and all the while, we all sensed that this meal was really a prelude to the real purpose of the dinner. When we had finished eating, I proposed that Jennie might come and take tea with me in the garden while we would leave the men at the table to have their talk.

The men talked for a long time. It was already beginning to get dark when John and Peter came out into the garden. As soon as they left, I was eager to find out what had happened.

"That is quite a clever young man," John began. "Not like some of those apprentices we have who never give a thought to tomorrow. I'm impressed that he takes nothing for granted."

"What do you mean?'

"He knows how fortunate he is to have walked into that business, so to speak. He can already see how it can be a stepping stone to other things. What I admire is that he's one of those rare people who knows what he doesn't know. That's why he came to me. I'm going to take him under my wing, Jemma. Help him along."

Not one to waste time, John arranged to take some time in the next few days to show Peter all the things that he was involved with; the land, the building, some of the business ideas. Peter took in all John's advice, but chose to move slowly. The Inn was a successful business and Peter and Jennie would prove to be as fine a team at running it as her parents had been. With John's help, it would become the foundation of a much larger enterprise. I sensed also, Jennie's steadying hand behind their plan to move slowly as they advanced.

In the months after the wedding, we were busier than ever. Somehow, John found the time to finish the design and supervise the building of our new house on York Street.

It was not until the next summer that the new house was

finished and our packing complete. We were ready to move in on a hot sultry morning in July. But barely a month after we moved in a fire broke out across the street. Thirty houses burned down. The fire spoiled the paint on our beautiful new house and the heat of it broke ten panes of glass.

Settling into the new house kept us busy that summer, with our apprentices, frequent visits from Ellen and the ever-growing Mountcastle clan. Toronto was growing quickly and we had so many projects that we were, at times, almost overwhelmed with work.

Sometimes, it seemed that it was almost too much for John. He would often come home exhausted from working in the office and being out supervising the construction of his projects. But even so, he had taken to going off by himself after supper, often taking the dogs for a long walk. "I feel the need to be on my own," he would say, "some time to think through all we have to do."

There'd been a time when we used to sit by the fire at night and review together all that had happened during the day. We used to laugh and say we were so busy during the day we hardly had time to speak to one another, but we always had that time at night. I missed the closeness we'd had, but I didn't want to press him. I knew only too well how John could push himself until he became ill. Then he would take to his bed and be forced to rest until he had recovered.

I have come up here to escape. The room, our guest room, is different. Someone has been up here, cleaning, moving things around and I wonder why.

I am so tense all the time, curled up like a little ball, a wild cat waiting to spring. I can't do anything right. When we were sitting at the table, I reached out for a pitcher of milk—a simple, ordinary task. My hands wouldn't do what I wanted them to and the milk spilled over everything, dripping onto the floor. Mary— or somebody—there are so many people here I can't keep track of them all jumped up and started wiping it away. There were the whispers again. John got up and stomped out of the room.

I ran up here to escape. Soon they will come after me.

I sink down beside the old chest again, memories shifting through my hands.

A yellowed page from the Colonial Gazette. The official announcement that John has been appointed to be the architect of the Provincial Lunatic Asylum.

I remember how proud we were.

I think, now, of that time. Knowing what I do. Knowing what would happen. I see now that I thought it was the happiest of times, but there was so much that I didn't know.

The Asylum

B ack in 1840, John had received the premium for his design for the Asylum, but like so many projects in the new city, nothing had come of it. Both the province and the city wanted to take on projects, like Market Square and the new university that would help the city to grow and give it a sense of importance. But when it came to putting the plans into action, there was never enough money to carry them out. We had resigned ourselves to the idea that it would be the same with the Asylum, but then John heard from Dr. Widmer and some other friends on Council, that the city was taking up the plan again, and soon would be naming a Supervisory Architect and starting to build.

Now his work began in earnest, to the point where it almost overwhelmed everything else we were doing. Sketches for the great building piled up everywhere. John sent for books and journals and read everything he could about the most up-to-date thinking on the treatment of the insane. The Asylum was always on his mind, and sometimes his ideas would burst out without any warning.

One morning, over breakfast, he suddenly stopped eating, a piece of toast literally half way to his lips. "Ventilation," he muttered.

"Pardon?"

"Ventilation, is what is needed. These people need to breathe. They shouldn't feel like they are prisoners."

Then he went on eating, but hardly knowing what he was doing. Over the months when he was so immersed in the project, I began to get quite used to his strange behaviour, but his preoccupation with the institution was taking over our lives. When Dr. Widmer lent him a book about hospitals for the insane by a German doctor, John devoured it as if he were reading that latest scandalous novel. He even read over dinner, stopping every once in a while to make notes or read passages out loud to me. Sometimes when he was reading along, he might stop and say aloud, "Imagine that!" as if we had been having a conversation.

Or suddenly he would burst out with, "Just what I was thinking!"

Or "Just listen to this, Jemima—" and he would read a passage about construction details. These held no interest for me at all; I did make an effort to look interested. I totally gave up any effort to channel the conversation in any other direction. We often dined late when John came home from the office, and if Alfred was with us, my nephew and I would sometimes exchange glances at these moments. What young Alfred thought of his uncle in those days, I never really knew.

Strangely enough, it was Alfred who asked the very question I had been puzzling over myself while all this had been going on. "But, Uncle, why does anyone want to build a place for all these lunatics anyway?"

"Ah," John began. How well I knew that look. It was as if John had just been waiting for the question, wanting to talk about all the ideas that were bubbling about in his busy head.

"Well, m'boy," he began. "That—is a good question. You see, we treat mad people very badly in our society. We lock them up in prisons—worse than prisons—chain them to the walls, beat them, treat them worse than animals. People used to say that they were possessed by demons and you had to beat the demons out of them. Or else we let them just wander the streets. But now, there are modern doctors who are showing us how wrong this has been. They're saying these people are sick and with help, they can be cured, just as if you have a bad illness and if you treat it properly you can get better."

As I write these words, I can see Alfred at our dinner table, still dressed in the school uniform he wore so proudly. He was only with us for a year and then went back to Clinton because he was needed at home. It was only a short time after he returned, that a terrible letter from Fanny arrived. Alfred—their first son— the sickly, little lad we had found on our first day—the boy we had both come to love—had died suddenly at only fourteen of one of the influenza epidemics that so often swept the whole province. John and I were devastated by the horrible news, and we could not even begin to imagine what it was like for Fanny and Sidney who had pinned such hopes on their bright, conscientious eldest boy. I wipe away the tears that still came when I think of him and turn back to my writing.

"But how can you treat them?" I asked, interrupting. "And what does this have to do with building an asylum?"

"It's everything, Jemima. We're building a place to treat them according to all these new ideas."

Reaching over for one of the many books he had been

reading, John opened it to a page marked with a leather bookmark. He read out a passage that explained how patients should be housed in a pleasant, airy building that had nothing prison-like about it. With help, John explained, they would learn to control their behaviour and get well. "We'll even have gardens where they can work outside in the fresh air and this too will help them to regain their health."

"But I'm still puzzled. We're a little city, just getting started. Do we really need such a place?"

"That's not up to me," John said. "But from what I've heard it comes right from the Governor. They wanted an asylum, in either Montreal or Toronto, and our Council made the best case for it. Gets these people out of the jails where they are mixed in with thieves and cutthroats, and actually help some of them. Seems to be the thing right now, every town wants to be modern and having a big, modern lunatic asylum seems to be just what is needed."

At the office, we were now, finally, able to hire an assistant. This young man named John Tully and John undertook a trip to the United States where they visited asylums in Utica, Syracuse, Boston, Philadelphia and New York. Everywhere they went, John interviewed architects, doctors and directors of the institutions then prepared his report along with drawing of what he had seen.

At the same time, John's vision for the grand building began to take shape. The city set aside a large piece of land for the project, far out in the country, west of Garrison Creek and between the lake and King Street. Since the building would stand on its own, John did not need to be concerned with having it fit in with other structures around it. He could give free reign to his imagination while planning his design. At last, he was ready to submit his application to Governor-General Metcalfe, which included letters of recommendation from Bishop Strachan, Dr. Widmer, who was on the Asylum Committee and other friends and clients.

All his effort paid off and in 1844, my John was named the Supervisory Architect to the building of the Asylum.

But nothing ever ran smoothly. Within weeks of John's appointment, we were beginning to hear talk that Thomas Young was going around saying unpleasant things about him. The next thing we knew, Young somehow got to some of the other younger architects in town and they actually wrote an article which was published in the British Canadian one of the local newspapers. Young and the others tried to claim that John did not have the ability to perform the task for which he was appointed.

"Treachery!" roared John when he heard about the piece. He threatened to go court and, as he bellowed, "Sue the whole lot of them!" Indeed, he and Thomas had faced each other in court over issues before.

"It will only stir things up more, if you do that." I argued. "The decision has been made. Let's pay them no more attention."

Fortunately, John finally agreed with me and it seemed that anyone who read the piece in the paper saw it for what it was—just sour grapes on the part of Young who could not even get his design in by the deadline and was never even under consideration for John's position. Young would soon face many other problems that were just beginning to surface.

The next few years passed by in a blur. The number of our commissions grew and we were able to hire more people to help us. Once he was named Supervisory Architect for the Asylum, John was busier than ever, travelling to Montreal to discuss the site, surveying and planning for the construction.

Finally, on August 22 in 1846, the official laying of the cornerstone took place. What a grand event it was! On that sweltering August day a great procession, led by Chief Justice John Robinson and including city officials, lawyers, the clergy and others marched to the site. A stage, hung with flags and bunting, had been set up in the middle of the field where the asylum would be built and John sat proudly at the centre of it, listening to the speeches. I sat with some of the other wives and dignitaries, on chairs that had been set up in front of the stage, ceremony, watching John with equal pride. When the final speech was over, Justice Robinson rose to lay the cornerstone. From where I sat, I could see bright flashes of sunshine dancing off his ceremonial silver trowel. In a loud and very formal voice, he then read out the words inscribed on a silver plaque mounted on the stone. It was truly a great moment for us and when the "British Colonist" published an extra issue to celebrate the event, we bought up every copy we could to send home to the family in England.

After the event, to celebrate, we went on a small trip. We planned to be away for a whole week—the first time we had been away in a long time. We went by boat to Hamilton, then by horse and chaise to Niagara Falls where we stayed at the Clifton House, a grand hotel that overlooked the falls. We went by steamer to Buffalo, to the theatre there, then back to Niagara where we visited the Ducats, the friends that we had met on the voyage to Canada. We had not seen much of each other over the years, but we kept in touch my mail and still felt the closeness that we had forged on that journey. We returned to Toronto by steamer, refreshed and ready to face a new challenge, the construction of the building and the implementing of all John's new exciting ideas.

The task of designing a grand project like the Lunatic Asylum seemed planned exactly for John. Every article he had read about new ideas, all those years of tinkering around and trying new kinds of equipment, all he had learned in his travels to institutions in the States; everything came together for him. The Asylum was to have hot and cold running water and a modern heating system like the one John had read about in the National Gallery in London. He took another trip to Montreal where this time he talked to engineers about how to install it.

I was fascinated as he explained how water would be pumped up from the Lake and stored in a huge water tank inside the beautiful dome that would top the centre of the building and be reached by a breath-taking circular staircase. John was very pleased with the fact that the dome would have an observation platform and act as a landmark, but it would also have a practical purpose.

All the time John was working on the Asylum, so much else was happening. Our business continued to expand and John had many commissions in Toronto, in many of the growing towns and villages in the province, and even a house on the mountain in Montreal. He had been appointed City Surveyor by the city, surveyed the harbour and made plans for an esplanade. Now that we had High Park and our house in the city, I thought perhaps that would be enough, but John continued to buy land; five lots on Strachan Street from Captain Strachan, two acres near our land from Thomas Ridout and a property on York Street from John Chewett. It never seemed to be enough. Hard as he was working on all his projects and commissions or him, he was also accumulating large debts on the land.

It still was not enough. It was as if something was driving him, a force I was powerless to stop. He joined the Odd Fellows, invested in ventures which often failed and helped to start up the Toronto Society of Art, becoming its Vice-President and Treasurer. The Society had an exhibition, similar to the one that they had held back in 1834. John exhibited many of his works. I submitted my paintings as well, and this time, my name was listed in the catalogue.

It was around this time too, that I had the first of a several strange encounters that I only came to understand much later.

One day, when we were terribly overloaded and no one else was available, I offered to take some drawings to one of our clients down in the east end, a part of town that I had never been to before.

As I walked, I had the feeling that someone was watching me. It was eerie—frightening—as if a hand stretched out and forced me to look around. I became aware of a woman staring at me from across the street.

Did I know her? Had we met before? She was clearly not someone I would have met in my circle. Frankly, not of my class. Her clothes were neat and respectable, but worn and showing nothing of fashion. Why was she staring at me so? The encounter left me shaken. For a long time, I could not get it out of my mind.

At the same time, the same troubles that had plagued John for years returned, but he continued to ignore them. Finally, he became so ill with constant stomach trouble, that he was unable to leave his bed for weeks on end. Dr. Widmer came and applied leeches to his head. I spent countless nights up nursing him. The doctor prescribed all sorts of techniques to help cure him: castor oil, a boiled starch with laudanum. John seemed to improve, and then a few weeks later, he became ill again. This time, Dr. Widmer himself was sick and a different doctor gave him an odd concoction of powdered chalk, with opium and aniseed, which caused him a lot of pain, but seemed finally to help. He was very weak and I was exhausted, having had so little sleep and so much worry.

I thought perhaps John would step back and give himself time to rest, but all too soon he was back at the office, busier than ever. We now had a number of people working for our office, including the assistant, John Tully, who supervised the work on the Asylum and two articled clerks who were living with us as well. When John was so ill, and I, so busy looking after him, they managed between them to run the office quite well without us. So many things at home had been neglected during John's illness, that I took some extra time away from the office to put everything in order. One morning, as I sat at my desk, writing letters and doing our accounts, I realized that for the first time in all the years that we had been working together, I was not looking forward to my return. I did go back, of course, but I sometimes found myself looking around at everyone busily working on drawings and plans. There were plenty of people there to look after things without me. Perhaps I had earned some time to myself.

Not long after that, I broached the subject to John. To my surprise, it turned out that the same idea had occurred to him.

"When I was ill," he said. "It was so pleasant having you at home with me, less hectic than the way things usually are. I thought about suggesting a short retirement to you, but I wasn't sure how you would feel about it."

"I think it would be lovely," I said. "Lessconfining."

He looked at me with a little twinkle in his eye. "I hope you won't give us up entirely," he teased. "We might still have to come to you for help, you know. And you'll have time for your painting. It's been a long time since you've done that."

And so it was decided.

It wasn't as if I now had nothing to do. We now had the two clerks living with us, one who had already been with us for a year, and a new lad, William Boultbee who was just sixteen. I needed to arrange two new beds for them, with mattresses, bolsters and pillows and generally look after them.

How often over the years, I had longed for time to myself.

179

Now, as so often happens in life, I had what I wanted, but after a while, it seemed that time often hung heavy on my hands. I missed the bustle of the office. I missed the work. I had always enjoyed working on the plans and drawings, although I had often looked at the piles of papers on my desk and complained about all I had to do.

Now, my easel sat empty, my paints and brushes idle. I seemed to have lost interest in starting a new project.

Ellen

As always, we were busy. There was the constant round of visits and dinners and we continued to include Sara Tuton, who had now been a widow for several years, and her daughter in our activities, often inviting them to tea after church on Sundays. They also came with us to the Lunatic Asylum Ball. At that wonderful evening which was held to raise money for the project, John and I were treated as special guests. There were balls and concerts as well, and even in the winter, we went out to the Lodge on Sundays and often invited friends to accompany us.

We kept up our friendship with other people we had known for a long time, like the Rowsells, the Cherwetts and the Wakefields and now we had expanded our circle to include new acquaintances as well. Almost from the moment we met, we became close to Jacob and Margery Anne Hirschfelder, a young couple who had arrived in Toronto in 1842; she from Montreal, he originally from Germany. The Hirschfelders created quite a splash in the city; people said she was a "Montreal belle" and everyone spoke of Jacob as a "bon vivant." Jacob had come to Toronto to seek work as a tutor of Hebrew and German and was soon appointed as lecturer in Oriental Studies at King's College and soon made his name as a Biblical scholar. It would seem that

British Colonist.

Sometimes, we were able to arrange to visit Jennie and her family. Ellen would take the children off to play and read to them so Jennie and I could have a visit. Once, as we were chatting, Ellen remarked that she would like one day to have her own school.

"If you are really serious about this," Jennie had responded, "perhaps you might like to practice on my rambunctious lot. Find out whether you really want to do this."

"Could I really?" Ellen had cried.

"Absolutely," she said. "The more I think about it, the better I like it. Young Peter has just started school, but I am so busy, I rarely have enough time to help him with his letters, and you could begin to teach little Sarah as well. She's a bright one and she wants to catch up to her brother."

What started out almost on a whim, turned out to be an excellent arrangement. In addition to her own school work, Ellen would go to Jennie's several times a week to help the children. Jennie surprised her at the end of the first visit by giving her a small payment.

"Mrs. Martin, I can't possibly accept this," Ellen said, as she told me later.

"You must," Jennie had insisted. "I wouldn't have it any other way."

So Ellen was now proudly earning on her own for the first time.

"Of course, I'll send it on to Mother," Ellen told me.

I knew, of course, that it would be a help to Fanny, but I tried to convince Ellen to keep back a small amount for herself.

"No," she said. "It will mean a great deal to Ma. She tries so hard not to let on and works so hard. But I know how much she worries."

Although she was busy with her school and dancing classes, Ellen was just the companion I had imagined. During the winter, we went out for sleigh rides together and often in the evening, when John was out at his meetings, we would read or play cards together. Ellen came out shopping with me and often came along when I went out to visit friends.

Now that I was no longer going to the office, I did not pay close attention to our business, but John still brought specifications home for me to finish. He was still often ill, but continued to drive himself in spite of my pleadings and the advice of Dr. Widmer. I even tried to persuade him to take a trip to England. Since steamships now plied to ocean, I knew that our journey would only take a week, instead of the grueling three month crossing that had brought us here all those years ago. Still, such a journey would be strenuous and I hoped that we could do it before we grew much older.

John would not hear of it. "With all I have to do," he said, emphatically. "I could not possibly spare the time."

Sometimes, it was as if I hardly saw him at all. After breakfast, he dashed to the office or out to supervise a project. By now, the Asylum was almost finished; the outside walls were completed and work was proceeding on the interior. John often stopped by the site in addition to supervising all his other projects and then often worked at home quite late into the night.

Then there were the meetings; the Masons, the Odd-fellows, the Artists' Society and when John was appointed a Justice of the Peace, he often had cases to attend. So often, when he finally did return home, he was so weary that he could hardly speak. I worried that he was taking on too much, but there was nothing I could do to stop him.

I wake up... not in my room... not in our bed.

That Irish woman—the nurse—is sitting there sewing. She looks up when she hears me stirring. There is no warmth in her smile.

"Are ye awake then, dearie?" she says.

Who is she to call me dearie? I don't like her. I don't want her here.

What has happened to me? Why am I here? I try to make myself remember. I scrunch up my face. I clench my fists, trying to force thoughts into my brain.

They gave me more of that medicine ... I know that ... probably more than usual ... so they could do what they wanted.

I close my eyes, feign sleep. The medicine will wear off and I will feel like I am climbing up out of a deep, murky pool. I will be able to think about this.

She is gone—that person. I don't even know her name, but she is always there, lurking around me. I climb gingerly out of bed, not knowing how long I have been lying here, afraid of not being steady on my feet. The bare floor is cold as ice.

So, this is what has been going on, all that rustling and hammering. Make a place for Jemima. Put her out of the way.

Chilled, shaking—with cold—with rage, I make my way around the room Bars on the windows. A lock on the door.

I crumple in the corner, in despair.

When the mist in my brain clears, as it still does, I am able to sort things out. I have a vague memory of being lifted out of my bed and being deposited here, hands that were rough, not gentle. I think even in my drug-addled stupor, I must have fought against them. I clawed at them until my hands were sore. My nails are broken. There was the sound of howling, unworldly. I think it came from me.

I know so much more than they think I do. I wonder how

much of this confusion is the drugs they give me and how much is the fading away that has been going on now for so long.

The old trunk is still here. Trembling, I crawl over to it and open the lid. Everything—my notebooks, my pens, the one remaining bottle of ink—is still here. Safe. I get up, dust myself off and figure out what to do. I stuff papers under the mattress, hide the pens and ink close by. I will have to be wily now, to find treasured moments when I am alone. But I will go on writing... as long as I can.

The Great Fire

1849

There was nothing I could do to stop John when, one April night, we were suddenly awakened by the clanging of bells all over the city. We jumped out of bed and ran to the windows. People on King Street, some still in their nightclothes were running down the road, shouting to one another or standing staring into the night sky which was glowing a hot red. We dressed hurriedly and joined the others standing in the street. To the east, in the strange light smoke billowed into the sky. Although it seemed that the actual fire was quite far away, the air was already becoming heavy and people were coughing and sputtering. Before I had time to stop him, John raced to the stable and dashed downtown to find out was happening.

I joined the other neighbours standing in the street and watched helplessly as crowds surged down the streets and smoke belched over the city. The fire grew so huge that we could actually see flames leaping into the sky, like meteors flying through the air. Around three o'clock a light rain began to fall and we all breathed a collective sigh of relief, knowing the rain would help to prevent the fire from spreading any closer to us.

It was morning before John returned home, his face covered

with soot and his coat reeking of smoke.

Later in the day, we went down together to view the damage caused by the fire. The streets were full of people, many with their faces still streaked with smoke, some seeming to be in shock.

Walking east along King Street, we saw the first buildings only damaged by the smoke. But soon the beginnings of the destruction, and then, to our horror, we saw that St. James Cathedral, our church, had been completely destroyed. We heard later that there had been time to rescue everything of value from the church; the library, the organ, even the hymn books in the pews. It was said that the open space around the church saved the city from the danger of the fire spreading even further than it did. Still a shocking swath of land east of the church had been levelled by the fire which still smouldered that morning. Although homes, shops and public buildings had been destroyed, we learned that only one person had died in the fire: Richard Watson, the publisher of the *Upper Canada Gazette,* had gone to help rescue type from the Patriot building and had been unable to escape.

I could see by the look on John's face that he was already beginning to think about what needed to be done. Quite soon, the City would come and ask him to help. I knew he would not refuse even though I didn't know how he could possibly take on anything else. As always, there would be nothing I could say to make him change his mind.

And certainly, within days, John's advice was being sought. Along with George Cumberland, an up-and-coming architect in town, John was hired to assess the damage caused and submit a report. Later, along with William Thomas, another architect we had come to know, he inspected the cathedral and reported on the damage there. I held my breath. All the architects in town were invited to submit their plans to replace this important city landmark. I was terribly afraid that John's old spirit of competition might drive him to join in. But several days later, as we were talking about fire, he told me that he had been hired as a consultant for the competition that would follow. "I'm much too old to do anything else." He laughed and I breathed a sigh of relief.

But there was something else. A feeling I could never identify, a sensation that was always there. Although I never really admitted it to myself there was a change in John. I don't know when it started to happen, but it seemed as if he had withdrawn from me. Sometimes, I would catch him, sitting at his desk, staring into space. When I asked him what he was thinking about, he caught himself, gave his head a little a shake. "Just the work," he muttered. "Just the work."

I told myself that was the way things were, when you had been married for a long time.

Shortly after the fire, I saw her again, that strange woman who had stood in the street and stared at me so oddly. I was on my way home, walking along King Street, not far from the office. She had a small boy with her this time. Holding him by the hand, she stood on the other side of the street, staring at me, just as she had before. Even from a distance, her look was so intense, it made me shiver. I shook myself, as if to rid my skin of something clawing at me.

Who was she? Where were they going? There was something about them I couldn't name.

The image of that encounter never left my mind.

My head is beginning to ache. I rub my temples, but it does little to help.

The empty page stares at me. I know that I have put off writing this for so long.

To tell this part of the story is to relive it.

It is so hard to begin.

I remember.

"I'm just out for a bit of a walk, Jemma. It's a lovely morning."

"I'll come with you."

"Another time, my dear. Just need to do a bit of thinking, just myself and the dogs."

Something had been lost between us for a long time, but I had willed myself not to see it.

I remember.

It was one of those surprising spring mornings that start off quite chilly, then suddenly burst into an almost summer-like heat as the day progressed. That morning I still worked on specifications when we were very rushed. That morning I was working at home on some specifications that John sold that afternoon. As the morning went on, it became warm and stuffy in the room. I got up and opened the door to let some air in.

And then I heard them—Mary and Edie chatting as they went about their work, their voices carrying down the hall.

"So then, it's true, what they say?"

"Sure as I'm standing here. I seen them with my own eyes!"

I suppose I shouldn't have paid any attention. But there was something, something that made me shiver. I leaned closer to the door.

"What's she like?"

"Plain as can be, but shameless. Walking with her arm in his as if she were the missus."

"Did he see you? Mister?"

"Oh heavens, no! As soon as I saw them, I ducked out of the way down the nearest alley. My heart was beating like a drum I tell you."

"Poor Missus. If she knew her heart would break."

And so I knew. And my heart did break. Not then, at that moment, but in bits and shards, as time went on.

I stood for a while at the top of the stairs, transfixed. Paralyzed.

There had been moments over the years. Those strange encounters that I could never explain, but haunted me. Now I understood them at last.

Downstairs, I heard the familiar sounds of the house. Pots clanged. Brooms swished. The servants went on about their work. I did not think they could have known that I overheard them talking—about me.

Mechanically, I went down the stairs and out the door into the street.

I looked at the faces of people I passed.

Does everybody know?

I thought of conversations that had stopped when I entered a room. I remembered of the rustle I heard in church when people turned to look at me.

Did they all know?

John must have come home with the dogs while I was out and then gone on to the office. He was there, working at his desk when I brought the drawings I had been working on. I stood at the door, watching him. He was in his shirtsleeves because of the hot day, his jacket draped across the back of his chair. I looked at him hunched there, the familiar way he leaned in slightly as he worked, the curve of his back.

"Well, you took your time, this morning," he called out without looking up.

"Here," I said, dropping the drawings on his desk with a slap. He looked up in surprise, but said nothing.

How can I do this? I wondered. *How can I come to this place where we sat at our desks facing each other for so long? How can I go on as if nothing has happened?*

Somehow I got through the day, mechanically going on about my work. When John came home, we had our supper, chatting as always. I pretended nothing had changed. Later, John said he was going off to a meeting, as he had done so often. I had never thought to question before. In fact, I had always been faintly amused by all the joining John did. There had never been any reason to question where he was going.

But now, I was beginning to question everything. Including myself.

Had I heard right? Perhaps, I was mistaken and the maids were talking about someone else.

No. I knew that I had heard and understood what the girls were saying. I sat alone in our parlour, that night, thinking about what I had heard, waiting for John to return and wondering, for the first time in our lives together, and questioning, for the first time in our lives together, where he was.

The next day, I remained at home, waiting for the afternoon. I knew that there was only one person I could turn to. Jennie, with her ear for gossip and her interest in the news about town would be sure to have heard something if what the girls had said was true. And Jennie was the only one I could trust. She would tell me the truth. I knew that the inn would be quiet in the afternoon and we would be able to talk.

I walked slowly, wanting to know, but dreading the moment, afraid of what I would hear.

I found Jennie alone, sitting at a table where the afternoon light streamed in the through the window of the dining room. Account books were spread out in front of her. She rose quickly when she saw me, a big smile on her face. But when she saw my expression, she froze. She offered me some tea. I declined. This wasn't a social visit. She stared at me, quizzically.

I plunged in, without so much as a greeting. "I—I have something to ask you."

She waited.

"About John." I heard her catch her breath.

"What is it?" she asked, hesitantly.

There was no turning back. "I know, there is something. I heard the maids talking. Please, Jennie tell me."

She looked around the room, as if for an escape. A guilty thing caught. She was my dear friend and I had put her in a terrible position.

"Please."

Her face clouded.

"Please, tell me," I said again. "Tell me."

I don't know how long we sat there, Jennie with her eyes cast down.

Finally, she raised her gaze to meet mine. She stepped toward me and took me in her arms. "Oh, Jemima," she whispered. "I'm so sorry."

"Then it's true?"

She nodded.

I began to cry, sobs bursting out of me, growing stronger and wilder as she held me. Finally, my cries subsided.

"Tell me what you know. Tell me all of it."

Jennie led me to the sofa and sat down with me. "What do

you know?" she asked.

"I heard the servants talking today. One of them saw John... with ... with a woman. She said, I seen them, as if this were public knowledge. As if they had talked about this before."

"There is a woman, Mary Williams. She calls herself a widow. Who knows?" She hesitated, then continued. "He has set her up, with a house."

Jennie stood up and walked to the sideboard on which there were several bottles and decanters of liquor and wine. She poured two small glasses of brandy and turned back to look at me sadly. I felt cold. We had never had a drink before. What could be so terrible that she felt we need to be fortified?

"There is something else I have to tell you," she said. "There are children—two of them!"

The room began to swim. I could hardly breathe. I gasped.

And then, I remembered.

The woman holding the hand of a small boy as she stared at me. The thing I wouldn't allow myself to think of. He had John's face ... in miniature. John's face, his eyes. Some part of me had always known.

I felt Jennie sit again beside me. She put her arm around me and made me drink a little of the brandy. It burned my throat, but seemed to calm me a little.

"How...how do you know this?" I whispered.

"My mother heard, as always. I guess someone talked to her, knowing that we know you. Probably trying to find out more. You know how people are."

"So," I said, miserably. "Everybody knows."

"Probably. Mr. H has quite a name in town, you know."

"Two children. So it's been going on for a long time."

Jennie nodded.

Again, we sat in silence.

So there it was. I had asked and now I knew the truth.

"Jennie, what am I to do?" I asked at last.

"Nothing," she said. "There is nothing you can do."

She was right, of course. I had a brief vision of my confronting John like a scene from a melodrama. He would lie, say it was only idle gossip. Or worse, he would admit it, and then, what...?

"I will leave," I said, with resolve. "I will pack up and leave."

Jennie, ever practical said, "And then what? Where would you go?"

"To Fanny, I could help her with the children."

"Fanny can barely look after her own. She can't take you in."

"I'll go back to England. I'll find work."

But even as I heard myself saying those words, I knew it would never happen.

"Just go on, Jemima. As if this had never happened. He's a good husband. You have a good life."

I laughed bitterly. "A good husband! With another woman and two children with her."

"You must, Jemima. There is nothing else to do."

Somehow or other, I got home. I don't remember walking along the streets. I don't recall what route I took. Did I wander through the streets not seeing where I was going? Were there crowds of people around me or was the road empty?

Was I crying or muttering to myself?

Did people think I was mad?

I came to myself, sitting in the parlour, no fire in the grate, no lamps lit.

I didn't know how long had been there.

Jennie's words echoed in my brain, going around and

around like a ball bouncing off a brick wall.

There's a woman.

There's a woman.

It was as if I heard the words, but they could have been in a foreign language that I was struggling to comprehend.

Then, it was as if a mist was lifting.

Figures seemed to move through a fog, becoming clear as they approached, until I began to understand what I had only sensed before.

A distance—I had sensed that.

John staring into space.

His remoteness.

It was not as if I hadn't noticed. But I had told myself it was all the work. Preoccupied, I had said. Obsessed, I thought when it made me angry. I had felt that the asylum had taken over our lives, the hours, the days and nights spent on planning and design.

And then, the endless time spent on supervising the building, coming home, exhausted, being so tired he could hardly speak. It had been that.

And it hadn't.

I struggled to put what I was feeling into words.

"Years," she'd said. "It's been going on for years."

I kept turning my memories over in my mind. It was like a kaleidoscope. With each twist, colours scattered and new patterns formed. I didn't know what was real anymore.

Later, when the truth began to penetrate, I found myself looking back, dispassionately, seeing everything that had happened to us like a hall of mirrors when images seemed to be reflected over and over, but each reflection was somehow changed.

I thought of the trips he had taken, those business trips to little towns to supervise the building of churches and jails, the banks and the courthouses. I was the one who noted the times, recorded the expenses in the account books. Had he lied?

Were the trips longer than they needed to be? I never asked. Did "she" go with him? Would I ever know?

We worked together in the same office, our desks facing each other. We spent our days together.

When had it started?

How?

The days passed. I said nothing. I found myself analyzing everything. I listened to everything John said wondering what was behind the words. I questioned every action. I needed time to think, but I was afraid to be alone.

Who else knows? I wondered. *Do people look at me with pity, shake their heads as I go by?* I became watchful. I looked for signs. A wrong word, an arch tone of voice and I began to suspect even my closest friends. Toronto is a small, gossipy town. People must have known.

It was the thought of the children that was tearing me apart. If it were only a woman, this Mary Williams, I could perhaps have accepted it, in time. I was not naive. I knew, of course that these things happened. The town was ripe with gossip and there were always stories about husbands with other woman tucked away somewhere. We had after all grown up in an England where the Prince Regent flaunted his mistresses at the world and the broadsheets were filled with scandal. Perhaps, in time, I too could have accepted it.

But the children! In everything I did in those terrible days, it was all that could think about. I began to look at women walking on the street with children and peering at them, wondering is that her? Is that them? No matter how I turned and twisted my thoughts, I was completely unable to understand.

Of course, John had wanted children just as I had. But we

were never able to talk about it, even after I lost the baby and was so terribly ill. I thought back over the years; there had been a word here, an observation there. Although it was unspoken, I knew that we had both cherished the thought that coming to Canada would make things different. We had been unable to share our disappointment when nothing changed.

But the children! John Howard! John Corby! I remembered all those years ago before we were married, how the old aunties gossiped about him. Even my father, fond as he was of John, was openly not happy with my choice, telling me that "I could do better," and asking me right up to the wedding if I was sure of what I was doing.

I remembered John, so self-conscious, embarrassed, telling me the truth about his background so that I wouldn't hear it from someone else, afraid that I might change my mind.

And John's story continued to haunt him. I remembered how the gossip surfaced when he was on the Committee for the Arts Society and those nasty, unpleasant letters appeared and how it took the intervention of the Lieutenant-Governor himself to squelch it.

Even afterwards, it continued to follow him. A hint dropped here. A comment made there. The implication that although he might do work for the Jarvises, the Ridouts, the Baldwins, and the other "great" families of the city, that although he might buy all the land he could, and join all the clubs and societies in town, he would never really be part of the upper echelon of Toronto's little society. He would never attain that recognition that he craved.

Illegitimate! Born on the wrong side of the sheets! It had haunted him all his life. How could he bring that fate to three children!

I stumbled through the days like a wooden thing; a puppet

with no strings. The office hummed with activity. The business we had built up from nothing now thrummed along successfully, but now it meant nothing, as if I hadn't been there at all. Our house felt like a shell; all the things we had chosen together—it all meant nothing. We went to visit friends; I sat silently, scarcely able to look at anyone without wondering; Do they know? Are they looking at me with pity? Do they think that I am a fool?

Jennie was right, as always, there was nothing to do, or say.

At first, I was sure I would leave him. I couldn't continue to share a life with a man who had so betrayed me, could I?

But then, I would try to picture in my mind, my life without him. I saw only a life of loneliness, a small, dark cold room somewhere, an empty house.

I would be a woman alone; not a widow, not even a spinster. A kind of a freak.

And so, I chose to stay. I would go on, knowing what I did, seeing everything that happened as the days and then the years went by, as if through a magic mirror.

I would go on, pretending that nothing had changed in our lives and that I never saw the truth or heard the lies.

As I had when I lost our child, I learned to silence my thoughts, to drive them away. Again, I hid them away in a box and tied up the string. Again, I imagined myself hiding the box away in a closet. Now in the attic of my mind, there were two locked doors. To open them would destroy me.

And so began my double life.

I am alone here, at the top of the house, in a solitary room with a low, sloping ceiling and narrow dormer windows peeking out over the woods.

No one comes here.

For years, until they made a space for me—a solitary bed, an old sofa, a scratched table—it was only a space where we discarded things for which we no longer had any use. Under one of the windows, I stored that old battered chest, the last remnant of all the things we had brought with us when we came to Canada so long ago. If you look carefully, you will see traces of the faded, yellow label with the number John assigned to it before our voyage.

Why this, of all those boxes and cases we carried with us? Why did this small chest become a memory box, moving with us from house to house? I remember it in the attic room in that first freezing winter, filled with the blankets and shawls that kept us warm. It moved downstairs to our first apartment to become the place to hold all the rough sketches as we worked so hard on John's portfolio for Sir John Colborne. Later I got into the habit of using it to squirrel away souvenirs I wanted to keep; newspaper clippings, programs, letters, drawings. Down at the very bottom, in a small bag, I hid the tiny bottle that Marie had given me, as if unable to give up that tiny glimmer of hope. The chest followed us as we moved,, and once, when John had looked at it with a frown and said, "Isn't it about time we got rid of that old thing?" I had one of the servants bring it up here and stash it out of the way.

Now, sometimes, when there is no one to notice, I sit here on the floor beneath the narrow window and one by one, I look at all the old treasures. And here underneath everything, I hide my writing, a growing stack of notebooks.

England

1853

N othing changed on the outside. John was busy with his work and his meetings or so he said. I had never questioned anything he did before and I said nothing now, even though I always wondered where he was really going.

In the time that Ellen spent with us, I watched her grow into a polished young lady. But finally, it was time for her to return home and the house was quite empty without her. We continued with our busy rounds with our ever-growing circle of friends, but now I found myself watching them, trying to guess which of them knew. What were they saying behind my back?

Sometimes, I was able to put it behind me. Toronto had changed much over the years and now there was so much more for us to do. We went to concerts and the theatre on our own or with friends. There were the balls, especially the annual Lunatic Asylum Ball where John was always honoured as the architect of the great building that now dominated the west end of the city.

Once the asylum had been finished at last, we went together to watch patients being brought to their new surroundings and sometimes we were able to go to watch them as they went about their days in their bright new surroundings. Just as John had envisaged, the Asylum became quite an attraction as visitors to the city came to see it and write about their impressions. We were especially pleased when the well-known author Mrs. Moodie wrote a very flattering description of it that appeared in the new "Globe" newspaper. We bought up many copies of the edition to send home to England.

But there was a change in John, hardly noticeable at first. There had always been something frantic about him, that habit of driving himself when faced with a deadline. Over the years I had become used to him working ceaselessly into the night, eating little, stopping to rest only when he could absolutely go no longer. Now there were no more deadlines. The Asylum was completed at last. Other commissions flowed in and he had a well-trained staff to help. We had reached a point in our lives when John should have been able to slow down and rest, but now his behaviour was more frantic than ever.

He had taken to pacing the floors, being up at all hours of the night, sitting at his desk, pouring over account books, muttering away under his breath.

I longed to take the books back from him, to go back to the way things were when this was my domain and he did not have to take on so many worries.

"Are you sure there is nothing I can do to help?" I asked finally one night, setting a cup of tea down beside him, to get his attention. "What is it? What is worrying you so much?"

John, uncharacteristically, slammed his fist down on the table. "It's that damn Samuel Jarvis!" he shouted. "He'll kill me yet!"

"What? What has happened? You must tell me."

Samuel Jarvis—I should have known. John had mentioned to me that he was doing work for Jarvis, again. I should have said something at the time, but I let it go because I was no longer really involved with what was now 'his' work.

Years ago, when we were just starting out, we had been thrilled when Jarvis hired John to design shutters and a cornice for his grand home called Hazelburne, just outside the city. Newly arrived in the little town of York, we had known nothing of what was called "society", but the masters at the College had told John all about the notorious Jarvis family. Samuel's father, William had come up with Governor Simcoe and as one of the first families, he had been given land grants and the position of Provincial Secretary in the colony. In spite of these advantages, he was soon hopelessly in debt and was accused of misappropriating government funds. Young Samuel had fought in 1812, but just a few years later, he had killed eighteen-year-old John Ridout in a duel and went to jail for manslaughter. But then he was acquitted by Chief Justice William Powell, the man who became his father-in-law when Jarvis married his daughter Mary.

The lurid stories about the Jarvis family were of no concern to us, since we saw this small piece of work we had been hired for as an entree into the important families in town.

Much later, when Jarvis was appointed as Chief Superintendent of the Department of Indian Affairs for the province, John encountered him again, when Jarvis commissioned him to design and build a number of Anglican churches in Indian towns. Jarvis held the position for a number of years, but rumours always swirled about him. People were shocked, but not really surprised when accusations surfaced about Jarvis and the Department. Not only was he accused of fraud and other wrong doing, but an examination of his books revealed unexplained withdrawals of funds allocated for the Indians. The government accountant determined that Jarvis was in debt to the Indians for ten thousand pounds, lowered that to four thousand and finally suspended him from office.

We should have been warned. I should have intervened as soon as I heard.

Without work, Jarvis decided to subdivide and sell off property from his large Hazelburn estate which stretched all the way east of Yonge Street, from Queen to Bloor. He hired John to do the survey work and become his exclusive agent for a term of five years.

John took on the project, even though he was in the midst of designing and building the Asylum. He surveyed the land, laid out the streets and named them; George, Mutual and Jarvis—the grand, tree-lined boulevard that would run the whole length of the property.

It was all too much: the Jarvis work, the Asylum, all the other projects and commissions. And the land—John's never ending obsession with acquiring more land, buying and selling houses, getting involved with new businesses. As always, there was nothing I could do to stop him. John became so ill and exhausted that Dr. Widmer begged him to go to Saratoga Springs in New York and take a month-long rest cure. I tried to convince him to go, but it was to no avail.

I had been trying hard to get him to talk to me, to let me help, but it was not until that night when he became so angry, that he finally told me what had been going on.

"He hasn't paid me anything, not one shilling!" he raged. "I wrote him a stream of letters which he never even deigned to answer. Can you imagine? And then it became worse. Seven months later he actually wrote to say that he had never entered into an agreement for more than one year. He accused me, me if you can imagine of—and I quote—"overstepping my authority!"

"Oh, John," I cried, embracing him. "Why haven't you told

me any of this?"

"What would have been the use?" he asked sadly. "It would only have made you worry even more."

There was something about the tone of his voice that made me truly fearful.

"Is there more?" I almost whispered.

There was a long pause. He shook his head, sadly.

"We—I—we owe a great deal of money...."

"I don't understand. We have always done so well. You have so much work. More than you can manage."

"It's just as you always said—and I—I never listened. The land, all those lots and the buildings. I borrowed to buy them—and now, I can't make the payments on what I owe."

"And Jarvis won't pay you what he owes?"

"And there it is."

"Can't we sell some of the land?"

"Believe me, I've tried. There just do not seem to be any buyers."

"I don't understand. Everyone talks about how the city is growing, so many people coming here."

"But not to the west end, at least not yet. I've tried to interest buyers in Sunnyside, but nothing happens." He paused. "I'm even thinking of putting High Park, the house and all up for sale."

"Oh, John. No. There must be another way."

John did put High Park up for sale, but there were no buyers. He continued to write to Jarvis, hoping to avoid having to go to court to get the money we were owed. When finally, there was no other remedy, John sought arbitration, but even though Jarvis was a scoundrel and as many still said, a murderer, he still had all the power and connections. John was awarded two lots on George Street as payment for all his years of work and billed an arbitration fee.

By the time Samuel Jarvis died not long after this, William Lyon Mackenzie had been given a pardon, returned to Toronto and started up a weekly newspaper. For once, I absolutely agreed with him when he wrote, "Jarvis embezzled many thousands of dollars of the money of the poor Indians whom he was paid to protect. Of course, the government winked at all this."

It didn't help us, but at least we weren't the only ones who had suffered at the hands of Samuel Jarvis. I kept that issue of the paper with all the other bits and pieces in the old trunk and it still makes me angry to this day.

The struggle with Jarvis and all the work he had taken on took its toll. John became more and more ill. For weeks on end, he got little or no sleep. He was either pacing the floor with worry or experiencing such great pains that he was unable to rest. I was up with him every night, trying to soothe him, trying to find something that would take away the pain. On days when he dragged himself to the office, I tried to get some rest, but I found that I too was growing more and more tired as the days passed. I was worried that I might become ill with all the strain as well.

Sometimes, when John was resting, I went out by myself for a walk. It was only then, when I had some time to myself, that those thoughts would claw themselves into my mind. Was she still there, that woman? Had he given her money, set her up in a house somewhere? How much did she have to do with the torment in our lives?

Dr. Widmer called every day, looking at John with a furrowed brow, shaking his head with concern. Finally, out of desperation, he bled John with leeches which seemed to bring some temporary relief.

When John finally fell into a sleep, Dr. Widmer took me aside, saying, "I must speak with you."

I made some tea and we sat down together in the parlour. Christopher Widmer, usually so elegant and calm looked weary and almost nervous.

"Mrs. Howard," he began, "I've known Mr. Howard— John—for so many years. He's not just my patient, he's my good friend. As are you, my dear."

"Of course," I agreed. "You've been such a help to us in so many ways."

"Then, you will understand the urgency with which I speak. You must do something about this, Mrs. Howard. If John continues on with his business at this pace, it will kill him."

It was true Widmer had been our doctor and our friend for many years. I knew that he would not make this threat lightly.

When John recovered a little and seemed a little stronger, I began what I thought of as my campaign. In all our years together, we had rarely quarrelled, and then only about small unimportant things. But then, I had never really opposed him about anything, even when I felt that he was making a poor decision.

This time, with so much at stake, I finally took charge. For a long time, I had cherished the thought of taking a journey back to England. Some of our friends, who now, like us, were established and could manage to take the time away, had done just that. I envied them and kept dreaming of going. I had tried to get John to put away money for the trip, showed him letters from our friends and pieces about travel in the papers. Usually he ignored my suggestions, but now I decided to make John see how much good such trip would do him.

I began by going to Rowsell's bookshop and buying the latest English papers. With the faster steamships plying the Atlantic, mail came much more quickly from England. These papers were only a month old. I casually left one of them, folded open to an article about London, on the tray which I brought to John with his breakfast.

The next time I stopped by Rowsell's for the paper, Henry looked at me curiously.

"A sudden interest in England, Jemima?" he asked curiously

There was something about Henry's tone that made me stop and think for a moment. We had been friends with the Rowsell's since out earliest days in Toronto.

I felt that I could confide in him.

"You know how ill John has been," I began.

He nodded.

"I am trying to interest him in taking a trip to England, getting away from everything for a while. I thought reading the papers might help."

"I can do more than that," Henry said, leaning over his counter, almost conspiratorially.

It turned out that the Rowsells had been thinking of sending their young son over to England to meet his relations there and had been hoping that someone they knew might be planning such a journey. Our plan would be the perfect opportunity.

"And there's more," Henry added. "We could arrange a meeting with Charles. I'm sure we could tempt John with that."

John's sister, Sarah, had married the architect, Charles Barry, who had recently been selected to design the new houses of Parliament in London and had just received a knighthood for his work.

"I'll come and speak with him, if you think it might help," he offered.

We agreed that I would begin to broach the subject of the trip with John, and then Rowsell would come by for a visit and casually mention the topic as well. All our friends were concerned about John and many had come by to visit, bringing books and newspapers, keeping their talk light with town gossip and family stories, trying to keep away from anything serious.

Rowsell did drop by for a visit and afterward, I found John eyeing me somewhat suspiciously.

"Well," he said. "It seems as if travelling to England is suddenly all the rage."

"What do you mean?" I tried to pretend I had no idea what he was talking about.

"Come now, m'dear. You have been going on about it. And now, suddenly, there is Rowsell wanting to send young Robert over home, telling all the latest news about Barry."

I really had thought that I was being quite subtle, but John had seen right through my plan. There was nothing to do but have a straightforward talk about it.

"Imagine, you'll be far away from everything. You'll be able to rest, we'll see our families, perhaps travel a little. John, we've worked so hard all these years. Surely we can manage to do this."

At first, he raised all sorts of arguments.

"Who is going to look after the office? Tell me that? It's not going to run itself, is it? And what about the College? Who will teach my classes? And how can we possibly afford such nonsense?"

I just smiled. There was something in his voice that told me that he was gradually warming to the idea.

Being so ill had severely weakened him. Even when he tried to get up and go back to work, he could not manage more than a few hours in the office. He would come home, exhausted, falling immediately to sleep. I knew that his illness had frightened him, although he would never admit it. The thought of a recurrence was unbearable for both of us.

At last, John finally agreed to the journey. He set up a plan to manage the office, arranged for a fellow architect, William Thomas to take over as City Engineer and asked John Tully who had once worked with us, to teach his classes as the College.

John decided to take five whole months away. We were really going to go to England.

If you had asked me, I would have said that I was only thinking of John's health, that the desire to take a long journey to England came only from wanting to take him away from his work, from anything that would give him stress and worsen his condition. But I knew, even then, that there was another reason.

Five months away and an ocean between them, was it too much to hope that he would forget her, forget them? Without daring to put it into words, I allowed myself to hope that if we were far away, things would once again be as they had been between us.

In early May, twenty years after we had arrived in Canada, we finally started off on our journey home, taking young Henry Rowsell along with us. We carried a letter of introduction to Sir Charles Barry, gifts for our families, letters and packages from Fanny to both our family and the Mountcastles. Clara had drawn sketches to show to everyone: portraits of the members of the family, pictures of their farm and the little village of Clinton. What would it be like? I wondered. After all those years of letters crossing back and forth, how would it be to finally meet again?

For twenty years, we had lived in Canada, but England had always been a part of us; we always spoke of it as home. How we waited eagerly in those early years for those letters that would take three months to arrive, so difficult to read, written as they were on both sides of thin paper to save postage. We would be so anxious to read the newspapers, sharing them with friends, not caring if the news was old and important events long since

Excited as he was, John was still feeling unwell. Through our friends we were able to make an appointment with the famous physician, Dr. Copeland. When he examined John, he informed him that he was suffering from overwork and needed to rest. Although, it was, of course, exactly what Christopher Widmer had told him, I thought perhaps, the advice of a famous London doctor might carry more weight with him. But John would have none of it. He had planned so much for London and was soon busy making appointments and filling his days with activities.

Henry Rowsell had written ahead to his brother-in-law, Charles, and John was invited to dine with him as soon as he arrived. It was a great thrill for John to spend the evening talking with the now famous architect who showed him his drawings for the Parliament Buildings and shared his stories about the work.

It was not surprising that John had exhausted himself so much in those first days in London that he had to visit Dr. Copeland again. This time, the doctor advised John in no uncertain terms that he had to rest. He recommended a visit to the Isle of Wight. Although we had planned to visit our families outside London, we now had to change our plans and the members of both our families came to visit us instead, before we went away to Wight.

How shocked I was when I saw my sisters for the first time. On the outside, we were smiling and embracing one another. Inside, a voice was asking, who are these old ladies with their grey hair and lined faces? I knew that they were asking the same questions as they looked at me. Twenty years. A lifetime had passed by. And then, as we talked, as I heard the old, familiar voices, the accents I had grown up with, it was as if the years slipped away. They were, again, the sisters I had missed so much for all these years.

There was so much to catch up on. I was filled with pride,

and yes, even a little smugness when we told our family and friends about our life in Toronto.

With a flourish, John had rolled out a plan of High Park, showing them how our land stretched all the way from the lake to Bloor St.

"All that land!" his brother had exclaimed, "You have done well for yourself." Everyone marvelled at the drawings he showed them, especially those of the Asylum. And they were clearly intrigued when John explained all the ideas he had incorporated in the design. We had also brought some of John's sketches of Colborne Lodge, and they huddled over them, eager to know all about our life there. When I brought out Fanny's gifts and the sketches Clara had sent, the subject of the Mountcastles and their troubles was unavoidable. The family had, of course, heard of the difficulties Fanny had faced over the years and now they wanted to hear about it all again directly from me.

"The girls are getting on," Martha observed. "Is there anyone for them to meet in this Clinton where they live?"

I felt as if they were criticizing Fanny, for Sidney's failures, for the girls' lack of prospects.

"It's difficult," I said, trying to change the subject. "We had Ellen come to stay with us, arranged for her school and dancing classes. We saw that she went to dances and parties."

"But nothing happened?"

"No, often she comes to us. She and her sisters. But they don't seem to be settling."

"Fanny writes to say Clara is showing great talent."

"She is. John is quite taken with her painting. He wants her to come to us and have lessons."

Martha shook her head. "I hope he doesn't fill her head with nonsense," she said.

As we talked of Fanny's children, I could sense something

hanging in the air, unspoken. Felt by all of us. My sisters were married and they had their children. Martha was already a grandmother. But never in our letters, in all those years, was there ever a mention of our own childless state. It would not be mentioned now.

My father had always been fond of John, even though he did have some doubts about my marrying him. Once, as we were looking at the drawings, he pulled me aside and said, "He's certainly found his way in life." Though he was old and frail now, my father still had in his eyes that sparkle that I had always loved. Now he turned to me with a smile. "Of course, all those days of trailing me in the studio might have had something to do with it."

"Oh, Papa. I had nothing to do with any of this." I protested.

"Nonsense, my girl." he answered. "Where would he have been without you helping to get him on his feet? Don't you ever forget that."

My father's words would always stay with me. I never really thought much of my part in getting ourselves established. Sometimes, it seems, that you have to see yourself through another's eyes.

Martha and John's brother and their spouses were able to make arrangements to accompany us to the Isle of Wight where we rented rooms in Ventnor, a pretty town which has become known as a health retreat. The landscape was breath-taking and the climate so restorative, almost Mediterranean as some people described it. Here John was under the care of a Dr. Martin, who recommended gentle rides along the beach.

So John, at first sputtering with embarrassment, went for rides each morning on what was called an 'invalid's pony.'

"Me," he roared, on the first morning. "With a whole stable of horses at home!" But he had to admit, the easy rides and the fresh sea air did seem to help. Soon he was beginning to feel much better and began to get quite restless. Time was passing and we wanted to move on.

Dr. Martin felt that John had greatly improved and was able to travel. He gave him a letter to the landlord of the Hotel de l'Ile d'Albion, a hotel in Paris frequented by British tourists, asking him to give John a tumbler of a certain vintage of wine before getting out of bed in the morning.

How we laughed together at what we began to call "The French Cure," but it worked. In three days, John was himself again, full of energy, dashing about Paris with his notebook in hand checking off all the famous buildings he had always wanted to see, including a trip out to see Versailles. At night we would find a charming little restaurant, order excellent wine or champagne and talk about our day. We even shopped together, with John encouraging me to buy fashionable French dresses and helping to choose gifts to take home. We were so happy together in those days in Paris. It seemed like a dream.

Sometimes, in moments of stillness, when John was napping or reading a newspaper, I would catch myself staring at him. I hardly dared to put my thoughts into words. It was a long, long time since we had been so close and shared so much together, I almost dared to hope that it would last.

But then, something would happen, just a brief moment that would shatter my fragile happiness. Once, as we browsed in a delightful toy shop, I suddenly noticed John lagging behind. I turned back. He was standing quite still, absorbed in thought and unaware of me. Did I imagine it or did I see longing in his face as he looked at boys' building sets on the counter in front of him? I couldn't shake the cold chill that crept over me, like a fog rolling in before a storm. Even here. Even in Paris—was he thinking of them.

All too soon, however, we returned to England, and now

that John was well again, we were able to do some travelling there as well. We set out to visit friends and relatives who lived outside London, and even played at being tourists in England, to visiting towns and places that we had always wanted to see, going to art galleries, museums and stately homes. In the flurry of visits and touring, it was so easy to be complacent, to simply enjoy the moment. But then, there it would come again. We rarely thought about what was going on at home in Toronto, but we had arranged for letters to be sent to John's brother to keep us in touch. Was it just the suspicious nature I had developed, or did John anxiously almost grab the mail from Canada before I had a chance to look at it? Did he seem, once, to be shoving aside a letter he was writing when he heard me coming into our room? Even here, even on the other side of the ocean, I knew he was thinking of her.

Soon, five months had passed and it was time to return home. It was so hard to bid farewell to my parents and sisters, to John's family, and our friends; somehow even harder than that first time all the years before. Then, we were filled with a spirit of adventure. Now, we were all growing older. We would never again make such a journey, never again see each other. Everyone sent us off with packages; gifts for all the Mountcastles, and remembrances for us. People we met in London gave us letters and gifts for friends and relations in Toronto. We had collected souvenirs everywhere we went and shopped in Paris and London for the latest fashions, the newest books and all sorts of things that we would never be able to buy in Toronto. We were sailing home with much more than we had brought with us. Robert Rowsell, who had been staying with his relatives all this time, was similarly laden with a great deal of additional luggage.

This time, we would travel on the *Arabia's* sister ship, the *Africa*. It was a rough crossing and John was seasick again for most of the voyage. I found myself weary and looking forward to being back in Toronto, however wonderful our visit to England had been. In those last days alone on the *Africa*, all that I had willfully ignored during our vacation began to surface again. Those days in England had been the happiest time of my life.

As the *Africa* drew nearer to New York, I felt a sense of darkness descending around me. In those five months away, I had been so happy. For the first time, in so long, except for those few fleeting moments I was able to push out of my mind, nothing had stood between us. There had been no double life for me.

And now, after a short visit to New York, we would be going back to Toronto.

Would we now slip into that strange half-life again?

Clara

We had barely settled in at home when we gave in to Fanny's pleas for a visit.

She and the children were thrilled with all the letters and gifts that the family sent them. How eagerly she clung to everything I had to tell her, craving to imagine, to share every moment I could remember. I could see in the sadness in her eyes as I talked. I knew that she was thinking it would never be possible for her to undertake such as journey.

Hoping to cheer her, I raised the idea of having Clara come to stay with us, something we had often talked about before. This time, I insisted and soon it was all arranged. Clara would go to school, just as Ellen had, and John would see to it that she had art lessons as well. She would come to us just after Christmas.

Clara, my clever, talented Clara. Of course, I loved Ellen and it was always a delight to have her with us. But Clara was special. At eighteen she was a serious young woman with no giddiness about her. She was tall and sturdy with that strength you see in women accustomed to hard work on the farm. Her hair was a dark, glossy brown and her large, dark eyes always seemed to be watching, taking in everything around her. Even as a little girl, she had always stood out in the family with her noticeable drive and energy. In the midst of a busy, noisy household, you could often find her scribbling on whatever scraps of paper she could find or painting little pictures to decorate the drab farmhouse walls. Often Fanny had to draw her away to help out with the household tasks. That her talent as an artist emerged so early in such unlikely surroundings always fascinated me, as did Clara's own awareness of it.

Where did that spark come from, I often wondered. Life had not been easy for Clara, a middle child of a large family who had lost her beloved older brother, Alfred and several other younger siblings as well. As Sidney tried one thing after another, the Mountcastles had moved often, uprooting Clara from her home, interrupting what little schooling she had. As she had with all her children, Fanny had somehow managed not only to make sure Clara had kept up with her studies at home, but also had taught her to paint as well. But when I thought of Clara growing up a farm, in Goderich or the even smaller town of Clinton, I marvelled at her ambition. She shimmered with talent and with dreams and I found myself caught up in them.

We enrolled Clara in the same girl's school to which we had sent Ellen. It was now run by a woman who had taught at the school before. As for the Deslands themselves, they had strangely disappeared after running the school successfully for two years and nobody knew what had happened to them. Far from being behind the city girls, Clara found herself quite beyond most of them. Unlike them, she took her studies seriously, wanting, I think, to make up for the rather haphazard schooling she had had. She had little time for the other girls, most of whom she felt were just marking time until they found a husband.

It was, however, the prospect of proper art lessons that clearly thrilled her. I remember how nervous she was the day of her first lesson with John Chatterton, an English artist of John's acquaintance who had settled in Toronto.

I remember how she returned home, glowing. "He quite liked my work, Aunt," she had exclaimed. "I thought he might just think I was some country girl, painting trees and fields, but took me seriously. He is going to help me in working from nature."

Clara had brought her sketch books with her and eagerly set to work producing paintings for her weekly lessons. Although we wanted to encourage her to meet other young people, to go to dances and parties, Clara made it clear that she was in Toronto to work; she had little interest in what she called, "frivolities."

As I had with Ellen, I wanted to take Clara shopping and treat her to some new fashionable dresses. But Clara had little interest in fancy clothes; she was clearly happiest in her paint-covered smock completely immersed in her work. She was, however, very pleased when I took her to Rowsell's, and introduced her to Henry.

We went off with an armful of the newest journals and some of the latest books that had arrived from London and New York. Whispering to Henry as she browsed excitedly through the shelves, I arranged to open an account for her, so that she could come buy books and art supplies whenever she wanted.

One afternoon, I came into the parlour to find Clara looking intently at my painting of "The Dying Soldier", the painting I had contributed to that first Art Exhibition so long ago.

"You don't paint anymore, do you?" she remarked as she heard me enter the room.

"Not really. When I stopped going to the office, I thought I might take it up again—but, no ..." Her question left me flustered. I didn't know how to respond.

The walls of our parlour were filled with paintings, John's, mine, other works that we had purchased over the years. Clara walked slowly around the room, looking carefully at each work.

"You were quite a good artist," she said thoughtfully, "You and mother, both of you. It's a shame you never pursued it."

I laughed. "We were just amateurs. I would never have even thought of myself as an artist."

"Well, I do," Clara said emphatically, her voice quivering with emotion. "I am going to be an artist, and successful. You'll see."

I remember smiling at her, an almost patronizing tone in my voice. "Of course, dear," I had said. "But you'll be married soon, and then there won't be any time for such thoughts."

"Not me," she said. "I will never get married."

There was such determination in her voice that I knew this was something she had thought a great deal about.

"Life as an artist, alone, will be very difficult. How will you make a living?"

"I've already thought about that. I plan to find work as a teacher and still have time for my own work."

"Well, you always were determined."

Clara burst out laughing. "I know, you're going to tell me that story again."

I joined in the laughter. I knew exactly what she was talking about—my "Clara story" that had become almost a staple in the family. I smiled and remained silent, but I couldn't help thinking about it.

Clara must have been just about five or six years old when I went to visit the Mountcastles who were then back on a farm. There on the floor of the log cabin they were living in at the time sat little Clara, wearing a hand-me-down dress that her older sisters had worn till it was threadbare. She had put some paper on the floor in front of her, held the stub of a crayon in her hand and was deeply absorbed in a picture she was making. When one of the other children called out to her, she looked up, scowled and shook her curly mop of hair. "I'm busy!" she had snapped, going back to her work.

When we talked about that surprising comment later, Fanny said, "You were just like that, I remember. Father used to beam so proudly when you showed him your "work." Then she added wistfully, "He never took me seriously."

"But he called you his 'little Sprite.' We all thought you were his favourite."

"Quite a Sprite," she said, looking down at her calloused, work-hardened hands and torn, grubby fingernails.

We shook our heads. There we were, two middle-aged women, still remembering our childhood rivalry, that rivalry that still existed as I envied Fanny her family and she envied me our comfortable life. We loved each deeply and knew how lonely it would have been to live in Canada without any family nearby, but still, those childhood slights never went completely away.

Sometime, later when I thought about Clara, I couldn't help but wonder what lay behind her plans for the future. Was it only her ambition to be an artist or was it something more? She loved her father, of course, and would never have said a negative thing about him, but even at eighteen, she had shrewdly analyzed how being dependent on the whims of a husband could determine her life. She had seen her mother worn down by the demands of a large family and constant worry about how to provide for them. Clara was determined not to let that happen to her.

With Clara with us, we finally settled down again in Toronto, our wonderful holiday far behind us. Although, as City Engineer, John took on work for the city and a few new commissions, I think that even he knew that he could no longer work the way he had in the past. He went back to his teaching at the College, but soon retired and slowly he began to wind down the work at the office. At the same time, we began to make plans to move back to Colborne Lodge which we had always seen as the place where we would retire.

servants will still have to carry the hot water upstairs, but I'll figure out how to solve that one too. You'll see." Then John lifted the page to reveal another drawing.

"I don't understand," I said, staring at the drawing. "What is this?"

"It's the privy. It's going to be inside—the newest thing. I've been reading all about it."

John explained how there would be a tank filled with rainwater upstairs. "See here. There will be a lever, push it and water will come down from the tank and *whoosh!*... Down to the pit below."

I was quite speechless. This certainly was not something we usually talked about, not even with John and not even with all the years of his illnesses. "Are you sure about this? Is it... is it healthy... having it in the house?"

"Ah, you're thinking about the miasma."

I nodded, thinking about the dreaded cholera epidemics we had experienced in England and after our arrival here. It was believed that it was caused by the miasma—the night air that came from waste. Privies were thought to be safer away from the house.

"I've just been reading here about a Doctor Snow in England who says he's found the cause of cholera. He's shown that it comes from waste in the drinking water. There is no such thing as the miasma... And, anyway, everything will drain properly away."

"But look." He turned to another drawing. "Just so people don't start talking about us, I'm making a secret door into the bathroom. The wall and the door will all be papered, you won't even notice it, and no one will know it's there. No one but us."

So John was able to try out all his new ideas and our new life in the country was generally peaceful and happy, settled in our now quite grand home with rooms for friends to come from the city to visit and even stay for a while. With the farms well established, we had fruits and vegetables, milk and eggs and chickens and could manage quite well without having to go to the city markets all the time. There was now an omnibus that went into town and the journey became much easier. We could arrange for John, the groom, to drive us to the main road and come back to pick us up at an appointed time.

But every so often, something would come to shatter my serenity. John often went into the city on business; we still owned a great deal of land, houses that were rented out, lots that needed to be sold and I never questioned those days when he went away. He still had his clubs and his meetings to attend. But still, sometimes, there was something else. The tone of his voice when he mentioned that he was going out; the late hour when he would return.

She was still there; I knew that. And sometimes, I thought about those children, grown up now. Did he see them often? Did they think of him as their father?

It was always there. A kind of miasma.

It was *a kind of a miasma—a poison that surrounded me all those years, appearing when I least expected it, sinking its claws into me, suffocating me. But once—only once—it brought something good out of its contagion.*

High Park. Our gift to the city.

Even now, as I sense the walls closing in, I know what we have done—what I have done. There are no children, but there will always be something of us left behind.

And I did it. I was the one who found a way for us to live on.

How long has it been? It is cold in my little room, so cold. There is a small stove, but it doesn't produce much warmth. Somehow, it is locked so I cannot touch it and sometimes, the fire dies down and no one comes to stoke it. I gather a shawl around me and climb to look out of the window.

It must be a hard winter. There is so much snow, it blankets everything, covering the gardens, heaped high on the roofs of the barn and cottage, weighing heavily on the branches of the trees which seem about to crack under the load. It is as if there is nothing alive out there; no sight of any animals, no sound of birds, no one about working around the house or venturing out into the cold.

John comes to see me. Sometimes, if it's a good day, he sits and talks with me and I remember it.

I think he comes often, perhaps every day, but I can't be sure.

Others come and go, but mostly I am alone.

I have forgotten so much, but I remember, so clearly, the moment when that little spark of an idea first came to me. It had begun one afternoon, the year after we had returned from England. It had been a lovely summer, warm, sunny days but plenty of rain to set the garden ablaze with colour, bright zinnias and blue hollyhocks, orange day lilies and tall, golden sunflowers. Although, it was still quite a long difficult journey to come out to High Park, especially with three young ones, Jennie came often. The children could run freely in the woods and fields, ride the horses, go paddling in the pond and sometimes John would take them out in his canoe.

That day, while John was busy with the children, Jennie and I sat together on the verandah, quietly, drinking our tea. It was often like that with us; no need to fill a silence with aimless chatter, just that pleasant sense of relaxing together. Jennie had been little more than a child when we met, and I had watched her grow up over the years, until now I saw her as my equal, a friend, but more than that. My confidant. The only person I could really talk to about the secret we shared. In her thirties now, and after three children in quick succession, Jenny had become a little stout, but it became her. Happy in her marriage and motherhood, she radiated a confidence, a sense of well-being.

That day, my thoughts spilled out, unbidden, turning into words what had only been as unformed ideas, nagging at the corners of my brain.

"I sometimes wonder," I said, turning to her, "what will become of all this, when... we are no longer here."

I gulped, shocked that I had expressed these thoughts aloud. These thoughts I had so often. *What would happen to our land? Would John find a way to give it to* her? *To those children?*

There must have been something in my voice that suggested my meaning to Jennie. She turned to me, peering thoughtfully. Jennie did not seem surprised. Perhaps this had been on her mind as well.

"Have you and Mr. H ever talked about it?" she asked.

I shook my head. It seemed that we never talked about anything very much, anymore.

"Do you ever think of selling some of the land?'

"We've tried that, back when we had our troubles. But we were still so far from the city, there wasn't much interest. And now I don't think John would ever even consider it. He loves this land. It's the first thing we ever bought."

"And you?"

"Not so much. We're talking about moving back here, retiring. But I will miss our house in the city. It's lonely here, even with the girls coming so often to stay."

I paused. A thought unspoken hung in the air.

It was Jennie who put it into words.

"And you think about *them,* don't you?"

"Oh, Jennie, you know I do. Perhaps it's wrong, but I can't help myself."

How often in my loneliness had I looked out over the land and thought about them, his children. It was such beautiful land, with its hills and streams, the view over the lake, the farms, the orchards and gardens we had made. Had John thought about it, had he decided to leave it to them in the future?

It was still woodland and difficult to reach, but even now the city was growing closer and closer. John's own Asylum had been out in the country when he started to plan it, but King Street had been extended along between his building and the lake, running almost to our land. Lot Street, now called Queen Street, was no longer the north end of the city and new buildings were springing up along it all the time. One day, we could imagine High Park being surrounded by the growing city.

"But he wouldn't just leave it to them, would he? He'd have to tell you, wouldn't he?" Jennie asked.

He's a tough old bird, for all his illnesses. He's going to outlast me, for sure. And when I'm gone, he can do as he wants."

Would they divide up my land between them? Would they live in my house? The thought had tormented me for so long, but it was hard to believe now I was sitting here, coolly discussing it with Jennie.

Jennie turned to me, reached over and took both my hands

in hers. "Then you have to do something to stop it," she said.

I laughed bitterly. "So easy to say. But how could I stop something I'm not even supposed to know about?"

The conversation kept buzzing around in my brain. Out gardening, I looked over my carefully planted flowers and thought of their fate. Out walking, I found myself wondering who would walk on these paths when I was gone. It was like an itch that wouldn't leave me alone.

Was it just a coincidence, or was it fate? John himself gave me the answer a short time later, although, of course, he would never know what he had done.

He came home from the city one day, with the latest papers under his arm. It was still light and warm and after dinner we took our tea and sat on the verandah to read.

Suddenly, I heard John muttering. He leaned over, almost shoving the newspaper at me.

"Look at this, Jemima. They're doing in New York exactly what I have been trying to get this city to do!"

"What are they doing?"

"Setting aside a big piece of land for a park, that's what."

He pointed to the paragraph about the plan for what was to be called Central Park, a large tract of land just north of the city. On our return from England, we had stayed in New York for several days. After that very rough crossing, we had been very tired and found the city crowded and quite overwhelming. I remembered someone telling us about a settlement called Seneca Village not far from the city in what was still open country and thinking how odd it was that so many people were crammed in a small space at the tip of the island of Manhattan while just a little farther north, there was still all that farmland and forest.

John had been trying for years to get the city Council in Toronto to give some thought to building a park. He had presented a plan for a park on the island and tried to convince them to develop the Esplanade. But his plans had always fallen on deaf ears.

A *Park!* We were, I realized, at that moment, sitting in the middle of a park, Our Park!

What if? Would it be possible?

Could I somehow find a way for us turn our park, High Park, into a place for the city?

I said nothing. Just waited.

John reached for his pipe, lit it, and sat quietly smoking, staring out over the garden which was growing dark quickly, now that the sun had set.

For most of our life together, I had followed along with whatever John wanted to do, moving to Canada, setting up our business, buying and building High Park. But once, when I felt his very life depended on it, I had set about on what I thought of as my campaign to convince him to leave his work behind and set off on our trip to England.

My strategies, my arguments and hints, my planting of tantalizing bits from the English papers had all worked. Now, I had to find a way to do the same things again. For me, the stakes were higher. I was fighting for what was mine; for what would never belong to those children. That night I found a way to make sure that would never happen. I was going to convince John to give High Park to the city of Toronto forever.

I never forgot my plan, scouring the papers from London and New York for any reference to parks. Sometimes if I was lucky I would find articles about new designs and ideas for them. I would leave the papers folded casually, open to the articles that John might catch sight of.

I held my breath when John started thinking again of subdividing the land and trying to sell it off. Fortunately, we were still too far from the city for people to think of settling on land that was so rugged and hard to reach. There were no sales.

I listened in when people talked about problems in the city and what could be done about them.

I waited for my chances to plant the idea for my grand plan.

The next time I saw Jennie, I managed to catch her alone and tell her about it.

"Yes," she said, nodding her head. "It's a wonderful idea. Such a gift to the city!"

Then she leaned over, looking at me intently with those piercing blue eyes of hers.

"And what have you done about it?"

"Well I... I haven't really done anything... not yet."

"You should you know. Mr. H might come up with a different idea from yours and it will be too late."

It was Jennie who never forgot this conversation. I tended to get caught up in the moment; working on the house and the gardens; entertaining our friends. But Jennie kept after me. Whenever we met, there always came a moment when she would peer at me closely and whisper, "Well, have you done anything?"

I have no clock or calendar. I have no sense of time passing. I know only when it is dark and when it is light. Now even the little patch of blue I see from my windows has changed. No longer that pale, almost insipid blue of the winter. The sky has a new brightness.

They have put an old cot beneath the window so that I can climb up and peer outside. The snow is beginning to melt at last. I can see a corner of our garden from up here. It is that ugly moment of spring when everything is brown. Bare bushes and dry grasses lie somehow exposed. We would be starting to talk of the garden now. What needed to be done. What new things we wanted to plant this year. Does John care so much about our garden, now that he must look after it alone?

I am running out of paper. I found some old sketch pads in a corner and now I am writing on the backs of all the pages.

There is so much I want to say and so much I have avoided. I cannot hide any longer.

Retirement

T he thought of retirement conjures up an image of a sleepy, old couple nodding by the fire or out on the verandah snoozing in their rocking chairs in the summer sunshine. For us, our lives were so busy once we had settled into Colborne Lodge that I often welcomed the winter as a time to slow down a little.

For John, the house with its gardens, parkland and farms was a never-ending project.

Over the years, he made constant alterations to the house; installing lights and a glass roof, building shelves for the dining room and the upstairs bedroom and even making furniture just as he had when we were just starting out. He set up a workshop out in the barn where he could work on his projects. As much as we loved the house, its location on the height of land close to the lake meant that it was subject to extremes of weather; the rooms upstairs were often bitter cold in the winter when the howling wind would rattle the windows and shake the walls. Snow on the glass roof was always a danger and had to be constantly cleaned away. John installed double windows for the winter, set up a stove in the dining room and although he tried various ideas to make our bedroom warmer, there were times, especially in the cold of January, when we had to move back downstairs to keep warm. There was a storm in February of 1868 that brought the deepest snow we had ever seen in all our years in Canada; it was as high as the gateposts and kept us snowed in for days and all the trains were stopped.

That same year, a terrible storm in May brought heavy rain and hailstones so large they broke the windows over the stairs and in the greenhouse. The rain was so heavy it brought down the plaster in the library, soaking the papers lying on the desk. John spent months repairing the damage to the windows and the roof. Later when Clara came to visit, he asked her to help him wallpaper the hall and bedrooms.

After years of an ever-changing stream of servants who would stay for only a short while and then move on, we finally found a couple, James and Phoebe Duff, who would work as our groom and cook and live in the servants' quarters downstairs. James also helped John in many ways and Phoebe and I came to work well together to maintain the house, doing the cooking and looking after all the guests. There was also Mr. Rhodes who lived nearby and would come often to help John with the heavy work about the house and gardens and we had a woman who would come in to do the laundry.

Routine repairs to the house, roof, windows and out-buildings also kept John busy, but for both of us, it was the garden that occupied much of our time all year. Even in the depth of winter, we spent many happy hours planning, going over the gardening books that I kept and deciding what we wanted to do for the coming season. Early spring, found us busily at work sowing seeds for vegetables and flowers in the hot bed that John had made and readying the flowerbeds in front of the house and along the lawn.

From the time the first daffodils and tulips bloomed until well into the fall, the garden would be a blaze of ever-changing colours. Roses and honeysuckle grew around the verandah, fruit trees sprang into blossom and then produced their apples, cherries, pears and plums. There were rose trees and peony bushes, banks of flowers everywhere and carefully planned flowerbeds.

Summers kept us busy constantly weeding and maintaining the gardens. We had a large vegetable garden which provided us with everything from watercress which sprang up early in the spring, through the berries and all sorts of green vegetables Phoebe and I gathered all summer, to the potatoes and root vegetables which kept us going all winter. We loved to experiment and tried many different varieties of crop; potatoes, cabbage, peas and beans. Phoebe and I preserved plums, quince and one summer we made eleven gallons of currant wine. John planted grape vines, developed ways to water them and John and I made sweet wine and claret. In the fall, we harvested all we had grown, giving food away, selling some things, putting down as much as we could for the winter.

Summers meant a constant stream of visitors. Now that we had extra bedrooms, we could invite friends more often, knowing that they could stay with us and not have to make the long journey back into the city late at night. Jacob and Margery Hirschfelder came often. Now their family had grown to eight children; Fanny, their eldest, often stayed with us for long visits and when she and her younger sister Rosamund became engaged to be married, John and I happily joined in the celebrations. John enjoyed the company of the older boys, Rudolph and Alfred and there were two little ones, Charlie and little Florrie who were born when Margery was in her forties. Then there were the Rowsells and their grown-up children and Chewetts, (James was the son of William, our first client and dear friend.) William Thomas, now an important architect in town, and many other friends also visited with their young children and other relatives. Jennie and Peter came often, sometimes staying over or just bringing the children out for a day in the country. What great times we had; in the summer we sailed or rowed on the pond, went for long walks, east along the lake or west along the railway tracks. The men often went off shooting, giving the women a chance to simply sit and chat and enjoy the gardens. John had built a boathouse down by the pond and he loved to take the visiting children out for trips on the pond in the rowboats or canoes. In the winter we skated on the pond or took everyone out for sleigh rides. Sometimes, it felt as if we were running an inn with me spending much time planning large meals and supervising the preparations. But Phoebe was always a great help, managing to cook for large numbers of visitors. Sometimes, it was necessary to have some of the tenant's children to come and help out.

In the summer, Phoebe and James would often set up a long table in the garden and after all the day's activities, we would all gather together for dinner. I remember one Sunday when the Rowsells with Kate and Lizzie and the Chewitts and their children came to visit along with some other friends. Phoebe had cooked chickens from the farm and a duck from the pond. The beans, peas and asparagus were all freshly picked that day and I had baked fruit pies with our own cherries and raspberries.

After dinner, Henry looked thoughtfully at the guests assembled at the table, and said, "Do you realize that we have all known each other for thirty years?"

There were murmurs and a shaking of heads.

"It can't possibly be that long," I said.

"Ah, but it is. It's 1864 after all and we all met shortly after we arrived."

Now we were nodding our heads and you could almost see what we were all thinking. It was John who put the thoughts into words. "It is quite remarkable when you think of it, all the things we've survived—the agues, influenza, even that cholera when we first came..."

"And the terrible winters and insufferable heat," added Lizzie Rowsell. "Do you remember, we lived above the shop on King Street and you were just down the road, upstairs from Ducat's drugstore?"

Then Henry chimed in, "And all those ups and downs in business and that mad rebellion. We've done well, all of us." We were drinking the wine that John and I had made the year before. He raised his glass in a toast and we all joined in.

We had done well; Henry with his bookstore, library and successful publishing company, John with our business and most of his other ventures. We all knew others who had not been so fortunate. The thought of all the struggles of the Mountcastles crossed my mind.

"We're pretty spry for folks of our age," said Henry, continuing his reflections.

"Now, now!" I shook my finger at him.

"My dear Mrs. Howard," he said with a laugh, and a bit of a bow. "We are, all of us, sixty if we're a day. And look at us! You are still riding. We shoot, we skate." He shook his head. "And just coming out here, to your wilderness so often is no small feat. Even though you two come and go at the drop of a hat," he added. He'd been making sly jibes about our "wilderness" and "Howard's Folly" since that very first picnic in the wilds. But they were just meant in good humour and the Rowsells had always been among our most frequent guests.

It was in those years that we began to welcome people from the city to enjoy the outdoors. There was the annual picnic of the Oddfellows which grew to be a huge event. One year, a tent was set up on the grounds and three hundred people attended; by the next, there was even a band and dancing and John set up rides for the children. We had James stand watch to make sure no one picked our flowers. Church groups and schoolchildren came as well.

Always, in the back of my mind, when we hosted such events was that dream of the park; a vision of the future.

In addition to the house and gardens, we had the farm that John had dreamed of all those years ago, with its sheep and cows and chickens. We had had many tenants over the years, but so often they didn't work out and we had to hire people to come and sheer the sheep and look after the fields. It was in 1864 that a young couple who lived in Bond Head north of the city enquired about renting the farm. The former tenant had left the farm house in such a state that we invited them to stay with us until it was ready.

We became friends instantly. We leant them furniture and milking equipment to help them get started and shortly after they moved into the house, the young girl they hired came running to us for help for Mrs. Cope was in labour. John sent for Dr. Richardson and I rushed to help her. The baby, a little boy they named Percy became like a grandchild to us.

Right from the beginning, John took a shine to little Percy. He bought the Copes a baby carriage and gave Percy a little wheelbarrow for his first birthday. When the wheels on the carriage kept breaking, he offered to fix it in his shop. One afternoon, after he had been in the shop for a long time, I walked down to bring John some tea.

The door was open and John did not hear me come in. He was standing at his work table, his hand resting on the little carriage, lost in thought. From where I stood at the door, I could see his face, but he hadn't noticed me. I had seen that look before, once, long ago, in a toyshop in Paris; the look of longing as he had looked at the toys; the look as he stared down at the baby carriage. As if he had telegraphed his thoughts, there was no mistaking what he was thinking. I knew that after all these years, he was still thinking of them, the children, of her.

There were other times, glimpses, momentary lapses that I tried to ignore. The time when I walked into the library and surprised John sitting at his desk, writing a letter. He fumbled and pushed the paper aside. The morning when Phoebe was busy with other tasks and I decided to tidy the library while John was outside working. The litter basket was filled to the brim—on top, bits of paper shredded into little pieces. Some perverse urge, the suspicion that was always there, made me pick up one of the pieces. A strange hand, letters crudely formed from someone not used to writing. I couldn't stop myself. I plowed through the scraps until I found the proof I didn't want to see. Her name—Mary—at the bottom of the letter.

Most of time, I schooled myself to shut these thoughts from my mind. Our life was full, I told myself; a whirl of work, and friends and sometimes almost frantic activity. Then something would surface and that fortress that I had created for myself collapsed. I would be devastated, barely able to carry on. Sometimes, I took to my bed, pleaded some sort of illness, drew the curtains, and lay alone in our darkened room until I could force myself to go on. John's other life was always there, hovering and I had to go on pretending that I didn't know.

But there was usually little time to brood. Now that there was an omnibus that went into town, we could arrange for James to drive us to the main road and come back to pick us up at an appointed time. We were forever rushing into town to visit our friends and shop. Although we were still out in the country, we never missed any of the events happening in the city, the balls and parties, concerts, and exhibitions at the Crystal Palace on

King Street, which was a smaller version of the famous Crystal Palace that we had visited in London. Plays and travelling exhibitions, like General Tom Thumb and Commodore Nutt at the Music Hall. Now that we had the railways, it was much easier to travel. From the station in nearby Mimico, John and I took the train to Goderich to visit the Mountcastles and the journey which used to take several days could now be accomplished in just five hours. We were away quite often in those years and Eliza would come and look after our home while we travelled.

Meanwhile, Toronto was changing, certainly everyone agreed with that; but not everyone thought it was for the better. The population had grown to fifty thousand people. Sometimes it felt as if the city was almost like a child outgrowing its clothes as soon as they were put on. As soon as a boundary was established, the outskirts of the city quickly stretched beyond it. Houses were built north of Queen Street and west of Bathurst. Streetcars like the ones we had seen in London finally came to the city and tracks were laid along Queen Street all the way to the Asylum which had once seemed so far out of town. John sold the land where our Toronto house had been and helped the Rossins, two brothers from Buffalo—to build their grand hotel there at the corner of York and King Streets. Railway tracks were laid along the lakeshore, even on some of our land. The new railways brought tourists, new businesses and industry to the city.

But there was another side to the city, a rougher less pleasant effect of all the growth.

There had always been poor people in the city; people who lived in the rougher areas of town, down in the east end near the Don. There had always been drunks in the city, even back when we first arrived and people talked about the fact that in the tiny, new settlement there was a tavern on every block. Life was hard there, and not everyone who came to the new colony succeeded in making their way.

It is difficult to say just what had happened, but it seemed to almost everyone that drinking was now a far greater problem than it had been before. Even Jennie talked about it.

She and Peter had built a grand house in town and became known for their glittering parties and good work they both did. Intrigued by politics when she was young, Jennie had turned that concern for others and energy into playing an important role in many women's and church groups in the city that were trying to help the city's poor and hungry, Jennie became known as one of those women who get things done. She was always in demand when any new cause came up and was always very busy with them and with new friends the couple made as they moved up in society.

With John's help, Peter had expanded the original Grey's Inn, bought other taverns as well. He'd started his brewery and bought land and houses in the city. Jennie no longer went to Grey's, not just because she was busy with other things, but as she explained to me, that business had changed.

"It's not a place for a woman anymore," she had said. "It's strange. When Ma and Pa ran the inn, it was quite a common thing. There were women on their own, widows sometimes who took over the business when their husbands died; those independent types who started up on their own. No one thought anything of it. But today, it's different. A woman working alone in a tavern ..." she shook her head.

"It was a different time," I remarked. "We were all just getting started here. Women just had to pitch in, I guess."

"And you did too," Jennie said. "But it's different now. I... I wouldn't feel safe." She tucked a strand of hair behind her ear. "Strange. I grew up, living upstairs from a tavern, with Ma behind the bar like as not. Now, Peter keeps a few strong men on hand, just to keep order." Jennie laughed wryly. "I know I almost sound like I'm Temperance. Me, an innkeeper's daughter and an innkeeper's wife. But you know, something has to be done."

Some people said that drinking was only a problem with the poor, but, in truth, it affected people everywhere. Shortly after I had had this conversation with Jennie, we heard that Thomas Young had died suddenly. Of apoplexy, it was said, but everyone knew the truth.

Young had been John's great rival, of course, getting commissions that John competed for and losing to John in things that Young clearly wanted. Like John, Young had also taught at the College, shown his paintings in the exhibition John had organized and helped to build the city. But then, we began to hear, more and more that something had happened to him. He lost work, he quarrelled with people. His commissions were taken over by others. Then the rumours started to spread about his drinking. At one point, we heard that he had left his wife and taken the youngest child with him. Then, he and his wife were reconciled and another child was born, but the marriage did not last.

There was no sense of triumph when we heard of his death, only a feeling of sadness and waste. I always remembered his obituary in the *Toronto Daily Leader* which caught that feeling so well in the words "the seductive but destroying influence of liquor" which had led to the end of a promising career and death.

It wasn't just Thomas Young. We saw it in workers that we hired and in our tenants. Once, John had sent a young man off to the city on an errand, and when he didn't come back for three days, there was nothing to do but let him go when he finally did reappear. Another time, one of our barns was set on fire and much of the crop was destroyed. Once again, it turned out that the men had been drinking.

John and I weren't Temperance ourselves. We liked a little wine with our suppers and we even tried our hand at making it ourselves, not doing too badly, if I might say so.

But I did attend several meetings with my friends and afterwards I kept thinking about what I had heard. People spoke not only about the need to prevent people from drinking by banning the sale of liquor, but also of the need to provide healthy activities instead.

Outside it is spring.

From the window, I can see the garden, our garden, bursting into life. At first we wanted an English garden, but soon we learned, sometimes painfully, with great disappointment, what would live and what would die in this harsh climate.

There are the daffodils, just beginning to raise their heads and nod up to the sky. The tulips seem to be hesitating, their swaths of colour not yet turning the flower beds into an artist's pallet. Soon, little bluebells will stretch their carpet over all the flowerbeds and it won't be long until the lilacs are in full bloom.

I breathe deeply, almost able to imagine the sweet spring air.

Inside there is no time.

I pace around my little room, back and forth, around and around.

There is nowhere to go.

I sink down beside the old chest again, memories shifting through my hands.

Alone

I had no one to talk to. For years, I had relied on Jennie, but now there never seemed time anymore for those long, intimate talks. Even when I visited her in the city or she came out to see us, our conversations would be light and amusing; her eldest daughter's stream of eligible young men, then her engagement and then the plans for her wedding, the parties Jennie went to with Peter, the entertainments they held at their grand home, the important work she was doing in the city.

There was no place in our conversations for my sordid, little story about John's other family and Jennie wasn't one for gossip anymore anyway.

But the dream of the park had always stayed with her and she never stopped pestering me about it. When through her own work in the city, Jennie became involved with church groups and clubs which would bring poor, city children out for a day in the park, she became even more insistent about making it a reality.

Jennie came out with the younger children, in the late summer, on what would be her last visit. She was distracted, worried. As everyone was preparing to leave, she put her hand on my arm and drew me aside. Speaking quietly, she said, "We haven't spoken of this for a long time, but have you done anything about the land?"

I shook my head, somewhat embarrassed.

"Don't let it ride, Jemima," she said insistently. "Time passes. You have to do something about it."

Although I had never done anything about it, I had kept my dream of the park alive, watching for an excuse to turn John into thinking my way. I couldn't believe my eyes, when one afternoon, I opened up a new garden journal that John had brought from Rowsell's. Now that we had time for our garden, we liked to read everything we could about designs, gardening hints and advice and profiles of famous landscape designers.

There, in a large spread right at the beginning of the journal, was an article about the designers Frederick Law Olmstead and Calvert Vaux who had won the competition for the design of the new park in New York. It was to be a breath-taking project with a lake, and esplanade; a wonderful place for the people who were crowded into tenement apartments to escape the heat and crowding of the city. Excitedly, I showed it to John. He was immediately intrigued by the article.

I was careful. I didn't want to push too hard. Once in a while, John again tried to sell off some of the land, but there was no interest. We were still too far out of town for most people to think of living here.

Without Jennie, I might have turned to the girls. Ellen, Eliza and Clara continued to visit us, often staying for weeks at a time. Of course, they were wonderful company and a great help to us, but I had never confided in them, nor them in me. Their visits always left me saddened. The years were passing and they were getting older. It began to seem as if life had somehow passed them by and there was no longer any chance of marriage for any of them. Ellen began to spend more and more time with us and both she and Eliza were beginning to help in managing the house.

As they became more comfortable in their new roles, we began to feel we could be away more often. Once, when I had injured my shoulder, I went off to the hot springs in St. Catherines for a week leaving Ellen in charge. Later, Eliza came several times when we went away on short trips.

Ellen travelled a little, found work as a teacher in Maine for a while, but soon came back to Clinton and talked of opening a school. Except for the times she spent with us, Eliza stayed at home.

Clara, who had always wanted to be independent, found a job teaching art in the girl's school in St. Catherines. She said it was a pleasant but undemanding position which left her time for her own work. Clara now thought of herself as an artist and when she submitted her drawings to a Provincial Art Exhibition and won five prizes for her watercolours, everyone had to admit that she had clearly earned the right to be taken seriously. We all had great hopes for her.

I had tried to do what I could for the girls, but coming to stay with us and have a bit of schooling did not really seem to have made much difference in their lives. Sometimes, when I thought of them, I couldn't help but compare them to the Hirschfelders. Fanny and Rosamund had both married well and already had children. The older brothers, Alfred, Frederic and Rudolph were bright, ambitious young men who would clearly make their mark in the world. The little ones, Charlie and Florence, were likely to do just as well. The Hirschfelders had become almost like family to us and John and I delighted in their successes. But a part of me always watched and thought of Fanny.

She too would have loved to have seen the girls happily married, to have welcomed grandchildren just as Margery Hirschfelder had done. Instead, wondering what would happen to her daughters and how they would manage to make a living was added to all Fanny's other worries. Was it just luck? When Fanny chose Sydney from all her other suitors, she had every reason to believe that their lives would turn out well. They had tried their hands at so many things, and Fanny had always gone along, loyally, with Sydney's schemes. It broke my heart that things had turned out so badly for her and the girls.

Although, we often visited the Mountcastles and Fanny spent much time with us, there seemed to be an almost unspoken agreement between us, an understanding about those things we would never discuss. I never talked to her about the girls; if she knew anything about John's secret life, and she probably did, she never said anything to me about it.

On July the first, 1867, Canada became a Dominion, an independent nation. There were huge celebrations in the city, but John and I did not go in to join them. Living out in the country, we had long since withdrawn from politics and found the noise and crowds of the city harder and harder to deal with. We rarely went in to town for large events anymore. The thought of joining the huge crowds with marching bands and fireworks was just too much for us. Instead, we invited friends to come out to visit and celebrated on our own.

The constant stream of visitors that summer kept me so busy that sometimes that I hardly had time to think. Letters piled up unanswered and newspapers went unread as I tended to our guests. I never realized that it was a long time since I had heard from Jennie. We had attended the wedding of Lizzie, her eldest daughter, and recently we went to the christening of Lizzie's first child. One morning, when I had decided, at last, to tackle the mail, I was surprised to see a letter from Peter, not Jennie. I was not sure when it had arrived.

Opening the letter, I was shocked to read that Jennie was ill and that he thought she would very much like a visit. I put aside the mail and made plans to go to town that afternoon.

The Martins had built a lovely large house in the newly growing west end. It had a large verandah surrounded by extensive gardens, a riot of colour on this late summer day. When I knocked on the door, it was opened by a maid I remembered from previous visits. Usually cheerful and energetic, I noticed immediately how worn she seemed to be.

As I entered the house, she stopped and turned to me. "Mrs. Martin is very unwell."

She swallowed. "You will be shocked when you see her."

Despite her warning, I was completely unprepared for the state in which I found Jennie. I entered the parlour, usually a bright, airy room with large windows overlooking the garden. On my previous visits, Jennie had chattered excitedly as she showed me their newest acquisitions, the paintings, the grand piano, a new gilt clock in a bell jar on the mantle. In her pleasure, I would often catch a glimpse of the little girl I once knew. Now, the drapes were drawn and the room was in darkness. Jennie lay on a sofa propped up on pillows and wrapped in a shawl even on this hot day. She struggled to sit up when she saw me.

I rushed to her and clasped her in my arms. The last time I had seen her, which would have been at Christmas, she had been healthy and robust, very much the matriarch of her growing family. Now she was just a shadow of herself, painfully thin, her face pinched and even her once glorious hair lying lank and thin to her shoulders. Her eyes were dull.

I was in such shock, I could hardly put my thoughts together.

"Jennie... I... I... didn't know. Why didn't anyone tell me? I would have come sooner, if I—"

She reached out and put a finger to my lips. Even her voice

was faint. "It happened so fast. You're here now..." Even that effort caused her pain. She gasped and lay back on her pillows. Words came out in fragments. "Just a few months ago. At first I thought it was something I had eaten... it would just go away. But then, I was ill, all the time. Then the pain started..."

"But surely there is something..."

She shook her head. "We've been to every doctor. We even went over to Buffalo, someone had heard of a doctor there. There is nothing anyone can do."

We sat for a while and talked, of her family, her first little grandchild and another on the way—of our friendship, how much we had meant to one another.

I could see soon that she was tiring. It was an effort for her to speak.

I got up to leave. "I'll come back and see you very soon."

Jennie looked at me sadly with those dull eyes. In that moment, we both knew how unlikely that was.

With a great effort, she sat up, reached out and grabbed my arm. Even her hand had become thin and bony, almost like a claw

"The park," she rasped.

At first, I couldn't understand what she was talking about.

"You must... have that park. Time... time goes so fast."

I held her in my arms. She was so thin that I could feel the bones in her back jutting out underneath her parched skin.

Still in shock, I left the room and let myself out the door. As I stepped out into the harsh summer sunshine, the light after the darkness of the parlour felt like a physical assault.

Jennie died in the fall, not long after my visit. When John and I attended the funeral, I could hardly bear to look at Peter standing there, bereft, surrounded by his children; Lizzie, clutching her young husband; Harry, their youngest, clinging to his father, uncomprehending. Much of the city came out to mourn

Jennie; her own large family, Peter's partners and many of his employees, members of many well-known families and the clubs and organizations Jennie had belonged to, her numerous friends, and at the back of the church, those nameless people she had quietly helped over the years who sat at the back of the church.

Afterwards, they said she died of cancer. She was not quite fifty years old.

All that winter, I grieved Jennie. She was so much younger than the rest of my old friends from our early days in the city. It seemed so wrong; so unfair. I would think of something I wanted to share with her, and shudder when I remembered that she was gone. I would notice a book or a trinket she had given me and burst into tears. She had become gracious, and elegant and known for her good works, but I still remembered the little girl in pigtails who had kept us so amused and cared for us in the first terrible winter so long ago.

In the spring, just as I was beginning to recover, I was struck with another blow.

I had gone into town with John to do some shopping and visit Margery while he was attending to some business. Rosamund and Fanny were both married now and were going to come over with their babies. I was walking back along King Street when I saw her.

It was the woman I had seen all those years ago, staring at me on the street—the woman with the child who looked like John. Of course, now I knew that her name was Mary Williams. She was older, of course, grey hair, stout, and somewhat stooped over. But she was still the woman who had stood, staring at me, mocking.

A tall young man walked beside her, slim, pale, just as John had been all those years ago when we were young. His face was John's face, as it had been once long ago. A pretty, young woman walked beside him. And two young children! They were smiling and laughing and skipping ahead.

Grandchildren! John's grandchildren! The children who should have been mine!

Something inside me snapped.

I was meeting John at Rowsell's, where we would catch the omnibus home to High Park together. Somehow, I managed to make conversation when I arrived at the bookstore. I even purchased a few new books and a newspaper. Somehow I climbed on board the omnibus. We chatted on, and I managed to keep myself under control for the long journey home.

James was waiting for us when we reached the edge of the park. My fists were so clenched through all that journey that my hands ached by the time we reached home and I could hardly stretch out my fingers. I said that I had a headache and went upstairs without saying anything more.

I pulled the curtains and lay down on my bed, fully clothed. I don't know how long I lay there. I heard John calling me to dinner. Phoebe rapped lightly on the door. I called out to say I was ill and couldn't come downstairs. Sometime later, she brought me some tea and toast. I sat up, had a few sips of tea, and lay down again.

How long have I been standing here, staring out my window?

All summer I have been writing, the words just pouring out of me. It is becoming harder and harder to find time alone. I have nurses now, like a child. A constant stream of them. I never know who will be there, sitting, sewing when I wake up.

I ask for Ellen, for Clara. They pretend they don't know what I am talking about. Have the girls been sent away. Or do they no longer care. Have they abandoned me?

I am still clever; I find ways to convince them that I am fine. I coax them, ever so sweetly to take a rest. "Oh, it's such a lovely day," I say. "Wouldn't you like to take a little walk? I will just have a little rest while you are gone."

I am like a small child wheedling for treat. And then, I soon as they're gone, I find my book and scribble away, writing as fast as I can, knowing that the time is running out for me.

Something had happened to me. I'd had these episodes many times before—whenever I was confronted with her—or the unavoidable evidence of that other life John led, but always I had snapped back. But now, it was as if something fragile that held me together had fractured. I was a violin that could no longer be played, something inside me was broken.

If only I could have talked to Jennie, but she was gone and I was all alone. In the past, I had always been able to pull myself together; to get up out of bed, to force myself to go on. Now, I had little reason to even try.

I lay in my bed, in the dark, for days on end. I kept seeing those children—running and playing—those children who looked like John. It was a nightmare—but I was awake and it would not end. And then strangely, as if something was forcing itself into my consciousness, I began to hear Jennie's voice. I saw her parched, bony hand reaching out to me. I heard her whispering to me.

"You must do something... Time goes so fast."

It was that, only that dream that gave me the strength to get up and go on.

That summer, John and I worked in the gardens just as we

had always done. We made wine from our grapes and I put up our preserves and compotes with the fruit from our fruit trees. But I was growing old. I no longer had the energy I once had and dreaded doing the tasks that had once given me such pleasure. More and more, I found myself stepping back and letting Phoebe do most of the work.

Just as Jennie had warned me I felt my time was running out. Somehow, I had to find a way to broach my idea to John, to somehow make it seem as if it had all come from him. I was always watching for my chance. In the summer when there was picnic for the children, I made sure to talk about my wish that we could have events like this more often. When I saw an article in the Globe about how poor children needed fresh air, I tried to start a conversation about what we could do to help.

One winter, when John came down with a very bad cold and was in bed moaning about the trials of getting old, I saw an opportunity. I brought him a cup of steaming, hot lemon tea and sat down beside him on the bed. "You know," I began, "we are getting on. It's time we started thinking about what we are going to do." I waved my hand around, "with all this."

But John didn't take my bait.

In the end, it was John himself who found the answer. One evening sitting by the fire reading, I heard him muttering to himself as he read the paper. "Look here," he said, waving the Globe at me, "Maybe they're finally going to listen." He read aloud a part of an editorial which made a strong argument for the need for public parks. John had made proposals for an esplanade and parkland along the lake, but no one in the city had listened.

His face suddenly lit up. "You know, Jemima. I've been mulling this over. What is going to happen to all this land? We can't sell it." He stopped, as if about to say something else, then went on. "That's it, Jemima. We can give them their park! We're not New York, you know, with their Central Park. They'll never do it on their own here."

I pretended not to understand. "What do you mean, give them their park?"

It was almost as if I could see John thinking this through, turning the idea in his mind.

"We'll turn High Park over to the city, the house, the land, and the farms. Everything. It will be our legacy. It will take some doing, but we'll figure it out."

John's old fire began to come back. Suddenly, he was reading everything he could about public parks. He began making designs, filling notebooks with ideas, grabbing my arm as we walked through the fields, pointing out how he could imagine the park taking shape.

It wasn't long before he was talking to William Boulton, his lawyer, and coming up with a plan.

"Listen to this, Jemima," he declared, after a day of meetings in town. "This is brilliant. We've found a clever way to give the land to the city and get them to look after us as well."

"And how on earth is that going to happen?"

"Look," he said, reading from the papers he had brought home. "We'll convey the land to the city, all of it, except for the land around the house. There's a way for us to continue to live in our house and get the city to pay us twelve hundred dollars a year while we look after the park for them."

John leaned back in his chair, grinning at his own cleverness. Bursting with new energy, he rubbed his hands together, just as he had as a young man working on his first projects.

Together, we hammered out more of the details. One night we read a report about a a group of young men who, being very drunk, had gone off on a spree and caused a lot of damage. The incident made us think about the sort of place we wanted our park to be.

"I would hate to see that happen here," I remarked. "A gang of these louts spoiling it for everyone else." I thought back to the time when Jennie had talked about how things had changed in the city, how drunkenness had become such a problem that she almost found herself siding with the Temperance movement. I thought of Thomas Young dying of drink.

Together, we decided that we wanted High Park to be a place where families could come and enjoy the out-of-doors, have their picnics, swim in the pond walk in the woods and be free of drunkenness and the brawls and rowdiness that so often went along with it. It took some doing, but we were able to get the city to agree. We were able to write into our agreement with the city that there would be no taverns built in High Park and that liquor would ever be sold in it.

I thought we had just about finalized our plans, when one night I head John muttering in the library. I looked in and saw him pacing back and forth, talking under his breath. He turned, and strode over to his desk, slammed his hand on the papers scattered there, everywhere. "Then, that's it," he said emphatically.

He looked up and saw me standing at the door. Our eyes met. Was it just my imagination, or could I almost read his mind? Was he struggling with our decision, thinking of those others, the other family, who could lay claim to the land?

The next day, I went with John to see Boulton and hammer out the final agreement and then John went into town to present our proposal to the Mayor.

And so it was done. In November, in 1873, we conveyed our land, one hundred and twenty acres of land, from Bloor Street to the railway tracks and road that now ran along the shore, between the park and the lake.

We would live in Colborne Lodge for the rest of our lives, and then, it too, would be given to the city.

I had done it. John was very pleased with the arrangements, especially so since he was the Provincial Land Surveyor for the conveyance and was designated the Park Ranger in charge of the land. He always believed it had been his idea. He would never know how long before the idea had come to me, nor the reason why I feared for the future of the land.

Suddenly it is so hot. I long to be outside, working in my garden.

I want so much to walk down the hillside and look out over the lake. It will be so busy now, steamers puffing their way to Hamilton and Niagara, fishing boats darting back and forth. Once our land went all the way to the lake, Now trains run all day on the tracks at the bottom of the hill, their whistles breaking the silence and their smoke belching into the air. Everything so full of life.

The garden is a riot of colour now. I think the strawberries must be ready. I can smell them, I can almost taste that warm, tangy sweetness of the just picked fruit from our own patches. I remember when we planted the strawberries and waiting so anxiously for our first crop.

Here in my room, it is so hot, airless

Am I hiding my writing from myself?

I get up and pace around the room. It is so hot and stuffy and oppressive. Outside clouds are gathering in the sky. The air is growing heavy. I can almost sense one of those early summer thunderstorms rolling in.

When did it begin to happen, this feeling that I was beginning to slip away? I know only that after the time that I saw her, with "her" son and "her" grandchildren the strong walls that I had kept around me all those years begin to fall away. I could never stop thinking about it. Sometimes, I found myself talking to myself. I would catch myself, wondering if I had had spoken aloud.

It began to eat away at me.

If only I could have talked to him about it. Sometimes, I wished I could say that I understood. That I wished I could have known those children.

At other times I was consumed with anger, envy and shame.

She had what I could never have; me with my fine house filled with the paintings, the lovely silver, the china, the hard earned land, my good name, my proper friends. I would have given everything for the children she has.

It wasn't really so much that she existed or that it happened. Of course, things like that go on. Men like to think that women don't know, and we pretend that this is true.

And it wasn't even so much that it happened to John. All in all, in spite of everything, he hadn't really changed toward me. At first, we still worked together in the office, every day. At night, we still talked about his projects, shared our hopes and dreams. When we moved out to the Lodge, we worked on our plans together, gardened, rode, went visiting and had a house filled with guests at all times in the year. And sometimes, John would sit sketching and I would read to him, just as we did on those bitter nights in our attic that winter when we first came to Canada.

I think I could have borne it were it not for the gossip.

Was I not guilty of the same thing? This is still such a small town really, and everyone knows everyone else's business. How often I had sat at tea with friends and tittered over some juicy morsel. But to be the subject of it was a nightmare that had no end. At the beginning, when I went shopping on King Street, I felt that everyone was looking at me. In church, I would swear that women even turn in their pews to stare at us as we came in, fussing with a child here, brushing an imaginary spot from a husband's coat there, to mask a sudden look.

And now, now that I know about the grown children and those small ones, I know that behind my back, people still talk.

In the end, it is the children, the thought of those children that drives nails into my heart.

I remembered the time when I had seen her on the street with those two children. Now, I thought that she had planned it. The brazen hussy that she was, I thought. She did it deliberately. I know that. Parading them past the house, It could not be an accident. She had to show me—she had what I could never have.

For all we have done, all that we have built together. She knew that it was for nothing.

I don't know what is happening. I wake up and there is a bruise on my leg and I am in great pain, but I don't remember falling.

Ellen is staying with us, I know that. We go for walks together and sometimes out for a ride.

Or maybe not. Maybe I am just dreaming.

Sometimes, I wake up and I don't know where I am or how much time has passed. I went in the carriage to a place I had never been to before. There was a doctor, a Dr. Riddell, who talked to me a lot and gave me pills. Everyone seems to give me pills.

When we came home I went for a walk near the house, just

as I have always done. I remember that. And then, I was in the woods and it was raining. I heard voices calling me, but I couldn't call back.

And now, I am here in this room, all the time. I know that I have been writing, scribbling away for a long time. It is getting harder and harder to do this. Something is driving me, making me want to go on, to finish while there is still light.

And there is something else.

I have this pain, in my... in my chest. People come and look at me, probe, poke me. Ellen rubs something on it, where it is hurting, but the pain doesn't stop. They give me more pills. John takes me places. More people look at me. The pain digs into me. Sometimes, it seems pain is all I know.

Ellen has gone away. There are other people here, all the time, people I don't know.

Sometimes the faces of the girls seem to float before me. I am so lonely without them.

Eliza is thinking of starting a school. Ellen is going to teach. And Clara, my beautiful Clara has won prizes for her paintings and sold some of them. And still, none of them are married and time has passed by for them.

Perhaps it is my fault. I filled their heads with dreams. I wanted them to do the things I never did. I should have just married them off.

I blame myself, but then, John taught Clara to draw and paint, encouraged her just as I did, and even arranged art lessons for her.

Was I the one, did I make them into blue-stockings that nobody wanted? Or were they just poor, plain, bright young girls, but with nothing to offer a young man who was looking for a match that could help start him on his way.

What could I have done?

I was not their mother.

I was nobody's mother.

I just want the pain to end.

John is sitting in his chair beside me. He is always there.

Pen and notebook. He is always sketching. In the garret with the snow falling. Drawing.

No. Not now. He is old now. An old man with a beard and his cap on his head. Still drawing.

He looks up... and smiles.

The pain. It forces its way through the drugs I know they give me.

The mist is closing in again. Longer and longer.

Soon I know, it will close in forever.

But I have finished my story.

Afterword

Jemima Howard

M any of the events and characters in this story are real. They are based on various versions of the journals that John Howard kept throughout his life, several of Jemima Howard's letters, other information about the Howards and other historical figures and life in early Toronto from a variety of sources. Jemima Howard also wrote garden journals and kept up a correspondence with her sister Fanny and her family back in England. Unfortunately, with the exception of a few letters, her writing has been lost.

As for the rest—Jemima's young friend, Jennie, and her family, Jemima's struggles with infertility, the long and short term effects of her discovery of John's infidelity, the initiative for the donation of High Park—this is her story as I imagine it. I have chosen not to delve deeply into the tragic details of her last years, ending Jemima's own narrative before she would have become truly aware of what was happening to her.

At the end of her long life, Jemima Howard suffered from what we would now recognize as dementia and also from aggressive breast cancer. No one can really know to what extent she would have been aware of the tumour or her advancing madness. But John's journals reveal his efforts to care for her at the end of her life.

When her tumour became so advanced that it formed a visible lesion that ruptured, John Howard sent a sketch of Jemima's condition to a pathologist in England who concurred with the diagnosis given in Canada that it was indeed cancer. In addition, John took her to many doctors in Ontario in an effort to find a treatment. There was little that could be done for cancer in those days: doctors gave them ointments to rub on her breast as well as various pills and powders. The diaries mention other treatments such as dressing the breast with belladonna, taking aconite pills and a "carbonate of iron in honey with powdered alum and mutton suet."

It has been suggested that there is a link between the breast cancer and Jemima's dementia, but this is unlikely. Some have suggested that it was a result of addiction caused by painkillers given to deal with the pain caused by the growing tumour. A close reading of John's diary seems to suggest that her dementia was present before she would have been experiencing any pain from the cancer. Whatever the cause, caring for Jemima became increasingly difficult for John Howard. At one point he even made arrangements for her to be sent to a room in the "best" ward of his own asylum. A number of doctors advised him not to send her there, so he made arrangements for her to be cared for at Colborne Lodge. Because she had sometimes "run away", he set up a room for her upstairs in the lodge with bars on the windows and a false door, so that she would not be aware of the real door which was locked from the outside.

Recent research has suggested that there may be a link in women between long-term depression and stress and dementia. Since discovering Jemima's story many years ago, I always felt that it was ultimately the suppression of her reaction to John's infidelity, his long-term relationship with Mary Williams and especially the existence of those three children which eventually caused her descent into madness. While the Howards were living in the city, still busy with John's work and surrounded by many friends, it was possible for Jemima to go on with her life. At first, when they moved permanently to High Park, they were still busy and active and entertained a constant stream of guests. But as they grew older, I believe that Jemima might have become more and more isolated, would have had more time to brood and reflect on what might have been and may, perhaps have sunk into a depression from which there was no turning back.

Both Ellen and Clara Mountcastle came to help care for Jemima in her illness and, at some point, it seems that John paid them for their help in addition to hiring a number of nurses. There was, however, a falling out between John and the Mountcastle girls resulting in their being barred from visiting their beloved aunt even as her death approached.

Jemima Howard was seventy-five when she passed away on the first of September in 1877. She must have suffered terribly in those last four years and John wrote that at the end she was consumed with fever and had lost so much weight that she looked like a skeleton. Well into her sixties, she had lived an active life and certainly in her early years with John in Toronto, she had played an important role in his growing success. But far too often, any reference to her, seems to emphasize only those last few years in that locked room.

I will always see her, not as the "madwoman in the attic", but as quite an unusual woman for her time, out there on the shore of Lake Ontario laying the lines, riding along the beach or carrying her sketchbook with her, as she and her young husband go out hunting together. That was, when she was not busy running the office or worrying about business, finishing the specifications for their latest project or keeping those apprentices in order. Although I have created many imaginary events for Jemima Howard, I did not make up her involvement the family business. In the Baldwin Room at the Metropolitan Toronto Reference Library, I have held in my hands the letter Jemima wrote to Fanny after the Rebellion of 1867, in which she discusses the effects of the unrest on their business. The fact that that she writes about how their business had suffered during the disruption certainly proves to me how actively she was involved in that business.

With the onset of Jemima's illness, John began to design and build an elaborate tomb that would stand beside their home. In honour of Jemima's Scottish heritage, it has a stone cairn and is topped with a Maltese cross to mark John's Masonic membership. In 1874, John purchased and arranged for the shipment of the iron railings which had surrounded St. Paul's Cathedral and were designed by Sir Christopher Wren himself which he planned to use for his own tomb. The Delta, the ship that was bringing the railings to Canada went aground, but a portion of the railings was salvaged and sent to Montreal. John brought them to Toronto to be repaired and finally installed them around the tomb in the following year.

After Jemima's death, John planned an elaborate funeral and wrote a poem for her which concludes sadly:

Though oftentimes she knew him not
Still was the ruin dear to him.
And why should he now cling to life,
Now all worth living for is gone,
With nothing left but care and strife,
But man they say was made to mourn.

After Jemima's death, John sent her diaries, letters, photographs and most of her possessions, including even her "spectacles" to Fanny.

All have been lost, but I treasure the fantasy that one day they will all be discovered in the attic in some Victorian house in the country.

Until then, I have tried to give Jemima Howard a voice.

John Howard

A fter Jemima's death, John continued to live alone, with various servants in Colborne Lodge. As Park Ranger, he supervised the park, made many changes to it over the years and provided facilities for the city folk who began to visit it.

Over the years, he became quite a Toronto character and there are many stories about him and his activities. He continued to garden and kept detailed records of his work, tinkered about the house and kept making changes to it. In 1885, he published a book called *Incidents in the Life of John. G. Howard of Colborne Lodge*, which focused on the journey to Canada, early incidents in his life in Toronto and contained a record of much of his work as an architect. A city Alderman named Frankland visited

Howard in that year and wrote an editorial in the *Toronto Daily Globe,* praising Howard for his philanthropy and character.

For some reason, John quarrelled with the Mountcastles, perhaps initially over the care of Jemima. Towards the end of Jemima's life, he would not even permit visits from the girls who had been so close to her. Much later, when Clara came with a friend, attempting to see him, she was "made to sit outside waiting, while her friend was admitted." And yet, Clara sent him one of her paintings which he critiqued and then he sent her money to buy dresses. Over the years, while he seemed to keep up his quarrel, he also kept in touch, writing many letters to Fanny and also sending her money as well. In 1880, there is a reference in the journals towards "cruel" comments John made about the death of Fanny's son and also a suggestion that Fanny had tried to obtain money that had been left to Jemima from their father.

In 1832, that winter when he first arrived in Canada, John and Sidney went skating. Sidney fell through the ice and would have drowned if John had not saved his life. Although, John always seemed to be willing to help the family and offered Sidney many business proposals, it seems that this incident remained with John all his life. In his book, written fifty-three years later, John still writes that he is angered by the fact that his brother-in-law never seemed to be properly grateful to John for saving his life that day, Was this perhaps the root of John's strange relationship with the Mountcastles?

As he grew older, John suffered from many conditions. Cataracts caused him eventually to go blind, his back pain was so severe he was given opium pills and he often recorded many other ailments. The abdominal problems which plagued him all his life—and which we would probably call Crohn's disease—continued to be a problem.

His grand project, The Provincial Lunatic Asylum, was plagued with problems almost from its beginnings. By the 1970's it was known as the notorious 999 Queen Street and was demolished by the city of Toronto in 1975.

John Howard died on the third of February, 1890, at the age of eighty-seven and was buried beside Jemima in the tomb he had prepared thirteen years before.

John had three illegitimate children with Mary Williams about whom little is known: George 1843-1925, Douglas 1847-1885 and Anne-1852-1887. Although there are few references to John's children and grandchildren with Mary Williams in the dairies, John did recognize them in his will, leaving property and his gun collection to his son George, an antique dealer, and also an annuity to Mary Williams.

Reconciled with Fanny in the end, he also left her an annuity and provided for her children.

Along with High Park, John left his paintings and all the contents of Colborne Lodge to the City of Toronto, just as Jemima would have wished.

The Mountcastle Family

With the encouragement of John and Jemima Howard, Clara Mountcastle went on to have a successful career. Like many women who are forgotten now, Clara was known in her own time both as an artist and later on as writer. Such was her reputation, that she was one of the only Canadians to be included in a book called *Women of the Century* published in 1901 in the United States. Although her writing is unknown today, critics have compared her poetry favourably to that of her contemporary, Sir Charles G.D. Roberts, whose work used to be studied in Canadian schools.

Clara first became known as an artist. Her watercolours won five prizes when she exhibited her work in Provincial Art Exhibition in 1870. Of her painting, it has been said, that her landscapes prefigured those of the Group of Seven. Because she could not afford to go away and study in Paris, she was not influenced by Impressionism which was fashionable at the time. So, although she continued to exhibit her work, critics of the day dismissed it as being merely provincial and in 1897 her work was rejected by the Ontario Society of Artists where she had previously shown. On being rejected also in her bid to become a member of the society, because she was a woman, Clara wrote in a poem called "The Artist's Soliloquy", in which she said she was blocked by "the men who said me nay/ The rulers of the O.S.A."

They looked upon my work and found
No misty stretch of foreign ground,
But trees and bushes hung around
With richness of our scenery.

And said 'We have no need of these,
These Autumn-tinted glowing trees.
And vast tumultuous inland seas.
The French have no such imag'ry.

When failing eyesight caused Clara to abandon her artistic career, she turned to writing instead. Under the pen name of Caris Sima, Clara published *Mission of Love,* a collection of poetry in 1882, *A Mystery,* a novella in 1886 and an essay, *Is Marriage a Failure,* in 1899 in which she considered the use of Miss and Mrs. seventy years before the term Ms. was invented and began with this blunt assessment of marriage.

"I do not know how many women marry merely for the sake of being married and having the prefix "Mrs." to their name, but I do know that all such marriages must of necessity be failures."

The entry in *Women of the Century* states that she was highly regarded both in Canada and the United States and contains the fascinating statement that "Her platform work has included the rendition of her own essays and poems. She is a forcible and dramatic reader, a versatile author, and an artist of strong, varied powers."

Clara also taught art in a private girl's school in St. Catherines and later in the school that her sisters, Ellen and Eliza ran in Clinton where they remained all their lives.

Clara Mountcastle never married and died of cancer in 1908 at the age of seventy-one.

Ellen and Eliza also never married. They lived, along with Clara, in what has been called "genteel poverty." Ellen briefly ran a school in Goderich and tried other ways to earn a living. Both sisters were amateur artists and writers and, Eliza, also even studied medicine and was an amateur physician.

Both she and Eliza had long lives and died within a month of one another in 1922.

Ellen was 89 and Eliza was 87.

Fanny (Frances) Mountcastle died in Clinton, Ontario in 1891 at the age of 87 having given birth to twelve children, five of whom survived.

Other Torontonians

With the exception of Jennie and her family, the friends and associates of the Howards are real people, many with interesting stories to tell. Henry Rowsell opened a book and stationary shop and a lending library in Toronto in 1835 and was also an important publisher. His friendship with the Howards lasted throughout their long lives. Rowsell died in Toronto in 1890.

Christopher Widmer deserves a biography all his own. *The Dictionary of Canadian Biography* describes him as a "physician, surgeon, army officer, medical educator and administrator, justice of the peace, office holder, and politician." In everything I read from Henry Scadding's *Toronto of Old,* to an article on midwives in Upper Canada, his name seemed to pop up. When I first started to think about this story, I imagined Widmer as a small dapper man with in an elegant suit and a gold watch. A contemporary of his actually wrote that "Widmer dressed smartly" and was "an amazing favourite with the ladies". More than just their doctor, Widmer was a good friend of the Howards and supported John in his work.

And finally, there is Jacob Meir Hirschfelder, a German Jew who had converted to Christianity and arrived in Toronto in 1842 where he began as a Hebrew tutor and then became a lecturer in Oriental Studies when the University of Toronto opened in 1850. In addition to biblical Hebrew, he taught Samaritan Hebrew, Syriac, Arabic, and German, and had facility in Greek and Latin. He was a recognized Biblical scholar whose writings are still available today. Although much younger than the Howards, he and his young wife, Margery, who was from Montreal, became such close friends with the John and Jemima, that they asked them to be the godparents of their first two children. The two families remained close with John mentioning in his diaries their many visits to Colborne Lodge and the gifts he bought for the two eldest daughters on their engagements. The Hirschfelders had a large family all of whom became successful as adults.

In an interesting post-script to this story, I discovered that Jacob Hirschfleder's grandson was Alfred Hirschfelder Chapman, the architect who designed such diverse buildings in Toronto as the Old Mill Tea Room, Union Station, the Royal Ontario Museum and Holy Blossom Temple.

Jemima and Me

Twenty years ago, I was appointed to the Board of the Historic Homes of Toronto. At our first meeting at Colborne Lodge, the curator, Cheryl Hart, spoke briefly about Jemima Howard as she introduced us to the history of the house. Something about Jemima's story grabbed me that night and has never let go. Like so many women in history—indeed like her accomplished and successful niece, Clara Mountcastle—Jemima has been lost to history. If we hear about her at all, it is only as John Howard's wife or in reference to her final years, when in her seventies she was locked away in a room in her house, truly a "madwoman in the attic."

But what about that spirited young woman who arrived in the little frontier town of York, a settlement with only 9,000 people? What do we hear about the woman who worked alongside her husband to build a successful architectural practice? The one who worked on the specifications, helped to lay the lines for the surveys, and went to work in the office every day almost two hundred years ago at a time when we have always been told that women of a certain class didn't work outside the home at all?

We don't know anything about what Jemima did at the office, but is it only a coincidence that when she was no longer there, John Howard almost went bankrupt? Of course, there were other factors involved in his business problems: overwork, issues caused by Samuel Jarvis, and the cost of maintaining two households. But I am drawn to the idea that she likely ran that office for many years.

At a time, as we have been told, when women were mainly confined to the home, Jemima was out in wilderness around Toronto, going riding with John, shooting, fishing, and tramping around with her sketchbooks, drawing what she saw.

I thought of writing a novel about Jemima all those years ago, and even made a start on it, picked it up every once in a while, did a little sporadic research and then forgot about it again but never really made a serious effort on the project. Although I taught Creative Writing in high school for many years, I never showed my own writing to anyone until I became a facilitator with the Toronto Writers Collective and regularly shared my writing with our group. This led to my joining a writer's group in Florida and being invited to join a group of professional writers. It was when I finally read the introduction of the novel to others and received much interest and encouragement that I began to think that other people might be as interested in Jemima's story as I was.

Right at the very beginning, the character of young Jennie popped up in my mind and I could clearly see her and her whole family as, together, they worked and lived at the inn. Imagine my surprise when, in the course of my research I discovered a book called *In Mixed Company: Taverns and Public life in Upper Canada* by Julia Roberts who devotes much discussion to the role of women in that sphere. Women really did run inns sometimes with their husbands, sometimes alone. Families really did live 'upstairs from the store' and children really did help out in many ways. Jennie and the Greys could have been real.

I also learned a great deal from Sharon Vattay's study Defining Architects in Nineteenth Century Toronto and Thomas Young became not just a name, but an important character in the novel. The paper studies John Howard's career in detail, but it is disappointing to me that the only mention Jemima gets is a brief reference to her preparing the house for the apprentices.

Coincidences continued to crop up and just when I thought I had finished my research and my work was drawing to a close, yet another appeared. In reading an essay about an exhibition of the Pre-Raphaelite Sisters which I was fortunate to see in London in December 2019, I was startled to discover that Georgina Burne-Jones and Effie Millais *both read aloud to their husbands as they worked in their studios.* In addition, Georgina, Effie and the other wives managed the business for their artist-husbands, paid the bills, made or sourced the costumes and as in the case of Jane Morris was actively involved in the business side of the famous Morris & Co. This show was the first exhibition of the work of these women whose roles in the famous movement are only just now being recognized. Jemima Howard wasn't alone in the role she played in her husband's work or in the lack of recognition given to her for it.

Acknowledgements

For many years, this book remained a private project that I dabbled with from time to time and never shared with anyone. It was not until I shared the opening chapter with my writer's workshop at Wynmoor in Florida and received great positive feedback, that I began to think seriously of writing this novel.

It was Inkslingers and the Novel Approach Workshop which gave me the push to finally make this project a reality and I want to thank my fellow participants for their encouragement and insights.

Without Inkslingers and Sue Reynolds this book would not exist. Sue, I am so grateful for all your help, encouragement and inspiration.

I am also so grateful for the encouragement and comments of my readers Anne Clement, and Isaac Ezer and especially my daughter-in-law Emma Barnes who took the time to meticulously edit my novel while caring for a newborn baby, my grandson, Sebastian.

Thank you to Maureen Capotosto for all your help and for linking me up with my first reviewer, Gail Murray.

And finally a huge thank you to Joy Bullen for your superb editing, encouragement and advice and for managing this project.

Bibliography

Howard, John G., *Journals,* The Baldwin Room,
Metropolitan Toronto Reference Library

Howard John G. and Jemima, Manuscript Collection,
The Baldwin Room, Metropolitan
Toronto Reference Library

Howard, John G., *The Journal of John G. Howard,*
contributor, Shirley G. Morriss

Howard, John G., *The Life of John G. Howard, 1833-
1849,*Colborne Lodge, Women's Canadian Historical
Society, Shirley McManus, Metropolitan Reference
Library

Howard, John G., *Incidents in the Life of John. G. Howard,
esq. of Colborne Lodge, High Park,*
Copp, Clark, Toronto, 1885

Arthur, Eric, *Toronto No Mean City,*
University of Toronto Press, Toronto,1964

Brandis, Marianne, *Rebellion: a novel of Upper Canada,*Porcupine's Quill, Erin, 1996

Glazebrook, G. P. De T., *The Story of Toronto,* University of Toronto Press, Toronto, 1971

Goddard, John, *Inside the museums: Toronto's heritage sites and their most prized objects.* Dundurn Press, Toronto, 2014

Grey, Charlotte, *Sisters in the Wilderness.* Viking, Toronto, 1999

Guillet, Edwin C., *The great migration; the Atlantic crossing by sailing-ship since 1770.* Nelson and Sons, Toronto, 1937

Hale, Katherine, *Toronto; romance of a great city.* Cassell,Toronto, 1956

Kilbourn, William, *The Firebrand.* Clarke, Irwin, Toronto,1956

Kilbourn, William, *Toronto Remembered.* Stoddart, Toronto, 1984

Jameson, Anna, *Winter Studies and Summer Rambles in Canada, 1838,* Coles Publishing Company, 1972

Levine, Allan, *Toronto, Biography of a City,* Douglas & McIntyre, Toronto 2014

MacIntosh, Robert M., *Earliest Toronto,* General Store
Publishing House, Renfrew, 2006

Mays John Bentley, *Emerald City; Toronto Visited,*Viking
Toronto, 1994

Moodie Susanna, *Roughing it in the Bush,* McClelland and
Stewart, Toronto, 1962

Roberts, Julia, *In Mixed Company,Taverns and Public Life
in Upper Canada,* UBC Press, Vancouver,2009

Scadding, Henry, *Toronto of Old, edited by Frederick H.
Armstrong,* Dundas Press, Toronto 1987

Taylor, Doug, *Lost Toronto,*Pavilion Books, London, 2018

Thompson, Austin Seton, *Spadina; A story of Old Toronto,*
The Boston Mills Press, Erin, 2000

Walker, Frank Norman, *Sketches of Old Toronto,*
Longman's Canada, Ltd. 1965

West, Bruce, *Toronto,* Doubleday, Toronto, 1967

Vattay, Sharon, *Defining "Architect" in Nineteenth-Century
Toronto.*TSpace, University of Toronto, 2001

Articles

Franklin, Jill, "John Howard's Secret Children", *High Park Nature,* Summer, 1995

Franklin, Jill, "Jemima Howard - First Lady of High Park", *High Park Nature,* Winter, 1995

Franklin, Jill, "John Howard's Foray into Lunacy," *High Park Nature,* Winter, 1996

Franklin, Jill, "Howard and Jarvis", *High Park Nature,* Fall, 1996

Miles, Joan, "John Howard Gentleman Farmed High Park" *High Park Nature,* Spring 1995

Baehre, Rainer, "Pauper Emigration to Upper Canada in the 1830's," Department of History, Mount Saint Vincent University

Connor, J.T., "Larger Fish to Catch Here than Midwives", In *Caring and Curing: Historical Perspectives on Women and Healing in Canada,* edited by Diane Elizabeth Dodd, Deborah Graham, University of Ottawa Press, Ottawa, 1994

Dolski, Megan, "Museum staff take a close look at John Howard's john," *The Toronto Star,* Saturday, March 11, 2017

Fernandes, Roxanne, "Case Study at Colborne Lodge: Identifying the Undefined Contemporanity of Furniture in the Parlour Room", *Case Studies at the Royal Ontario Museum,* December 2016

Nessim,Daniel F. Jonathan, "260 Years in the Making: The Origins of Canadian Messianic Judaism,"in *Kesher; A Journal of Messianic Judaism,* January 2020